B&T 1.75

This Star Shall Abide

THIS STAR
SHALL ABIDE

Sylvia Louise Engdahl

drawings by Richard Cuffari

AN ALADDIN BOOK
Atheneum

J.
E

Published by Atheneum
All rights reserved
Copyright © 1972 by Sylvia Louise Engdahl
Published simultaneously in Canada by
McClelland & Stewart, Ltd.
Manufactured by Fairfield Graphics, Fairfield, Pennsylvania
ISBN 0-689-70458-5
First Aladdin Edition

This Star
Shall Abide

I

THREE ORANGE CRESCENTS HOVERED ABOVE THE FIELDS
and Little Moon was rising over the Tomorrow Mountains
when Noren and Talyra left the schoolhouse. Laughter
blended with the music of flutes drifted out across the stony
area as they walked toward the sledge.

"By the Mother Star, it's hot!" exclaimed Noren, as he
swung himself to the wicker seat and held out a sturdy hand
to the girl.

"Don't swear," she reproved gently, climbing in beside
him. "You never used to swear."

Frowning, Noren reproached himself for his careless-
ness. He hadn't meant to offend her, but it was hard to remember sometimes that she, so spirited in other ways, still
held the conventional beliefs on a subject about which he
had long ago formed his own. He'd planned to discuss that
subject on their way home, and he was already off to a bad
start.

He jerked the reins; the work-beast snorted and headed

3)

reluctantly down the sandy road away from the village. "We're free!" Talyra said exultantly. "How do you feel?"

Noren considered it. Their schooling was finished for good; having reached mid-adolescence, they were free citizens: free to claim new farmland or to seek any work they chose; free even to move to some other village. And they were also free to marry. So why should he feel less satisfied than ever in his life before? "I don't know how I feel," he told her.

She stared at him, surprised and a little hurt. Suddenly Noren was ashamed. This was not a time to worry about freedom, or knowledge, or the Prophecy. He let the reins fall slack and drew Talyra toward him, kissing her. But there was a restlessness in his mind that refused to slip aside. Talyra felt it, too. "You're angry," she accused. "Is it because of the Technician?"

"I'm not angry."

"You fume whenever you catch a glimpse of one of them," she said sadly, sliding over on the seat. "I wish he'd never shown up at the dance. I can't imagine what he's doing in the village tonight, anyway."

"What does a Technician ever do?" Noren retorted with undisguised bitterness. "He comes either to inspect something or to inform us of some duty to the High Law that we may not have noticed."

"That's not true. More often the Technicians come with Machines, or to hold devotions, or cure someone who's ill—"

"No one was ill at the schoolhouse." Noren's voice was sharp, for inwardly he knew she was right; the High Law was enforced not by men of the Technician caste, but by the village council.

"You're funny, Noren," Talyra said. "Technicians aren't unkind, ever; why do you hate them?"

He paused; it was a hard thing to explain. "They give no reasons for what they do. They have knowledge we're not

(4

allowed to share."

"Reasons? They are Technicians!"

"Why are they Technicians? They're men and women like us, I think."

Talyra withdrew her hand from his, shocked. "Noren, they're not; it's blasphemy to think of them so! They have abilities we can't even imagine. They can control Machines for clearing land, and quickening it, or for building road-beds, or—or *anything*. They talk to radiophonists from a long way off; they travel through the air from village to village . . . it's been said they can go to the other side of the world! And they've all sorts of marvelous things in the City. Why, they know nearly as much as the Scholars, who know everything."

"And tell us almost nothing."

"What would you expect them to tell us?" asked Talyra in surprise. The Scholars, as High Priests, were the acknowledged guardians of all mysteries. "We know all we'll ever need to," she continued. "You wouldn't want to go to school any more, would you?"

"No, I already know what the teacher knows," Noren agreed. "I've read all the books, and Talyra, I've worked out math problems the teacher couldn't even follow. But there is more knowledge than that. I want to know different things, like—like what Power is, and why crops can't be grown till a Machine's quickened the soil, and what good it does for Technicians to put clay into a purifying Machine before the potter's allowed to shape it."

"People aren't meant to know things like that! Not yet."

"Yet? You mean before the time given in the Prophecy?"

"Of course. The time when the Mother Star appears."

"Talyra," Noren said hesitantly, "do you believe that?"

"Believe in the *Prophecy?*" she gasped, her shock deepening. "Noren . . . don't you?"

"I'm not sure," he temporized. "Why should there be a time, generations in the future, when our descendants will suddenly know all the secrets? Why should knowledge be reserved for them? I want to know *now*."

"There isn't any 'why' about it; that's just the way it is. *'At that time, when the Mother Star appears in the sky, the ancient knowledge shall be free to all people, and shall be spread forth over the whole earth. And Cities shall rise beyond the Tomorrow Mountains, and shall have Power, and Machines, and the Scholars will no longer be their guardians.'* "

"How do you know that's true?"

"It's in the Book of the Prophecy."

Noren didn't answer. What he'd been thinking during the past years would horrify Talyra; but if they were to marry, he must not conceal it any longer. He was firmly convinced of that, though such an idea was no less contrary to custom than many of his other unconventional ones. Girls promised themselves to men they respected, and if they were loved and returned that love, so much the better; they did not expect to be told of a prospective husband's feelings on other subjects. Yet because he did love Talyra, he'd decided that he owed her the truth. He had also decided that this was the night on which he would have to tell her.

At the edge of an open field he reined the work-beast to a halt and threw himself flat on the straw that filled the sledge, pulling Talyra down beside him. For a while neither of them said anything; they lay looking up at the stars, the faint but familiar constellations with puzzling names from the old myths: the Steed, the Soldier, the Sky-ship . . . It was very still. A slow breeze rustled the grain and mingled dust with the warm, rich odor of growing things.

Soberly Talyra ventured, "Why couldn't you be happy tonight? Even before the Technician came you weren't having fun. Everyone at the dance was happy except you. I kept trying to get you to laugh—"

"I'm very happy." He fingered her dark curls.

(6

"Don't you care enough for me to share what's bothering you?"

"It's not easy to put into words, that's all." He must proceed slowly, Noren knew; he would frighten her if he came out with the thing before explaining the reasoning behind it. Probably he would frighten her anyway. "You say everybody at the dance was happy," he went on. "Well, I guess they were. They're usually happy; they've got plenty to eat and comfortable homes and that's all they care about. They don't *think*."

"Think about what?"

"About how things really are—the world, I mean. They don't mind not knowing everything the Technicians know. The Technicians bring the Machines we need and help us if we're in trouble, so they think it's all right for them to run things. They're content with being dependent."

"What's wrong with it? It's part of the High Law."

"Suppose we knew how to build our own Machines?"

"We couldn't," Talyra objected. "Machines aren't *built,* they just *are.* Noren, you're mixed up. Technicians don't run things in the village; our own councilmen do that."

"We elect councilmen to make village laws," admitted Noren, "but the Scholars are supreme, and the Technicians act in their name, not the council's. They're outside village law entirely."

"Has a Technician ever interfered with anything you wanted to do?"

"That's not the point."

"Then what is? Technicians don't interfere, they only give; but no matter what they did, it would be right. Keeping the High Law's a sacred duty, and the Scholars were appointed at the time of the Founding to see that it's kept. The Technicians are their representatives."

Noren hesitated a moment, then plunged. "Talyra, I don't believe any of that," he stated. "I don't believe that the earth was empty and that people simply sprang out of

7)

the sky on the day of the Founding. It's not—well, it's just not the way things happen. It's not natural. I think people must have been here for much, much longer than the Book of the Prophecy says, and to begin with they knew as little as the savages that live in the mountains—the ones we studied about, you remember; the teacher said they were once like us, but lost everything, even their intelligence, because they refused to obey the High Law?"

"Yes, but—"

"Let me finish. I think it was the other way around. You don't forget something you once knew, but you can always learn more. I think we were like the savages until someone, maybe one of the Scholars, found out how to get knowledge. Only he didn't tell anybody except his friends. He told the rest just enough to make them afraid of him, and made the High Law so that they'd obey."

Talyra sat up, edging away from him. "Noren, don't! That isn't true; that—that's heresy."

"Yes, it's contrary to the Book of the Prophecy. But don't you see, the Scholars wrote the Prophecy themselves because they wanted power; it didn't come from the Mother Star at all."

"Oh, Noren!" Talyra whispered. "You mustn't say such things." Raising her eyes devoutly, she began, " 'The Mother Star is our source and our destiny, the wellspring of our heritage; and the spirit of this Star shall abide forever in our hearts, and in those of our children, and our children's children, even unto countless generations. It is our guide and protector, without which we could not survive; it is our life's bulwark. . . . We will follow the Law until the time when the Mother Star itself shall blaze as bright as Little Moon—' "

Noren seized her angrily, swinging her around to face him. "Stop quoting empty phrases and listen! How could a new star appear when the constellations have been the same since before anyone can remember? And even if it could, how could the man who wrote the Prophecy know beforehand? How did he know there was a Mother Star if he'd never seen it?"

"Of course it's invisible now; the Prophecy says so."

"We don't need a prophecy to tell us *that*. We do need one to tell us that it will someday be as bright as Little Moon, since common sense tells us that can never happen."

"But the Prophecy gives the exact date."

"When the date arrives, there will be a new Prophecy to explain the failure of the old one. Can't you see, Talyra? It's the Scholars' scheme to make us think that their supremacy's only temporary, so that we won't oppose it. As long as we accept the story, they can keep their knowledge all to themselves and no one will protest; but if we rebel against it, we can make them give knowledge to everyone! We could have Cities and Power and Machines now; there's no point in waiting several more generations only to find that there'll be no changes after all."

"I don't want you to talk that way! What if someone should hear?"

"Perhaps they'd believe me. If enough people did—"

"They wouldn't, any more than I do. They'd despise you for your irreverence, they'd report you—" Her dark eyes grew large with fear. "Noren, you'd be tried for heresy! You'd be convicted!"

He met her gaze gravely, glad that she had not forced him to say it himself. "I—I know that, Talyra."

It was something he had known for a long time. He was a heretic. Decent people would despise him if he was found out. And eventually he would no longer be able to keep silent; to do so as a boy was one thing, but now that he was a man, his search for truth would take him beyond the safe confines of his private thoughts. Then, inevitably, he'd be accused; he would stand trial before the village council and would be found guilty, for when put to the question, he would not lie to save himself.

9)

And once convicted, he would be turned over to the Scholars. Under the High Law, the religious law that over-rode anything village law might say, all heretics were taken into the custody of the Scholars, taken away to the City where mysterious and terrible things were done to them. No one really knew what things. No one had ever entered the City where all the Scholars and Technicians lived; no one had ever seen a Scholar except from a distance, during one of the various ceremonies held before the City Gates. Noren longed to go there, but he was not anxious to go as a condemned prisoner. He'd awakened in the middle of the night sometimes, drenched with sweat, wondering what that would be like.

He reached out toward Talyra, more gently this time, suddenly noticing how she was shaking. "Talyra—oh, Talyra, I didn't want to scare you—"

"How could you not scare me by such ideas? I—I thought we were going to be married, Noren."

"We are," he assured her, hugging her close to him again. "Of course we are."

She wrenched away. "No, we're not! Do you suppose I want a husband who's a *heretic?* One I'd always be afraid for, and who—"

"Who could put you in danger," Noren finished slowly, chilled with remorse. "Talyra, I just didn't think—it was stupid of me—" He dropped his head in his hands, realiz-ing that in his concern for being honest with her, he'd forgotten that if he was ever tried for heresy, she would be questioned, too. She would be called to testify. Wives always were, yet she would be called whether they were married or not, for everyone knew they were betrothed, and she could no longer say that she knew nothing. "I've compromised you," he whispered in anguish. "You could be punished for not reporting me."

Talyra gave him a pained look. "Darling, don't you trust

me? Don't you know I'd never tell anyone? I love you, Noren!"

"Of course I trust you," he declared. "It's you I'm afraid for. It's not only that you'd be suspect because you hadn't told; it's that I've said enough to open your eyes. Before, you might never have thought of doubting, but now—well, now you're not innocent, and if you're questioned on my account, you'll have to admit it."

"What do you mean, I'm not innocent?" she protested. "Do you think I believe any of those awful things, Noren? Are you suggesting that I'll become a heretic myself? I love you and I won't betray you, but you're wrong, so wrong; I only hope that something will restore your faith."

Noren jumped to his feet, angry and bewildered. He had not thought she'd consider him mistaken. It had never occurred to him that Talyra wouldn't accept the obvious once it was pointed out to her. She was brighter than most girls; he'd liked that, and only because of it had he dared to speak of his conviction that the orthodox faith was false. To be sure, not even the smartest village elders ever questioned anything connected with religion, but he'd attributed that to their being old or spineless.

"I don't want my faith restored," he said heatedly. "I want to know the truth. The truth is the most important thing there is, Talyra. Don't you care about finding it?"

"I already know what's true," she maintained vehemently. "I'm happy—I was happy—the way we are. If I cared about anything besides you I could have it, and if you're going to be like this—"

"What do you mean, you could have it?"

She faced him, sitting back on her heels. "I kept something from you. I know why the Technician came tonight. He spoke to me; he said I could be more than the wife of a farmer or a craftsman. He asked if I wanted to be more."

"Well, so there are rewards for blind faith in the righteousness of Technicians!"

"He said," she went on, "that if I liked, I could go to the training center and become a schoolteacher or a village nurse."

Noren's thoughts raged. If he were to ask for even a little knowledge beyond that taught in the school, he'd be rebuffed, as he had been so many times, times when his harmless, eager questions had been turned aside by the Technicians who'd come to work their Machines in his father's fields. But Talyra, who seldom used her mind for wondering, had been offered the one sort of opportunity open to a villager who wanted to learn! To be sure, the training center vocations were semi-religious, and he was known to be anything but devout; yet it did not seem at all fair.

"I knew you'd be furious; that's why I didn't plan to mention it." She got up, brushing the straw from her skirt, and climbed back onto the seat. "When I told him I was pledged to marry, he said I was free to be whatever I chose."

"Even a Technician or a Scholar, maybe?" Noren said bitterly.

"That's blasphemous; I won't listen."

"No, I don't suppose you will. I can see how fraud has greater appeal than truth from your standpoint."

"*You're* questioning *my* piety, when you're calling the High Law a fraud? You had better take back what you've said if you expect to go on seeing me!"

"I'm sorry," he conceded. "That was unfair, and I apologize."

"Apologizing's not enough. I don't mean just the angry things."

Slowly Noren said, "I guess if I were to swear by the Mother Star never again to talk of the heretical ones, you'd be satisfied."

Her face softening, Talyra pleaded, "Oh, Noren—will

you? We could forget this ever happened."

He knew then that she had not understood any of what he had revealed. In a low voice he replied, "I can't do that, Talyra. It wouldn't be honest, since I'd still be thinking them, and besides, an oath like that wouldn't mean anything from me. You see, I wouldn't consider it—sacred."

Talyra turned away. Her eyes were wet, and Noren saw with sadness that it was not merely because their marriage plans were in ruins, but because she really thought him irreverent. She did not put a reverence for truth in the same category as her own sort of faith.

"T-take me home," she faltered, not letting herself give way to tears.

He took his seat, giving the reins a yank, and the work-beast plodded on, the only sound the steady whish of the sledge's stone runners over sand. Neither of them said anything more. Noren concentrated on keeping to the road: two of the crescent moons had set, and the dim light of the third wasn't enough to illuminate the way ahead.

What now? he wondered. He had intended to go to the radiophonist's office the next morning and submit his claim for a farm, but without Talyra that would be pointless. He did not want to be a farmer; he'd worked more than half each year, between school sessions, on his father's land, and he had always hated it. Since he didn't want to be a trader or craftsman either, he had thought farming as good a life as any; a man with a wife must work at something. He had planned it for her sake. Now he had no plans left.

None, that is, but an idea he scarcely dared frame, the exciting, irrepressible idea that although there was no way to get more knowledge himself, he might someday manage to convince people—as many as possible, but at least *some* people—that knowledge should be made free to everyone without delay. He was not sure how to put such an idea into action, much less how to avoid arrest while doing so.

He was not sure that arrest could be avoided. Noren was sure of only one thing: if and when he was convicted of heresy, he was not going to recant.

Most heretics did, he knew. Most of them, after a week or two in the City, knelt before the Scholars in a ceremony outside the Gates and publicly repudiated every heretical belief they'd ever held. And that was no great surprise, Noren thought, cold despite the oppressive heat of the evening. It was all too understandable, when the penalty for not recanting was reputed to be death.

It was close to dawn when Noren unhitched the work-beast in his father's barn and went in to bed, undressing silently to avoid waking his brothers. He did not sleep. Talyra . . . it was hard to accept what had happened with Talyra. He had never been close to other people; he had always felt different, a misfit; but he'd had Talyra, whom he loved, and for the past year he had looked forward increasingly to the day when he would have her as his wife. Now, with the day almost upon him, his one hope for the future had been dashed. If only he'd been less honest!

But he could not have been. It was not in him to live as a hypocrite, Noren realized ruefully. The only thing in the world that meant more to him than Talyra was . . . Truth. He thought about it that way sometimes—Truth, with a capital letter—knowing that people would laugh at him if they knew. That was the difference between himself and the others: he *cared* about the truth, and they did not.

Looking back, he could not remember just when he'd started to reject the conventional beliefs; he was aware of much he had not known in the beginning, and could not trace the development of his doubts, which at first had been only a vague resentment at the fact that knowledge existed that was unavailable to him. Perhaps he'd begun to formulate them on the evening the Technician had come unannounced to his father's farm.

That had been before his childish admiration of Technicians had turned to inexplicable dislike; he'd been quite a young boy, and the sight of the aircar floating down over his own family's grainfield had thrilled him. The Technicians who quickened the soil at the start of each growing season seldom arrived in aircars, for they simply moved on from the adjacent farm, pushing their noisy Machines back and forth over the continuous strip of cleared land. So with his brothers, Noren had run excitedly to meet the descending craft.

The man had asked lodging for the night, and had offered to pay well for it; Technicians never took anything without paying. Noren's father would have been within his rights to refuse the request. But of course it would never have occurred to him to do that, any more than it would have occurred to him to wonder why a Technician needed lodging when the aircar could have taken him back to the City in no time at all. Nobody ever questioned the ways of Technicians.

This Technician had been a young man with a pleasant smile and a friendly manner that had put the boys immediately at ease. He had allowed them to come close to the aircar, even to touch it. At least Noren had touched it; his brothers had hung back in awe, as people generally did in the presence of a Machine. He would have liked to climb inside, but that the Technician would not permit. Noren had to content himself with running his hand over the smooth, shining surface of the craft and, later, with fingering curiously the green sleeve of the Technician's uniform, so different from the coarse brown material of which ordinary clothing was made. And still more wondrous were the metal tools that the Technician carried, for metal was sacred and few villagers had opportunity to see it at close range; only if wealthy or especially blessed might one possess a small metal article of one's own.

15)

Those things, however, had not been what impressed him most about the Technician, for to his surprise Noren had found that this was a man he could talk to. Even in childhood he had found it difficult to talk to his friends about anything more significant than their day-by-day activities. Certainly he couldn't talk to his family. His father, though intelligent enough, cared for nothing but the price of grain and the problems of getting in the harvest; his brothers were stolid boys who spoke of happenings, but never of ideas. At times he'd felt that his mother had deeper interests than they; still, she was not one to go against women's custom by displaying such interests. She gave him love, yet could communicate with him no better than the others. The Technician was not like any of these people. The Technician spoke to Noren as if the use of one's mind was something very important. They had talked for a long time after supper, and Noren had felt a kind of excitement that he had never before imagined.

But in the morning, when the Technician had gone, the excitement had turned to frustration; and that day he had done a great deal of thinking.

He'd sprawled under a tall outcropping of rock in the corner of the field where he was supposed to be cutting grain, staring at his laboriously-sharpened stone scythe with the thought that a metal one—if such a thing existed —would be vastly more efficient; and gradually, with a mixture of elation and anger, he had become aware that Technicians were not the unique beings people presumed them to be. They were *men!* What they knew, other men could learn. Noren had been convinced, as surely as he'd ever been of anything, that he himself would be fully capable of learning it.

He'd also known that he would not be allowed to.

Someday, he'd decided fiercely, *someday I'll* . . . He had not let himself complete the thought, for inwardly he'd been afraid. Inside he'd already sensed what would happen someday, though he had not recognized his heresy for what it was until the following season.

He'd assumed that there was nobody in the world with whom he could talk as he had with the Technician, but he'd been mistaken. That year he had at last found a real friend: not just a companion, but a friend who had ideas, and spoke of those ideas. Kern had been much older than Noren, and in his final year of school; but once during noon hour, when Noren had asked to borrow a book not available in his own schoolroom, they'd discovered that they had more to say to each other than to their contemporaries. Instinctively Noren had avoided mentioning his opinion about Technicians to anyone else, but Kern he'd told freely and gladly, only to find that Kern was already far beyond him.

He had looked up to Kern as he'd never been able to look up to his father and brothers. Not that Kern had been considered admirable by the villagers, for he'd been a wild boy, a boy who laughed a great deal, belying the true gravity of his thoughts; and he had defied as many conventions as he could get away with. Though he'd spent much of his time with various girls—too much, their families felt—it was to Noren that he had turned with the confidences to which no ordinary person would listen. He'd been recklessly brave and proud of his secret heresies; he had said terrible things, shocking things that Noren had never expected to hear from anyone. He'd said that Scholars were as human as Technicians. He'd said that they were not immortal, but were vulnerable to the same injuries as other people. He had even said that they were not all-wise and were therefore unworthy of the reverence accorded them. But Kern had been careful to whom he expressed such views, at least until one night when he'd forgotten himself to the extent of telling a blasphemous joke within the hearing of a respectable tavernkeeper.

Noren had been in the village that night; he'd seen the marshals arrest Kern, and he'd seen the crowd gather around the jailhouse with blazing torches held aloft. There was to be a heresy trial the next day, but everyone had known that there could be no doubt as to its outcome. Kern himself had known, for once apprehended, he'd abandoned caution and vaunted offenses that even Noren had not suspected; he had gone so far as to boast of having drunk impure water—water neither collected from rain nor sent from the City—a claim few had believed, since had it been true he would most assuredly have been transformed into a babbling idiot. Having dared to laugh at an inviolable provision of the High Law, however, he'd incurred still greater contempt than heretics usually did.

Sick with dread, Noren had stood in the shadows watching the enraged mob. Kern would not cringe at his trial, he'd realized; Kern would laugh, as always, and when the Technicians took him away to the City, he would go with his head high. The terror of such a fate had overwhelmed Noren, but he'd tried very hard to look upon it as an adventure, as Kern surely would. They had often talked about the City, and there had been more to Kern's speculations than idle bravado. One time, in a more serious tone than usual, he had said, "There are mysteries in the City, Noren, but we mustn't fear them. Our minds are as good as the Scholars'. We can't be forced to do or to believe anything against our will. Don't worry about me, because if I'm ever condemned I'm going to find out a lot that I can't learn here."

Kern never did find out. He'd never reached the City; he'd received no chance to explore the mysteries and test himself against the powers he had defied. There had not even been any trial, for the mob was inflamed, the councilmen were not present, and though the High Law decreed that all heretics must be turned over to the Technicians, there were no Technicians present either. Somehow the thatched roof of the jailhouse had caught fire—Noren had known how, as had everyone, but there'd been no particular man who could be accused—and when the Technicians had come, they'd found only the blackened stones.

At first Noren had blamed the Technicians because they hadn't arrived in time to claim the prerogative given them by the High Law; later he'd blamed them for that Law itself. Who was to say that death by fire had not been the most merciful alternative? That thought had haunted Noren. School, which he'd once liked, became dreary, for having abandoned all friends but Kern, he was too absorbed in his bitterness to accept the inanities of his classmates. Besides, his liking for Kern was well known, and he was wary of talking much lest he arouse the suspicion with which, had he been older, he would certainly have been viewed. There had been little left for the school to teach him in any case. He began to seek elsewhere for answers, but soon learned that they could be found only within his own mind. The villagers were ignorant of things that interested him, and the Technicians who came to the farm were unlike the young man who'd once taken lodging there; they would not respond to his questions even when he bridled his resentment, approaching them with deference for the sake of the knowledge he craved. Sometimes it had seemed as if they were deliberately trying to frustrate him.

And then, the next year, his mother had died. She'd fallen ill suddenly while gathering sheaves at the outermost edge of their land, and he had found her lying there, her face contorted with pain, arms cruelly scratched by the wild briars into which she had fallen. The Technicians sent for had declared that she'd been poisoned by some forbidden herb, but Noren had been sure that she, of all people, would never have tasted anything not grown from seed blessed by the Scholars. They'd tried to save her, at least they'd said they were trying, but afterwards he'd never been quite certain. All knowledge was theirs; if they'd truly wanted her to live, surely they could have cured her illness as they did ordinary maladies. Or perhaps it was merely that they had again come too late. If he, Noren, had possessed the syringes they'd brought—if he'd known how to use them—he might have saved her himself; it was not right that such things should be only in the hands of Technicians!

He had said so to their faces, too stricken by grief and rage to care what they did to him. Surprisingly, they had not done anything. They had simply stated that he must not aspire to knowledge beyond his station; and from that moment, his aspirations had increased.

Yet as they'd increased, so had his realization that those aspirations could never find fulfillment. Soon he would have to choose a way to make his living, and there was no work he wanted to do. He despised farming; he was too inept at working with his hands to become a successful craftsman; he had neither the money nor the inclination to go into business as a trader. He had talent only for the use of his mind, and in the village that was more of a liability than an asset. The best he could hope for was that some trader or shopkeeper would hire him to keep accounts, since the few people who worked as schoolmasters, radiophonists and so forth obtained their posts only after appointment to the training center by Technicians. Noren had perceived that he would get no such appointment, for each year the school examiners had treated him more scornfully beneath their outward courtesy. They'd guessed his heretical thoughts, perhaps, though they could not take him into custody unless he was first convicted in a civil trial.

The world had grown steadily darker. Noren had turned still further inward after his mother's death, but because her loss was not his deepest pain, his grief had taken the form of an intensified search for some one good thing to make the future seem worth looking toward. And he had found it, for a time, in Talyra.

They'd known each other since childhood, for she lived on a neighboring farm, but he had not paid much attention to girls. Then all of a sudden he'd noticed her, and within a few weeks he had been in love. Never before had anyone cared for him, needed him, as Talyra did; nor had he ever received such joy from another person's presence. He'd no longer been lonely. He'd no longer considered the life of a farmer an intolerable one. His secret ideas had still been the core of his thought, but they'd been submerged, overshadowed by new and more powerful feelings. Underneath he had known that if forced to choose, he would not forsake those ideas, but he hadn't anticipated any choice. He'd told himself that Talyra would accept them, that he could share them with her as he had with Kern and, by the sharing, keep them from bursting forth to destroy him.

But it wasn't going to be that way. He'd been deluding himself, Noren perceived bitterly; he should have known that no girl, however deeply in love, would marry someone who admitted to being a heretic. Such a thing was unheard of. He had been selfish to ask it of her, for he had exposed her not only to possible peril, but to the scorn of the whole village even if her personal innocence was never placed in doubt. And she was indeed innocent. Why should she take his word against that of the venerated High Priests, the Scholars?

So it had come to a choice after all, and now the futile search would begin again; yet to Noren it would not be the same. He was a man now. He had nothing left to wait for. And he knew that from this night forward he would always be torn, for he still loved Talyra, and truth or no truth, he would never be happy without her.

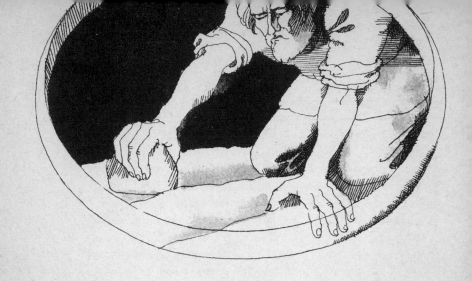

II

WHEN SUNLIGHT GLARED THROUGH THE WINDOW OPENING,
Noren rose and went out to wash his face. The air was
already hot, and the smoke of moss fires mingled with the
ever-present barn smells. Behind the farmhouse, the jagged
yellow ranges of the Tomorrow Mountains were flat against
a hazy sky.

At the cistern, he jerked the spigot handle impatiently
and water splashed onto the dusty earth. Noren paid scant
attention. It was wrong to waste pure water; his father
would be angry, for there would be a reprimand from the
village council if the family took more of what came from
the City than was usual to supplement the rain-catchment
supply, besides the extra trips to the common cistern that
would entail. But after this morning what went on at his
father's farm would no longer concern him.

That was the decision Noren had reached during his
sleepless hours: whatever happened, he could not stay at
home. Though he wouldn't claim a new farm without

Talyra, to continue working for his father was not to be endured. He would have to find some other way to earn his living.

He looked around him, surveying the place that for so many years he had found hateful. It was just like all other farms he'd ever seen, though perhaps larger than most, since his family had bought the adjoining one in his grandfather's time. The undulating grainfields, their ripened stalks orange in the sun, stretched away on three sides, and beyond, to the south, lay rolling wilderness of purple green. Close by, however, was the grayish fodder patch that surrounded the area bordering the road. That area was ugly, for nothing grew in it but a few scrawny purple bushes. It was reserved for buildings. There was the stone farmhouse with its thick thatched roof; the cistern, also of stone, topped by a huge, saucer-shaped catchment basin; and the wattle-and-daub barn where the work-beasts and the sledge were kept, along with the rows of wicker cages that contained fowl.

Noren grimaced. He disliked all farm chores, but in particular he despised the job of taking fertilizer from the fowl cages to the fields: filling the great baskets that hung on either side of a work-beast and then, with the same pottery scoop, sprinkling it between the furrows left by the Technicians' soil-quickening Machines. Worst of all was the digging in, which required crawling on hands and knees, as did cultivating. He'd often thought there should be an easier way to hoe; once, in fact, he had envisioned a long, stiff handle for the stone triangle, and had tried to improvise one. Like similiar experiments of his younger days, it had been a dismal failure. No plant existed with stalks strong enough not to bend under the pressure, even when several were bound together. His mother had remarked that since the purpose of all large plants was to provide wicker for the weaving of baskets, furniture, and the like, nature had done well to make them flexible. His

23)

father, more sharply, had declared that if hoes had been meant to have handles, people would have been taught to make handles at the time of the Founding, just as they had been taught to do everything else. His eldest brother had berated him for fooling around with plant stalks instead of getting on with his share of the work. His other brothers had simply laughed at him.

To Noren it did not seem reasonable that people could have discovered the best way to do everything all at once, whether at some mythical moment called "the Founding" or at any other time; yet he'd been taught in school that this was so, and he had found no evidence to the contrary. People did comparatively few things, after all, and no one had ever heard of their being done differently. Farmers planted, hoed, harvested and threshed; he'd learned from hard experience that the ancestral methods of performing these tasks could not be improved upon. Neither could the equally onerous ones of skinning dead work-beasts, preserving the hides and bones, rendering the tallow, and burying the remains in unquickened ground. Nor was there any imaginable way to make building less laborious: stones must be gathered and joined with mortar; the lightweight, porous softstone used for sledge runners and tables, among other things, must be slowly cut with sharper stone tools; wattles, thatch and wicker were as they were, and one could hardly handle them in a more efficient fashion. The village mill and brewery had existed unchanged since time out of mind, and so had the potter's shop. Even women's work remained the same from generation to generation. He had watched his mother, and later Talyra's, cut trousers, tunics and skirts from City-made cloth with stone knives, stitching the pieces together with needles of polished bone, and he had been sure that there *must* be a quicker way. But he could think of no such way—except one.

Metal! If knives, needles and other tools could be made of metal, that would obviously solve a great many problems. It was *wrong* that there should be no metal for anyone but Technicians!

He had wondered where the metal came from. It certainly did not come from the wilderness; the wilderness contained only dust, sand and stone, covered by mosses and other plants that didn't grow in quickened soil—some gray-green like the fodder patch, some purple-green, but none the bright, clear green of young grain shoots. He knew traders who'd gone far afield to collect the dry moss used for fuel, and they had not seen any metal either. The Book of the Prophecy said that all metal had come into the world during the Founding. Whispered legends suggested that some might be found in rock, but that couldn't be true; Noren had examined every kind of rock there was, and not a speck of it was in the least metallic. The Technicians, he'd concluded, must obtain their metal on the other side of the world.

A very few people did have metal articles: people whose ancestors had been specially favored at the time of the Founding, or who'd bought them from such blessed ones at great cost. Talyra herself owned a narrow silver wristband that had been bequeathed to her by her great-aunt. She, although in every way a pious and deserving person, had borne not a single child, and her husband, desiring a respectable-sized family, had had no choice but to petition the council for divorce. Over the years many had said that a barren woman was unworthy to have custody of anything so holy as a metal wristband, but Talyra had felt more sympathy than scorn for the old lady, so in the end the treasure had come to her. She had shown it to him, and she'd promised to wear it at their wedding, along with the blue glass beads that symbolized devotion to the Mother Star and the City-made red necklace he'd bought for her with the savings of past Founding Day gifts—red, the color of love tokens. . . .

Determinedly Noren wrenched himself back to the present. He must decide where to go. He knew of no open jobs or apprenticeships, but that was just as well, for there was too much restlessness in him to remain nearby; and besides, he could not bear to see Talyra if she was unwilling to marry him.

It was a temptation to leave at once, without seeing anyone, for there was bound to be an argument; yet Noren could not bring himself to do so. There was little love between himself and his father; still the old man had never treated him unkindly. He owed him a farewell. Resignedly, he finished washing, filled the pottery cook-jug, and went in to prepare breakfast.

Since their mother's death, the boys, having no sisters, had taken turns with the kitchen chores. This morning they were Noren's; his five brothers were already in the fields, and would be back soon, ravenously hungry and eager to joke with him about his impending marriage. They were expecting him to bring Talyra home, he knew, for the farm had been too long without a woman and he had not confided his plan to claim new land. It hadn't occurred to them that he would not ask his wife to be a drudge for the whole family, though their own willingness to do so might well account for the fact that the older ones had as yet found no wives for themselves. Talyra's coming would have helped in more ways than one. So they'd have been furious in any case, but he dreaded their derision now that she had turned him down. His being the first pledged to marry had given him a status among them that he, always the different one, had never before attained.

By the time they came in, he had the food ready: porridge, eggs, and large slabs of cold bread to be washed down with tea. Tea was expensive, since the herb from which it was brewed wasn't grown near the village and had to be bought from the traders, but Noren's father was not so poor as to give his sons unflavored water with their meals. Meals were monotonous enough as it was; it had sometimes occurred to Noren that it would be nice if there were some source of food besides grain and fowl.

From long habit the boys stood motionless behind their benches and raised their eyes upward while the words of the Prophecy were said: " *'Let us rejoice in the bounty of the land, for the land is good, and from the Mother Star came the heritage that has blessed it; the land has given us life. . . . And it shall remain fruitful, and the people shall multiply across the face of the earth, and at no time shall the spirit of the Mother Star die in the hearts of men.'* " Noren repeated them mechanically with the others. They meant nothing to him, yet in a way they recalled the presence of his mother, who had said them with warmth. He found himself thinking of the ceremony held for the sending of her body to the City, when he'd cried not because he was moved by the presiding Technician's intonation of the ritual phrases, but because she had believed them; it had seemed horrible for her to die believing something that wasn't grounded in truth.

The blessing complete, everybody sat down and turned noisily to eating. Noren had little appetite, but he knew he must take advantage of the meal, for it might be a long time before he could get another so plentiful. He had no money of his own. If he'd claimed land, he would have been paid in advance by the Technicians to cultivate it, in return for his promise to sell them most of the first year's harvest. Now, he realized, he would have to earn his keep day by day until he could find some sort of steady employment.

"Have you set the day for your wedding, son?" asked his father.

"No," replied Noren shortly, "I haven't." Everyone's eyes were on him, and he knew that there was nothing to be gained by delaying the inevitable. "There's not going to be a wedding," he continued resolutely.

"Oh, so you've lost your nerve?" remarked his oldest

brother, and there were good-natured guffaws. No one had taken the declaration seriously. Every man, after all, had occasional fights with his girl; but a betrothal registered with the village council was seldom broken.

"Perhaps he hasn't lost his nerve," suggested another brother. "Perhaps Talyra lost hers; maybe she decided she could do better for herself than to marry a lazy dreamer who sits and thinks when he might be working."

Noren clenched his fists beneath the table and did not answer. He was well practiced in controlling his feelings; he had learned from Kern's recklessness that one must not reveal one's inner rage at things, at least not if one expected to accomplish anything of value. So many more vital issues angered him that he was used to hiding fury, and taunts from his brothers were nothing new.

There was an awkward silence. "I'm leaving today," Noren announced abruptly. "I'll be seeking work in another village, I think."

"Work? You?" sneered one of them. "Who will hire a boy who has neither stamina nor skill?"

There was no use in pointing out that if he hadn't applied stamina to farm work, it was not from any lack but because he had never chosen to. "I can keep accounts," said Noren in a level voice. "Or—or perhaps I'll hire on with some trader who's delivering a load to the markets outside the City." This last was pure improvisation, but as he spoke he wondered why he had not thought of it before.

His father stared at him. "You can't do that. You're needed here. The harvest is just starting."

"I'm of age, Father. I finished school yesterday and that makes me a free citizen." As free as anybody could be in a world where one was barred from all that was reserved for Technicians and Scholars, he added inwardly.

"Two of your brothers came of age and stayed."

"They chose to work for wages on the farm, which was

their right. It's mine to leave it."

"Let him go, Father," the oldest brother said. "He never pulled his weight in any case; he wouldn't be worth a man's wage."

"He's my son, and however addlebrained he may be at times, I'll not have him ruin his life. The only sign of responsibility he's ever shown is his betrothal to Talyra; I'll not see him break it."

"There's little either of us can do about that," Noren admitted bitterly. "It's already been broken, and not by me." He did not say that his own honesty had precipitated the break.

"She changed her mind?" demanded his brother. "I must say, I'm less surprised than when she accepted you in the first place, though I'm disappointed."

"I don't wonder," retorted Noren, "since I won't be bringing you the housemaid you expected. But let me tell you that if I'd gotten married, I'd have taken my wife to a place of our own. Nothing's changed as far as you're concerned."

"*You* cultivate your own land, you who've spent most of your life with your head in the clouds?" the eldest burst out. "You're unfit for any work, least of all that. Talyra's well out of it."

"No doubt we're all well out of it," added the next-eldest. "I've doubted all along that she was the sort we should bring into the family. No girl could think this brother of ours a good provider, so it's clear she chose him for love, and she can find plenty of that without doing a farmwife's work. Once she tired of him, she'd have left to seek it elsewhere."

Noren's rigid control gave way; before he knew it he was out of his seat and his fist was swinging into his brother's face. All the pent-up rage of the past years went into the blow, and the older boy had no time to be surprised. As he slumped to the floor, the others grabbed

Noren's arms. They would not have interfered with a fight, but the blind fury in his eyes told them that he was scarcely aware that his opponent was already unconscious.

"1----I'm sorry, son," his father said helplessly. "That was ill-said; Talyra is a fine girl and would have borne you many fine children. I would have been proud to have her here." The other boys stood back, staring at Noren, realizing that they did not really know this brother who had always seemed such a weakling to them.

Noren hardly knew himself. He was numb, dazed; yet he was also free in a way he had not been before. His anger vented, he was sorry for all of them, sorry because they truly did not understand the thing they were lacking. They could not see that there was more to life than working, eating, and making love. "I'll go now," he said dully.

"I won't hold you, if that's what you want; but this will always be your home."

"You couldn't hold me. I don't need your consent, and as for a home, I don't have one. I never will." He turned and walked through the door, not looking back at them, not even stopping to think that he was taking none of his few belongings. He knew that what he had said was true; wherever he went he would be a stranger, for there was no home in the world for such as he.

He took the road toward the village center, not because he wanted to go there, but because it was the only road there was. To travel cross-country was dangerous, for the wilderness was full of forbidden things. Wild plants held peril: as he'd grown older, Noren had learned that the herb that had killed his mother had not been tasted, but had been a contact poison that attacked her through the scratches on her arms. Ordinarily Technicians with Machines destroyed any such herbs that could be reached from roads or fields, but that rare one had evidently been missed.

The farm was some distance from the village, more than an hour's walk, and the road was one of many spokes radiating out from that center. Whenever anybody started a new farm, the Technicians brought their Machines to extend some spoke road a little farther; his own land, if he'd claimed it, would have been several hours out, bordering the wilderness on two sides instead of one. There were also continuous roads that connected the various villages; a large map of them had hung between the schoolroom windows. Farmland on one of these connecting roads was not open to claim; it was already cleared and very expensive, particularly if it lay on a main radial, which was a direct route to the City.

Noren had spoken of traveling to the City on impulse, but once the words were out, he'd known that was what he would try. Traders did go there—not inside, of course, but to the great markets outside the walls—and one of them might well hire a man to drive a string of work-beasts or an extra sledge. Work-beasts were exasperating creatures, so slow and stupid that it was odd the Scholars were credited with having created them; one would think people would expect guardians of all wisdom to have done a better job of it. But he could put up with a driver's work if the City was his destination.

The City was beautiful; there had been a painting of it in the schoolroom next to the map. It had high lustrous walls, a ring of scallops, within which stood towers that were much, much higher, so high that the Technicians who lived in them must fly from top to bottom; and those towers had windows: not mere openings like ordinary windows, but sheets of what almost appeared to be glass. The towers of the City were made not of stone or even of metal, but of some sparkling silvery substance that Noren judged to be akin to the surface of the aircar he had once touched. He had always wanted to see them for himself, and there was no reason why he should not

31)

make such a journey.

A thrill spread through him, rousing him from the dazed state in which he had left the farm. The City! The City had more than beauty; it was where knowledge was. The Prophecy even said so: *Knowledge shall be kept within the City; it shall be held in trust until the day when the Mother Star becomes visible to us.* And that, at least the first half of it, was very likely one of the few statements in the whole thing that was accurate. The Scholars were keeping their knowledge safe within the City, all right, and though looking at the place from the outside wasn't going to get him any of that knowledge, there was a certain excitement in the idea of being so close.

But to reach the City, he must be hired by a trader, for it was a journey of many days, and were he to set out alone, he would starve along the way if he failed to find work at the farms he passed. He must therefore wait in the village until a trader came through who would take him on. Since it might be a long wait, he would have to have a means of paying for food, water and lodging while he was there. If he was lucky, the innkeeper, whose kitchen-maid was expecting a child soon, might have a place for him; he knew old Arnil for a kindly man, unlike the keeper of the brewery's tavern who'd denounced Kern.

Noren straightened and began to walk faster. As he did so, he was struck by the thought that he might never again pass over this road. Having walked it three days a week to school, except during the long season of harvest and replanting, he seldom noticed its landmarks; but if he was having his last view of them, he ought to. There were none he expected to miss, yet there was a pleasantness in the panorama of purple-clad knolls seen from the rise just before the softstone quarry. Then too, the pond where the work-beasts were watered, with its dense edging of rushes, held memories from his early childhood. Purple knolls; rush-lined ponds, springs, streams; spongy mossland; gray-green fodder plants and wicker plants and others with webbed stems; white rock, yellowish rock . . . on and on forever. . . . Was the whole world like this? In school he'd learned that the world was round and that it was all wilderness except for the circle of villages and farms spreading outward from the City; but did one piece of wilderness look like another?

The Technicians knew, he thought with rancor. The Technicians looked down on it from the air. No doubt they had already traveled beyond the Tomorrow Mountains, where the Prophecy claimed that more Cities would someday arise. The Scholars almost certainly had, for although it was rumored that they never left the City, it was ridiculous to suppose that they, who could do as they pleased in all respects, would not take advantage of the opportunity.

At the Gates of the City, Noren reflected, he might see Scholars. Robed in brilliant blue, they would appear as High Priests, not merely to conduct devotions as their representatives the Technicians did, but to receive the homage of the people. And the people would give it with gladness! On holidays like Founding Day, the periodic Blessing of the Seed, and the Day of the Prophecy—which celebrated the Mother Star's appearance in advance—hundreds walked to the City just to participate; and in the presence of Scholars those people knelt. Noren knew he could not look upon a Scholar without hating him.

And perhaps he might see more than just Scholars. Perhaps, he recalled in dismay, he'd witness some other heretic's recantation. . . .

Resolutely he set the thought aside. Ahead, over the next rise, he glimpsed the thatched roof of Talyra's house. A sudden, foolish hope came to him: might not Talyra have had second thoughts? Mightn't she too have spent a sleepless night, deciding in the end to marry him in spite of his heresy? Much as he feared the answer, he could not leave without finding out. When it came right down to it, Noren realized, he could not leave without seeing her once more.

He crossed the farmyard and stood by the familiar door. At his call, Talyra's mother drew back the matting. "Oh, Noren," she said, obviously flustered, "Talyra can't come out. She—she isn't feeling well today."

"She's not ill!" he exclaimed, panic-stricken.

"No—no, not really. Only she won't see anybody."

Noren dropped his eyes dejectedly. "Look," he persisted, "I'm on my way to the City. I don't know when I'll be back. I've *got* to see her."

The woman frowned. "Well," she said slowly, "I'll do what I can."

He sat at the scrubbed softstone table drinking the tea she gave him, hearing the low murmur of women's voices and, to his anguish, occasional muffled sobs. In the corner of the room was the wicker couch, its frame stuffed with moss and covered with softened hides, where he and Talyra had sat not many weeks ago to plan their marriage; now red fabric lay there, her unfinished wedding dress. Skirts of red, the color of love, were worn only by brides.

Finally Talyra's mother returned. "I'm sorry, Noren," she reported unhappily. "Though she's refused to tell me why, she says that—that you must not come back for her sake."

Mumbling something, he got up and strode to the door. "The spirit of the Mother Star go with you, Noren," Talyra's mother added with feeling.

The words, though customary, were an unfortunate choice. Once again Noren departed without a backward look, torn between distaste for the naive sincerity with which they'd been spoken and an irrational sense of hurt because his own father, in pronouncing him free to go, had not thought to say them.

(34

The village center was a cluster of unadorned stone buildings, facing upon a sanded street graced by neither shrubs nor moss. It was a gray place, enlivened by color only on festival days when people wore brilliant clothes instead of their ordinary brown ones: green for holidays, yellow and orange for parties, red-trimmed white for weddings and births. Blue clothing, of course, was never worn; blue was reserved for the Scholars. On this particular day there was no festival, and the village, deserted by everyone who had harvesting to begin, looked empty as well as drab.

Noren reached it just ahead of the scheduled rain. The first four mornings of each week, except during the final week of harvest season, it rained for exactly one hour, stopping at noon. In school he'd been taught that the Scholars arranged this; but lately he had wondered, for if there were no rain, would not all wild plants have perished before there were any Scholars? Whatever the facts, rain did not bother him; it was a pleasant contrast to the parching air. He walked down the street as the first drops spattered the sand, entering the inn less for cover than to talk to Arnil, the innkeeper.

"A trader?" Arnil said when Noren explained his purpose. "That's too bad, Noren. There was one here only last night looking for an extra driver. He planned to ask again in Prosperity."

Noren cursed inwardly; the village was not on the main route and there might not be another for days. "Could I catch up, do you think?" he inquired.

"Perhaps," Arnil told him. "He got a late start this morning and his two sledges were hitched together; besides, the road's past due for sanding."

"I'll try, I guess," Noren said. Work-beasts did not walk much faster than men, certainly not when hitched as a team—which they stubbornly resisted—and pulling laden sledges over a road that hadn't enough sand to make the runners slide smoothly. If he pushed himself, he could reach the next village, Prosperity, before the trader had time to find anyone there.

"If you miss him, come back," said Arnil. "You can work in the kitchen until my regular girl's child arrives; I can't afford to pay you, but I'll give you bed and board."

"Thanks," Noren said, "but I hope I won't have to."

He went on through the center, passing a row of craftsmen's shops: the potter's, the wickermonger's, the shoemaker's and the stonecutter's. Beyond was the shop that sold common City goods—fabric, thread, paper, matches; the powder one used to keep cistern water clear; utensils of glass and of the opaque material that resembled polished bone—as well as rarer products like colored glass necklaces and books. Books . . . Noren could never go by that shop without wishing that he had the money for just one book of his own. Maybe he'd been foolish not to have worked on the farm for wages at least until the harvest was finished; that should have given him plenty, though books, aside from the Book of the Prophecy, were even higher priced than the love-beads he'd bought Talyra. It was because so few people cared about them, the shopkeeper had told him. Books were heavy, and when there wasn't much demand, a trader wouldn't bring them all the way from the City unless he could be sure that they'd sell for enough to make the trouble worthwhile. Most families did little reading; they sent their children to school only because it was considered a religious duty. Why was it? Noren wondered suddenly. Why did the High Law *encourage* learning, and then withhold knowledge from people who did care? No book, at any price, would tell the things *he* wanted to know.

Chagrined, he turned away from the shop and headed quickly for the outbound road. He'd been daydreaming again; there was, he realized, some truth to his brothers' accusations. On the farm it might not matter, but if he

(36

wanted to catch up with that trader he must hurry!

He did not catch up. Some three hours later, thoroughly exhausted from a grueling trip during which he'd alternately walked and jogged without pausing, he arrived in Prosperity only to find that the trader had just left, having hired a driver without difficulty. Harvest season was already over in Prosperity; the main radial on which that village was located happened to be a seasonal boundary line. Long ago, Noren had heard, all villages had planted grain at the same time, but there were now so many that the Technicians could not take soil-quickening Machines everywhere at once, and the crop cycle was therefore staggered. Though he'd known that in theory, it was startling to find that in Prosperity it was Seed-Offering Day.

The village was jammed with people. Leaving the inn where he'd inquired for the trader, Noren walked toward the center, which in Prosperity took the form of a square. Nearly everyone in sight wore festive green. A woman with a basket approached him, smiling. "Will you have a Festival Bun, neighbor?" she asked. Noren accepted gratefully; he'd eaten nothing since breakfast, and Festival Buns, baked in fancy shapes and decorated with seeds, were always free.

In the square an aircar rested while a procession of farmers passed by, depositing clearly-labeled seed bags before the presiding Technicians. That seed would be taken to the City, where it would be blessed in an impressive ritual before the Gates and then returned; the Scholars would not keep any. The portion of the harvest charged for soil-quickening, along with whatever extra the Technicians had bought, was always claimed immediately after threshing, for in the City there were gristmills run by Power. Seed-Offering was different. The High Law declared that all seed must be offered for blessing, since unblessed seed would not sprout into healthy grain.

Noren scowled. The Scholars had power over even that,

he thought—even food, the one thing villagers could produce better than City-dwellers! To be sure, it could not be produced without the Machines that quickened the land . . . but did it really matter whether the seed was blessed or not?

Amid the light green of the crowd's clothing and the darker green of the Technicians' uniforms, flashes of color caught his eye. A group clad in red-trimmed white was approaching the aircar; it was led by a girl and boy, and from the girl's solid red skirt and headscarf he knew they were bride and groom. They, too, sought to be blessed. That, the High Law did not demand; weddings were performed by village councilmen, not Technicians; yet people always wanted a Technician's blessing on a marriage. Talyra would have wanted it, too! It would never have worked out, Noren thought in misery. He could never have brought himself to follow such a tradition.

The couple, surrounded by family and friends, stepped back, obviously happy with whatever the Technicians had said. Then, slowly, the aircar lifted; and as it rose, the crowd began to sing. Noren did not join in, though he knew the words well enough:

> "For blessing, now, we offer joyfully
> The seed of our abundant harvesttide
> To those who guard the heritage of the Star,
> That in our hearts its spirit may abide."

He turned disconsolately away from the square, wondering what to do. The people would celebrate all evening; soon the flutes would start playing, and everyone would dance. Noren did not feel like dancing. Besides, there'd be no work available here, and he had too much pride to beg a night's lodging for which he could not pay. There was nothing to do but return to Arnil's.

Back on the road, he walked blindly, not noticing his surroundings until he came to the stone arch that bridged a stream. The heat of the day was still at its peak; he was terribly thirsty, especially after the dry Festival Bun, and the water below the bridge looked cool and fresh. Not for the first time, he wondered why it should be wrong to drink such water.

And then, suddenly skeptical, he stopped. A new and daring thought came to him: *was* it wrong? Could Kern's fantastic boast have been true after all?

People did not drink from streams. Animals did; the work-beasts were often watered in them. But people, like the caged fowl whose eggs and flesh were eaten, were not allowed to touch impure water. From earliest childhood Noren had been told that any person whose lips it passed would be turned into an idiot like the savages of the mountains. The most sacred precepts of the High Law decreed that one must not drink. But why? It wasn't reasonable to think that drinking what animals drank could turn a man into an idiot! That the Scholars fostered such a belief to keep people dependent on supplementing rainfall with water from the City was far more likely, for as long as no one could live without that water, their power was assured.

He stared at the stream, excitement rising in his throat. Did he believe in his own ideas or didn't he? Logic told him that to taste it would be harmless. To be sure, the world abounded in poisons, but if poisons were in the water, there would be no need for a taboo against it; illness and death would be threat enough. Furthermore, escaped fowl never died of poisoning; they were slaughtered and the meat was destroyed, as the High Law commanded. Noren scanned the deserted road. The thought of becoming an idiot was more repugnant to him than any physical danger, yet what good was a mind he dared not trust? If he, a grown man, let himself be ruled by nursery tales, his convictions were not worth the sacrifice he had made for them.

Leaving the bridge, Noren flung himself flat on the mossy earth beside the stream and, defiantly, drank long and deep. The water tasted pure; it tasted better than cistern water ever had. Rising, he wiped his face with the back of his hand and looked up at the sky. He had not become an idiot. He was himself, and if anything, he felt stronger and wiser than before.

Perhaps he was not so helpless as he'd supposed against the formidable power of the Scholars. Perhaps, if he lived his beliefs instead of merely holding to them, he could really find a way to make people see.

III

THOUGH THE SUN HAD GONE DOWN WHEN NOREN RETURNED
to his own village, it was yet early and the inn's tavern was
not crowded. He sat at an empty table to eat the meal Arnil
gave him, thinking only of how tired he was. He'd had no
sleep for two days, and so much had happened . . . the
dance; the ordeal of telling Talyra his secret, followed by
their quarrel and the disruption of all his hopes; his long-
awaited departure from home; the grueling, futile trip in
the midday heat; the various disappointments and frustra-
tions of the past hours . . . and the triumphs. There had
indeed been triumphs: he'd at last proven himself not only
against his brother, but against the High Law itself! He had
drunk the forbidden water and was unharmed! Surely, in
due course, he would get to the City. . . .

His head drooped wearily; and since his back was to
the door, he did not see the Technicians until their dark
green uniforms loomed in front of him. There were two of
them: the middle-aged one who'd appeared at the dance,

and another who seemed very little older than Noren. "My greetings, citizen," said the first. "May we sit down with you?"

"I am pleased by your concern, sir," replied Noren. He was not pleased, but that was how one responded to the greeting of a Technician.

Arnil hurried over to serve the Technicians food and ale, and at their sign, placed a mug of ale before Noren also. "To the Scholars," said the young man, raising his.

Noren drank; it would have been unthinkable not to, though aside from his dislike of the toast he was unused to ale, having had neither the money nor the friends to spend much time in taverns. He found that it lessened his weariness. He looked across at the Technicians, irritated by the contrast between their situation and his own. It was unfair! Why should they have the right to know more than he did simply by virtue of their birth?

Wiping his brow, the young Technician declared, "Had I known the evenings were as hot as noon, I'd have been reluctant to stay the night."

Surely, thought Noren, these men could not think him so stupid as to suppose they'd chosen to sit at a villager's table merely to discuss the weather. "Is it less hot in the City, sir?" he asked.

"Since the Outer City is roofed over, its air is filtered," answered the other, "and it is therefore cool. My young companion has not lodged in a village before."

Noren had not been aware that the privileges of Technicians extended not only to education and the use of metal tools and Machines, but to unique physical comforts; his resentment grew. "You must excuse my ignorance," he said with ill-concealed irony.

The younger man smiled disarmingly. "Tell me, Noren, have you ever wished to learn more than you were taught in school?"

"More about what, sir?" The man's knowledge of his

name was proof that they'd sought him out with a purpose; no doubt they'd seen him enter the inn.

"About—well, about the Prophecy, for instance. Where it came from, how it is that we have a Prophecy."

"I've wondered, yes."

"And developed your own answers, perhaps?"

Noren hesitated. One was not supposed to develop one's own answers. These Technicians could well be trying to trap him into an admission of heresy, and here, in a public tavern, such an admission would be fatal. He was exhausted, both physically and emotionally, and it was hard to think clearly; yet he knew he must be very careful. "There's much in the Book of the Prophecy that needs to be explained," he said levelly. "To an ignorant person like myself, much of it seems to have more than one interpretation."

"Yet it's hardly your job to interpret it," the older Technician said. "What are you going to do now that you've got to choose your work? Does farming satisfy you?"

"No, sir, it doesn't," Noren replied frankly. "I haven't decided exactly what I'll do." Inwardly he was in turmoil. He'd felt for some time that most Technicians suspected him and were watching him, but why should they want to provoke him into revealing his thoughts? Logically, they should try to prevent any unorthodox opinions from being heard. Was it possible that he was a threat to them? Could this mean that there was some way in which he could expose the Scholars' deceit?

If so, then he must at all costs stay free to do it; still he must at the same time take a calculated risk. He must play along with them, let them think they were succeeding, in the hope of finding a clue to what they feared.

"It must be hard to come to the end of your schooling when there's still a great deal you'd like to know," remarked the younger Technician with apparent sympathy. "I would find it intolerable myself."

Noren almost choked on a swallow of ale. The implied

acknowledgment of equality astonished him; he had not thought they'd make such a statement publicly, whatever their reasons. Then, looking around, he saw that only two of the other tables were occupied, and that the men there were paying no attention to any talk but their own. Arnil was in the kitchen. For the moment, at least, they could not be overheard.

"It's indeed hard," he confessed. "I would give much for further learning."

"Villagers do learn more at the training center outside the City, where men and women are prepared to become radiophonists, schoolteachers, nurses, and the like. It is a virtue to so dedicate oneself."

"Are you offering to send me there?" Noren demanded. That was the proposal that had been made to Talyra; he had not expected it for himself, but crumb though it was, he would not reject such a chance.

"No," the Technician said. "Those to whom offers are made are chosen by the Scholars; we are merely envoys."

"How do the Scholars choose?"

"By school records, I suppose. They have everyone's school records, you know."

He hadn't known, but it was not surprising. There must be more to the choice than that, however, for he had led his class in school. Perhaps the Technicians actually weren't informed. "Don't the Scholars tell you?" he inquired casually.

"They tell us very little," the young man said. "We are trained in our work; that is all. Someone who does well can receive extra training if he wishes, but he is not taught the reasons for things."

The words sounded a bit rueful, and Noren was nonplused; he had not stopped to think that the Technicians themselves might long for more knowledge. Machines were obviously complicated and would require much wisdom to build. "Is it not necessary to know reasons in order to make

(44

the Machines function?" he asked.

"No, not at all. If a Machine is damaged, a specialist must repair it, and few of us do work of that kind."

Startled, Noren perceived that the men who operated the Machines might know very little about how they were made, though he had never before had cause to suspect such a distinction. "Do you choose the kind of work you want to learn?" he persisted.

"Yes, if it's available; we're as free as you are in that respect."

That seemed an odd way to put it. Maybe, Noren reflected, he'd been mistaken about these men's motive for sitting down with him; they were less patronizing than most, and it was possible that they were simply making conversation. Glancing over his shoulder, he saw that the room was still nearly deserted. He paused, wondering how best to make use of this opportunity, while the older of the two men refilled the mugs with ale.

"I myself would like to know reasons as well as skills," the younger man continued. "I can't see what harm there'd be in it."

Noren stared at him. Somehow it had not occurred to him that he might find allies among the Technicians. He'd lumped them together with the Scholars, assuming them to be equally calculating in their support of the High Law; but that was not really very reasonable. If they were men, they had opinions and feelings like other men, and they too must resent being deprived of the whole truth! For he saw that apart from the specific jobs they performed, they did not know nearly as much as he'd supposed. They were only tools. They probably took the Prophecy as seriously as did the villagers.

He must find out! Alone he was powerless; even if he should succeed in convincing a handful of other people, they could do nothing against the Scholars. But if *Technicians* could be won over . . .

45)

"You were asking me about the Prophecy," he said. "I've been told, of course, that it came to us from the Mother Star; but that's confusing. The Mother Star is not yet even visible. So how did it determine the words written in a book?"

"That is a mystery," said the other Technician. "We are not intended to understand such things as that."

He had said "we", Noren noted. And the more he thought about it, the more evident it was that the Scholars would not have confided in the Technicians. There were too many of them; if they suspected any fraud, they would no longer take orders. Technicians, being outside village law, were subject to the direct authority of the Scholars, whose power depended on their obedience.

"I suppose the Scholars understand."

"The Scholars understand everything," agreed the man.

"No doubt. Yet are they really more capable of understanding than wise men like yourselves? You, sir—" Noren turned to the sympathetic younger Technician with the tone of deference that he'd long ago learned to feign. "You have so much more knowledge than I do; I can't believe that there's anything you could not grasp if it were explained to you. Have you never wished that these mysteries were not hidden?"

"I have, sometimes," the youth admitted. "At times I'm weary of spending my days in the villages checking radiophone equipment; in fact I've requested Inner City work, which would give me opportunity to see the Scholars and perhaps learn from them. But that, for us, is an honor demanding self-dedication, as is the training center for you, and so far my request has been denied."

Noren was by this time wholly absorbed by the new and promising discovery he'd made; he had forgotten to watch over his shoulder. "Perhaps the Scholars fear you might learn too much," he suggested.

"Too much?"

"Maybe there are things you could indeed understand, but would make you less content to follow their orders. Would you be here in this inn tonight if you did not believe in the superior wisdom of Scholars?"

After a slight pause, the man dropped his eyes. "I—I never thought of it that way," he said, almost with chagrin. "No, I don't suppose I would."

"Nor would I," declared Noren. "If wisdom and Power and Machines were shared equally among all, as the Prophecy tells us will someday happen, we would both be freer and happier. Why should there be any delay?"

Abruptly, the Technician stood up. His expression had changed; he seemed stricken by a guilt he had not felt at first. "I spoke in haste," he said with evident distress. "We must discuss these matters with caution; the Prophecy covers them, and the Scholars are our betters—"

Noren too got to his feet, swaying unsteadily. He was in no condition to be cautious; his head was spinning with excitement, with prolonged fatigue, and perhaps with too much ale. "But Scholars are not our betters!" he exclaimed, unaware of how his voice had risen. "They're no better than you are, nor than the rest of us, either! Don't you see, the Prophecy's only an excuse; they made it up so that we wouldn't object to having them keep things from us."

There was dead silence. The young Technician looked positively ill, and following his anguished gaze, Noren turned to meet the scandalized stares of nearly a dozen men: those at the other tables, old Arnil the innkeeper, and in the open doorway, a newly-arrived group that included his own two elder brothers.

Noren's head swam dizzily. The room whirled, and for a moment he was sure he would collapse. It did not seem as if this could really have happened. How could he have been so rash as to say words that would condemn him?

Grimly, he reminded himself that he had always known

47)

it must happen someday. "Someday", however, was vague, and one's fears of it could be pushed aside . . . whereas this was *now*. The damage was irrevocable; he would be tried tomorrow, and the next day he would reach the City without the effort of driving a trader's sledge.

The Technicians moved quietly into the background, for it was not their business to arrest heretics; under the High Law they could neither accuse nor give evidence. They would take charge of him only after his conviction. For the present he stood alone, facing the villagers' enmity.

"I knew the boy was worthless," announced one of his brothers coldly, "but I hadn't thought him guilty of heresy. It's a good thing he no longer lives under our roof."

The public disavowal did not surprise Noren; few families would stand behind a self-proclaimed heretic, and certainly not his. The morning's fight with this brother had nothing to do with it. He knew, however, that they were all too pleased by his downfall.

The dread word *heresy*, once uttered, spread through the group like fire out of control. There hadn't been a heresy trial in the village for some time; and the last case had been an old woman, falsely accused of disobeying the High Law by making cook-pots of unpurified clay, who had actually been acquitted. There was no possibility of acquittal when the charge was brought by many witnesses. "I'll fetch the marshals," cried one of his brothers' friends excitedly.

Several men advanced toward Noren, and one of them spat contemptuously. "So the Scholars are not your betters," he growled. "You'll learn differently, boy, when they get you inside that City of theirs."

"Why wait for that," said someone in an ugly tone, "when he can begin his recanting here and now?"

His brothers and their companions moved closer, their intent obvious, and despite himself Noren stepped backward against the table, leaning against it for support. Ar-

(48

nil came to his side. "There'll be none of that here in my inn," he declared vehemently. "The boy's dazed by ale; he doesn't realize what he's said. I'm sure he's no true heretic."

Raising his eyes, Noren admitted, "I do know what I've said, Arnil. Everyone heard; you can't save me now, and you'll only cause trouble for yourself by trying."

"But Noren," protested Arnil, "you couldn't have meant it the way it sounded. Not about the Prophecy—"

Arnil, Noren knew, was a devout man who would never believe anything contrary to the Book of the Prophecy and would be deeply shocked by the idea that anyone else might; yet neither would he enjoy seeing a person hurt for it. "I'm sorry I got you involved," Noren said sincerely, "but I did mean it, and it wasn't the ale; it's something I've thought for a long time."

"What am I going to do when they call me to testify?" Arnil mumbled in anguish.

"You must tell the truth," said Noren resolutely. "I shall."

"You will indeed," agreed his eldest brother, "after we're through with you; you'll be begging for mercy before you ever see any Scholars."

Sick fear enveloped Noren; he was fair game now, and he knew that his brothers would take their revenge for the surprise punch. They were restrained not so much by Arnil's protests as by the presence of the Technicians, but they would have their chance later, for they were well acquainted with one of the jailers.

A crowd was already gathering outside the inn; Noren could see it when the door matting swung aside to admit the marshals. The night of Kern's death loomed vividly in his memory. He realized that he would not be murdered as Kern had been—he had neither a bad reputation nor any real enemies, and besides, while Technicians were lodged in the village not even the angriest mob would dare —but all the same, his heart contracted when he glimpsed the flame of a torch.

The marshals bound his arms with ropes and led him out into the torrid dusk. The jailhouse was some distance up the street, and the people followed them toward it, shouting. Most of the people had not heard what he'd said at the inn, and the story had grown rapidly; the present version of what he'd called the Scholars, of which he caught snatches, was not merely blasphemous, but ribald. All of a sudden Noren knew why these men could never forgive him. He had expressed what they dared not say! In misquoting him, they were echoing their own real inclinations; but they could not admit that even to themselves. Those noisiest in their denunciation were the ones most afraid of their own underlying feelings. To be sure, many villagers had no such feelings, but the people who didn't—people like Talyra, like Arnil—were not in the street.

Noren tried to keep his head up, he tried to bear the contempt unflinchingly for the sake of the truth that meant more to him than anything else, but he was unable to maintain much dignity. His exhaustion; his rage both at the world and at himself for having been caught without achieving anything; his irrepressible fear—together, they proved more than he could handle. Perhaps the ale did have something to do with it, but in any event, he stumbled and fell; and the marshals half-dragged him the rest of the way.

The jailhouse was fairly new, all but the stone walls having been rebuilt after the burning of its predecessor, but it was filthy, for it was seldom used and even less often cleaned. There was little lawbreaking in the village, and anyone convicted of a serious crime other than heresy was hanged without delay; so apart from men awaiting trial, the jail had few occupants. Marshals and jailers worked as such only when needed. On this particular evening they'd been called to the inn from the rival tavern run by the brewer, to which they were anxious to return.

Noren was thrown into the inner room, his legs tied as well as his arms, and the heavier-than-average door matting was lashed securely in place. The cell had no furnishings; he sprawled on a floor of rough stone. There were no windows, and the air, of course, was stifling. For a while he was too overcome to think rationally, yet despite his fatigue he could not sleep; the thought of what awaited him in the City would not let him. The hours passed slowly, till he judged it must be past midnight.

Eventually, as he lay there, Kern's words came back to him: *Don't worry about me, because if I'm ever condemned I'm going to find out a lot that I can't learn here.* To Kern it would have been an adventure. He too must think of it that way, Noren knew. Yet Kern, for all his bravery, had not felt the same sense of failure he did. He had not felt the compelling need to accomplish things, to *change* things, that had been growing in Noren of late. He'd been defiant, but he had not considered truth a trust that must be passed on. . . .

Hearing heavy, menacing footsteps, followed by the un- lashing of the door, Noren struggled to sit up. His brothers stood over him, flanked by the jailer who was their friend and another who'd relieved the one originally left on duty. They had spent the evening in the brewery's tavern and all of them had had more than enough ale. Noren was well aware of what was going to happen. His arms and legs were still bound tightly, and they would not be unbound. He was defenseless, for the Technicians were by this time asleep in the inn and though the High Law required that he be turned over to them unharmed, they would not in- tervene in a village affair unless he was in danger of serious injury. Perhaps if he yelled loud enough someone would come, since on the whole the people of the village were decent folk; but his pride was too great for that.

"Are you going to retract what you said?" his eldest brother taunted.

"No," said Noren. There was nothing else he could say. He bit down hard on his lip and took the beating with scarcely a sound, until at last, mercifully, the world went dark around him and he knew no more before morning.

When he awoke it was approaching midday; he could tell because before he'd mustered the courage to move, the sound of rain began. The trial, by long established custom, would be held an hour past noon, so he had two hours in which to prepare himself.

Painfully, Noren pulled himself to a sitting position. He was badly bruised, but as far as he could determine there were no bones broken. It could have been much worse; his strength had been so nearly gone at the outset, he judged, that he'd lost consciousness sooner than his assailants had expected.

The brutally-tight ropes with which he'd been bound had been loosened slightly, no doubt so that he would present a better appearance at the trial; the jailers must have grown fearful of the Technicians' censure. Noren flexed his fingers and found that they worked normally. While doing so he was abruptly overcome by nausea and, crawling to the clay pot in the corner, was violently, wretchedly ill. After that he lay down again, tormented by thirst and unsure as to whether his fortitude would be equal to the challenges ahead.

The outcome of the trial, of course, was a foregone conclusion. He had not asked for an advocate to defend him, as would have been necessary had he been falsely accused. The coming judgment was a mere formality, for he was, according to village law, manifestly guilty, and he had no intention of denying it. An advocate's defense would not help. There was only one defense: the truth. He had no illusions; he knew that no such defense could save him; but truth—Truth, in the special sense in which he had always thought of it—was in itself worth proclaiming. If he came

(52

out with it boldly, perhaps his words might influence someone, and that way his life would not be entirely wasted.

He had resigned himself to dying, though he knew no actual death sentence would be pronounced. The sentencing of heretics, unlike that of people convicted of other crimes, was not within the jurisdiction of the village council; it lay with the Scholars, and the Scholars were thought to be merciful. That was why the accused was sometimes murdered without benefit of trial, for never within memory had any heretic been sentenced to die. The passing of sentence, however, was part of the ceremony of public recantation —and Noren did not intend to recant.

Nobody had been told what happened to heretics who refused to recant—there were not many such, and in fact it was doubtful whether one could be mentioned by name— but it was commonly assumed that they must be killed. That, after all, was the only fate worse than the doom of those who did recant, for on one thing all rumors agreed: no heretic who had entered the City had ever been seen again, except during recantation itself where the chilling phrase "we hereby commute your sentence to perpetual confinement" invariably ended the ceremony.

The question of how heretics were persuaded to recant was discussed only in whispers. The threat of death presumably had a good deal to do with it, yet that could not be the whole story; many before Noren had been determined never to give in, declaring themselves entirely ready to die for their convictions, only to deny all those convictions a few weeks later. Enough strong men had done so to indicate that it was not merely a matter of losing one's nerve.

Determinedly Noren pushed such speculations from his mind. He must forget them; he must pull himself together for the trial. Drawing himself upright once more, he leaned against the wall of the airless cell, hoping he would prove able to stand alone.

A jailer—not one of those who'd come during the night

—brought him water and untied his bonds, making it plain that plenty of assistants were within call. After drinking, Noren cleaned himself up as best he could. Then he was taken under guard to the village hall. There were no hecklers in the street, for everybody who had a free afternoon was already packed inside. A trial was something few would want to miss. As he entered, Noren saw to his dismay that Talyra was seated in the front row. He'd feared they would force her to attend, and he knew that his most difficult task would be to protect her. Now more than ever, he cursed himself for having revealed his secret and thereby placed her in jeopardy. She was alone; her parents were not present, nor was his own father, who was no doubt unable to face the shame.

All eyes were on Noren as he took the place designated before his six judges, the village councilmen. At the sight of the bruises on his face and arms, Talyra bent her head in anguish, but his battered appearance was ignored by everyone else, including the Technicians, who sat in the back of the room. Both of them avoided his glance. His feelings were confused in regard to the Technicians; they might have been sent to trap him, still the young man's discontent had seemed genuine.

One by one the witnesses gave their reports of what had occurred at the inn. A number of them had short memories and related the street version of Noren's remarks rather than what he had actually said, causing most of the women in the room to turn pale with horror at the blasphemy; Talyra, staring at him, seemed about to faint. Noren found himself blushing for her sake, but as far as he was concerned it was a matter of small significance; he had not used words of that sort, but he could scarcely deny that he had thought them.

Arnil spoke last, and he gave a faithful account. That it was an ordeal for him was obvious; yet he had been required to swear by the Mother Star that his testimony would be true and complete, and he therefore had no alternative. Noren was glad when the old innkeeper was dismissed, and he himself was ordered to stand. The judges' table was positioned so that in facing them, he still met the hostile gaze of the spectators. It did not shake him. For the first time in his life he was free to say what he really thought.

"You have heard your accusers," the Chief of Council said to him sternly. "Do you dare to deny your guilt?"

"I deny that I've done anything to feel guilty for," Noren said steadily, "but I don't dispute the testimony. The charges are true."

A gasp arose from the spectators; they had not expected him to be so brazen. "Do you mean to say you see nothing wrong in blaspheming not only against our High Priests the Scholars, but against the Prophecy itself?" demanded one of the judges incredulously.

"There isn't anything wrong in it," Noren replied. "The Scholars, as I said, are no better than other men; in fact they're worse, for it's they who've done wrong in keeping knowledge from us. The Prophecy blinds us to the absurdity of the High Law through which they've established their power, and that's exactly why they wrote it."

At once the room was in uproar; several people jumped from their seats, shouting angrily for immediate condemnation. "Silence!" ordered the Chief of Council, banging the table with his fist. "I agree that the provocation was very great, but under the law—the High Law as well as our own—this boy must receive a fair trial."

"What need is there to investigate any further?" protested another councilman. "We have evidence of his guilt from his own lips as well as from those of ten witnesses, two of whom are his brothers."

"One of those witnesses, the innkeeper, felt that the boy was not himself and was unaware of the import of his words," reminded someone.

"That is belied by the statement he has just made," the

Chief of Council pointed out. "However, it is proper that we determine whether or not his heresy is of long standing." Turning to Noren he inquired, "How long have you held the false view you just expressed here?"

"It is not false," Noren declared calmly. "I have held it since childhood, but I never told anyone."

"Never? You have been a heretic for years and yet kept your pernicious ideas entirely to yourself? I would think rather that you might have corrupted others in secret."

Noren had known this issue would be raised, and he had decided how he must deal with it. The risk in telling the whole truth was less than that in attempting to evade it, for Talyra would be required to testify anyway, and she would not lie under oath; he must forestall any suspicion that she might have supported him. "As a child, I discussed my beliefs with another heretic who is now dead," he answered. "After his death, I was afraid. I spoke to no one until two nights ago. At that time I confessed them to my betrothed, whereupon she broke our betrothal and has refused to see me since."

Pain crossed Talyra's face: a look not merely of sorrow, but of deep hurt. Bewildered, Noren wondered why the truth should evoke such a look, for surely she knew that the fact she'd broken off with him was her best protection. And then he saw. She was blaming herself for his arrest! She thought he had not trusted her and had spoken in the tavern because he considered himself already doomed.

It was providential. He longed to say something reassuring, but he knew he must do the opposite. His greatest fear had been that although her refusal to go through with the marriage would be corroborated by both his family and hers, she would be suspect because she'd failed to report him; now, by one small but cruel lie, he could ensure her safety.

"She told me she wouldn't reveal her reason for calling off the wedding," he went on, "but I could see that her piety was stronger than whatever love she had once felt for me. After that there was little point in caution, for though she was kept home by illness yesterday, she would surely have denounced me as soon as she was able to."

Talyra turned away from him, her suffering obvious to all. "The girl's piety is indeed well known," one of the councilmen said. "It is plain that in betrothing herself to this scoundrel, she was the innocent victim of his deceit. I see no need to subject her to questioning, since he has already admitted his crime. I see no need to question anyone else at all. The case is clear-cut."

The Chief of Council nodded. "That's quite true. However, the boy himself must be examined further. Not only did he say blasphemous and heretical things, but he said them to Technicians! It is fortunate for him, and for all of us, that the High Law toward which he shows such disrespect does not in itself forbid the voicing of wicked ideas, and that its enforcement is left to us in any case; otherwise he would have been instantly struck down by those Technicians' wrath. We would not have them think us tolerant of whatever other heresies he may be harboring."

There was a murmur of agreement. "We of this village," the man continued, "are respectable, reverent people, ever mindful of the High Law's demands. We must concede that although we may forbid heresy in our own laws, it is not ours to chastise; yet should we fail to root out this boy's errors and censure him severely for them, our name would be forever tarnished."

Noren waited with newly-revived confidence. He had anticipated this and in fact had hoped for it; only under cross-examination would he be permitted to argue for his beliefs. He was fighting not for his freedom, which could not be won in any case, but to be heard; if this was to be his only chance, he was going to make the most of it.

All six of the councilmen glared at him reproachfully. "The Book of the Prophecy," one of them began, "tells us

57)

that at the time of the Founding, the Scholars in their wisdom made the High Law, and that although its mysteries will not be made plain to us until the Mother Star appears, we are nevertheless bound to follow it. It is possible that you are ignorant of the reason for this?"

"I am not ignorant of the reason that's given," said Noren. "It's claimed that without the High Law, people could not survive. But why should we assume that to be the real reason?"

"Because the book says so," declared the man, as if to a very stupid child.

Noren laughed. "That doesn't prove anything. When the Scholars wrote the book, they naturally put in a reason that sounded good."

"Have you no respect for anything sacred?" cried another judge indignantly.

"I respect truth," Noren said soberly. "I respect it too much to believe anything merely because some book or some person tells me I should. I want to really *know!* Maybe you'd rather accept stories that make you feel comfortable about the way things are, but I care more for truth than for comfort."

For a moment the councilman seemed incapable of reply. "I shall pass over the enormity of your arrogance," he told Noren after an ominous pause, "and simply point out to you that it is self-evident that we could not survive without the High Law. We live only by the grace of the Scholars. If they did not send us water, we would die of thirst. If they did not send Machines to quicken the land, no grain would sprout; and if they did not cause rain, the sprouts would die. For that matter, if the Scholars blessed no seed there would be no grain in the first place, nor would there be fowl if they had not favored our ancestors with the gift of fertile eggs. We would all starve."

"I too will pass over much," said Noren slowly, realizing that he could not possibly present the details of his thoughts about all these topics. "I will concede that we are dependent on the Scholars' knowledge and on the use of Machines. But knowledge and Machines should be shared by all of us. It is not right for them to be controlled by Scholars."

"Of course it is right! It is how things have been since the time of the Founding."

"I do not believe in the Founding," said Noren.

Once again the Chief of Council had to pound on the table to restore order, and this time it took quite a while to obtain it. No one in the village had ever heard of a heretic going so far as to deny the Prophecy's account of the Founding.

"Just how do you think people got here," inquired a councilman sarcastically, "if they did not come from the sky? Did they rise out of the ground, perhaps, like plants?"

With many interruptions, Noren attempted to explain his theory about the savages, noticing hopelessly that nobody was taking him seriously. "The savages are idiots," protested someone in an exasperated tone.

"Maybe our original ancestors were idiots, and as they learned more, became more intelligent."

That was the wrong thing to say. It was also a mistake to suggest that the ancestors of the Scholars and Technicians might have been idiots. Noren perceived that whatever secret support he might have gained had been wiped out; the spectators were now firmly united against him.

"You can achieve nothing by mocking us," the Chief of Council admonished. "You are exhausting our patience! Everyone knows that the savages are idiots because they disobeyed the High Law and drank impure water."

Noren hesitated only a moment; he had nothing to lose, and perhaps he could convince someone that in this respect at least, the High Law was foolish. "I doubt that," he asserted. "I myself drank from a stream only yesterday, and as you see I'm still quite sane."

There was an exclamation of horrified disbelief, and the judges scowled, as if they considered that last point to be somewhat questionable. "You are not an idiot *yet*," one of them conceded, "but we know nothing of how long the process takes. Any morning you could wake up to find yourself transformed."

"It's indeed fortunate that the boy was apprehended before his marriage," stated another coldly. "Some say that if a man should drink impure water and remain unchanged, his wife would give birth to idiot children."

Noren looked out at the people in surprise; that story was not prevalent, and he had never heard it before. He caught Talyra's eye, seeing that she was more shocked and wounded than ever. *Oh, Talyra,* he thought wretchedly, *surely you don't believe such nonsense!* But he knew that she did, and that she would never marry him after this even if he were to recant and be miraculously released. He also, for the first time, understood the real reason for Kern's murder; Kern had been all too popular with girls.

The councilmen huddled together; Noren realized that they were about to pronounce the verdict and that he would have little more chance to speak. Desperately he said, "Forget about the Founding! Forget all I've said if you wish, but is it not a fact that the Prophecy itself admits that it's not good for the Scholars to keep things from us? Does it not say that someday they will no longer do so, that knowledge and Machines will come to everyone and that *'the sons of men will find their own wisdom and choose their own Law'*? Why would the Scholars have made such a promise if not because they knew that's how the world should be? I don't deny that they're wise! They knew, and they also knew that the promise would keep us content to hope instead of seizing what's rightfully ours."

"The promise was not made by the Scholars," reproved the Chief of Council. "It came from the Mother Star itself. The Prophecy will be fulfilled when the Star appears to us and not a day sooner; to believe that things should be otherwise is the worst sort of heresy."

It was not the worst sort, and Noren, seeing that his case was lost, took the ultimate step of defiance. "I do not believe that there is a Mother Star," he stated honestly.

He expected pandemonium, but instead, the room remained hushed; everybody was speechless. Finally the Chief of Council mustered the composure to proceed. "We'll waste no more time here," he said, "for it's plain that you are past redemption. I grow cold at the thought of the punishments that will be yours when you enter the City! Are you not aware that the Technicians present in this room have a Machine wherewith they have recorded every word you have said? When you face the Scholars, Noren, you will be forced to listen to those words spoken by your own voice; and it will then be too late to plead for the forgiveness you will crave."

Noren hadn't known of the Recording Machine, but though startling, the idea of hearing his testimony repeated did not strike him as the dire ordeal it was evidently intended to be. "Do you think I don't plan to be truthful before the Scholars?" he demanded. "If my words are recorded, then I'll be saved the trouble of saying the same things over."

"You are insolent now. Your life may be spared once your insolence has been crushed, but I'll wager you'll be made sorry to be alive." The Chief of Council rose. "We have reached a unanimous verdict. We pronounce you guilty as charged, and hereby remand you to the custody of the Scholars as is required of us under the High Law, though I have never seen anyone less deserving of their mercy."

The marshals stepped again to Noren's side. As he was led down the aisle, Talyra's eyes met his, and she was in tears; he saw that despite her revulsion at his beliefs, she still loved him and would grieve for him. No one else showed any sympathy. Even Arnil lowered his head when Noren passed. From behind, one of the judges added, "May the spirit of the Mother Star protect you, Noren, for it's sure that you'll find no succor among men."

IV

NOREN WAS LODGED IN THE JAIL THAT NIGHT; THE TECH-
nicians, apparently, were not yet ready to take him away.
After some hours he remembered that he'd had no food
since the previous evening. Perhaps that contributed to his
faintness, though he felt no hunger.

Fear was rising in him again now that the trial was over.
He'd suppressed it while there'd been something he had to
do, but once alone, he could no longer keep it down. Too
many of his nightmares in the past years had been centered
on the unknown horrors that were about to confront him.
*We can't be forced to do or to believe anything against our
will*, Kern had said, but Noren could not help worrying.

The Scholars, he realized, would not view him as his
judges had. They, after all, knew even more of the truth
than he did; they would not consider it stupid or sinful
not to believe in things like the Founding and the Mother
Star. On the contrary, they would recognize the sharpness
of his mind. They would recognize it as a threat to their

supremacy. One way or another, they would have to silence him; it was no wonder that they required all heretics to be placed in their hands. Nor was it any wonder that no villagers seemed to care about truth, he saw with bitterness. Anyone who'd shown signs of caring had been trapped, as he had, and summarily disposed of.

His attempt to convince people at the trial had been an utter failure, Noren knew. Nobody had been impressed by his arguments; they had simply been incensed. Thinking of it, impotent rage burgeoned within him: rage at the defeat, the blindness of others, the whole injustice of the way the world was arranged. He strained against the tight ropes with which he was again bound until his wrists were raw and his body clammy with sweat. Was there no power that could stand against a system that was so *wrong?*

There was, he perceived suddenly. He would undoubtedly be hurt in the City; in the end he would be killed; but as long as he kept on caring, nothing could touch the freedom of his inner thoughts. With that one solace he fell at last into fitful sleep.

It was pitch dark in the cell when Noren awoke to the sound of voices and knew that the door matting was being unlashed. He sat up, thinking in despair that he had not the strength to endure another beating.

But the figure that appeared in the doorway was not one of his brothers, nor yet a drunken jailer. It was the young Technician.

He carried a lantern—not an ordinary one, but the mysterious kind that had neither tallow nor flame, being instead lit by Power—and as he approached, his face was illuminated; Noren saw that it was drawn. "Speak softly," the Technician cautioned, without formal greeting. "I've sent the jailer outside, but he's not far off, and I don't wish to be overheard."

"Are you going to take me to the City in the middle of

the night?" Noren demanded, startled.

"No. You'll be taken about two hours after sunrise, but I want to talk to you alone beforehand." The man's anguish was evident. "I—I'm sorry, Noren," he continued through white lips. "I don't expect you to forgive me, but all the same I had to come."

"What happened wasn't your fault," Noren said. "We both spoke rashly. You too could be in trouble if the Scholars found out all you said to me."

"You don't understand," persisted the Technician. "It was a deliberate set-up; I was instructed in what to say. At first I was only following orders, and then I—I found I meant what I was telling you, and I tried to stop the thing, but it was too late."

On the verge of fury, Noren paused. Despite the betrayal, this man might have had a change of heart, and if so, he might someday be able to actively oppose the Scholars; a Technician was in a far better position to do so than a villager. "Just what do you believe?" he asked slowly.

"I believe as you do," the Technician confessed. "I didn't know I did until I heard you testify today, but—well, that woke me up. It's wrong for the Scholars to conceal their knowledge! And it's wrong for you to be punished for saying what you think."

"Will you answer some questions?" Noren challenged. Above all, he needed information, and this was probably his one chance to get it.

"Yes, if I can." The Technician, to Noren's astonishment, drew the matting across the cell's door and without hesitation, removed the ropes by which his prisoner was kept helpless. Then he sat down on the dirty stone floor and placed the light between himself and Noren.

"Exactly what were your instructions?" Noren began.

"To watch you, wait till you were in some public place

65)

or else alone with your older brothers, and then trick you into an open declaration of heresy by pretending to sympathize."

Noren frowned; whoever had planned that had been very clever and very well informed. They had known his brothers would denounce him, and what was more, had been aware that he viewed Technicians as people rather than as the nameless, faceless beings most villagers considered them. The more obvious approach would have been to arouse his ire by an overbearing attitude, yet it had been foreseen that he'd be on guard against that. "Was the other man to do the same?" he inquired.

"I don't think so, but we were briefed separately. I assume he was told not to report me later for anything I might say." Meeting Noren's eyes, the Technician added painfully, "You'd best know everything. He admitted to me that it was hoped that offering your girl an appointment to the training center would upset your marriage plans, and perhaps make you vulnerable."

Noren clenched his hands, knowing that he could not afford to give in to anger, and demanded, "Were you told why they wanted me convicted?"

"Yes, at least they had an excuse that seemed plausible at the time. They claimed it was for your own good! They knew you were a heretic, and they said it would be better for you to get caught while we were on hand to see that you weren't harmed by the villagers."

"It would have been still better for me not to have gotten caught at all," said Noren dryly.

"They don't look at it that way. They think a heretic is happier after they've converted him, that he benefits from 'acknowledging the truth', as they call it."

"Recanting?" asked Noren with a shiver.

"Yes. I believed it, Noren! I've always believed it, but now—after what you said at the trial—I can't."

"Who gave you your instructions?"

"The Scholar Stefred." There was awe in the Technician's voice, as if the name was of particular and terrible significance. "He's the Chief Inquisitor, and he's in charge of all heresy proceedings. I'd never seen him except from a distance, at ceremonies, until he sent for me. He seemed to know a lot about me, Noren—and he knew *all* about you."

That fit, Noren thought; things had been too carefully planned for it to have been otherwise. "What will happen to me in—in the City?" he faltered.

"I honestly don't know. We don't have any more information about that than the villagers. Ordinary Technicians aren't allowed in the Inner City, the Scholars' part; when Stefred sent for me, I went to a conference room in the exit dome where the Gates are and that's Outer City. All I can tell you is that he'll make you recant."

"How? By torture?" Noren asked directly.

The young Technician averted his face. "I'm afraid it may be something like that," he admitted miserably. "When you talk to him, he doesn't seem like a cruel man, yet it's said that no heretic can hold out against him. I used to think he really convinced people, but I can see that wouldn't work with someone like you; and threats wouldn't, either."

"No," declared Noren grimly. "Look, if you know anything more specific—any rumors, even—go ahead and say so. Don't try to spare me, because I'd rather be prepared."

"I wish I could help. But there's—well, a strange sort of mystery about heresy. I don't know how to describe it except to say that we all feel there's some tremendous secret that's hidden from everyone but Scholars. Perhaps it's merely what you believe: that they made up the whole Prophecy to stay in power. I think there's more to it, though; I think it's connected with what becomes of heretics, both before they recant and afterwards. They're imprisoned in the Inner City, you see, and Outer City

67)

people don't have any contact with them."

Noren shuddered. The information he was getting was anything but reassuring. He was quiet for a few moments, then asked hesitantly, "Are you transporting me to the City yourself?"

"No," the Technician replied. "I can guess what you're thinking, and I'd like to let you escape; but it's impossible. They'll send an aircar for you. All we do is escort you to it, keeping you safe from the mob that'll gather to watch." There was an unhappy silence. Then suddenly he raised his head, saying in a low, excited voice, "If you were to escape, it would have to be tonight. Is there anybody who'd help you if I could get you out of here? Your family, maybe? I—I've just had an idea, but it depends on outside aid."

Noren thought. His brothers would not want to help him; his father would not dare. But Talyra . . .

Talyra loved him. She would not marry him, but neither would she abandon him to torture and death. To aid a convicted heretic would be a sin in her eyes; she would be torn; still, remembering her as he'd last seen her in the courtroom, he was quite sure that she wouldn't refuse him any help that was in her power to provide.

Yet he could not say so. His testimony at the trial had cleared her of involvement, and he dared not undo that. This Technician seemed sincere, but he had tricked him once; there was no real assurance that he would not do so again. The whole episode, including both the confession of remorse and the frightening suggestion of some unspeakable mystery in regard to his fate, might be a trick to get the names of other potential heretics; the Scholars' design was obviously complex.

"No," he said. "No, there isn't anyone."

The Technician's distress, whatever its cause, was unquestionably real. "I don't believe that," he said slowly, "but I can't blame you for not trusting me. Noren, you don't need to! I won't have to know from whom you get help. What I'm proposing is that you change clothes with me, here and now, then tie me up and simply walk out."

Noren stared at him, completely and utterly astonished. That a Technician should make such an offer was incredible even in the light of his own unprecedented view of their humanity. "But—but what would happen to you?" he stammered.

"Nothing. The aircar will take me back to the City, where I'll be recognized. The other Technician will recognize me first, of course; but the villagers won't, and to save face he'll put me aboard quickly, without letting them notice that I'm not you."

"Won't the Scholars punish you?" Noren protested.

"I'll say your ropes were loose and you overpowered me. That can't hurt you even if they recapture you, since under the High Law they can't accuse a villager of any crime for which he hasn't been convicted in a civil trial."

It made sense, Noren saw. They would certainly be more likely to believe that a heretic would overpower a Technician than that the Technician would voluntarily change places with him!

"In any case," the man went on, "they'll be looking for you before I get back; the aircar has radiophone equipment, and I'll have to let the pilot use it. That's why you'll need help. You've got to get other clothes and be well away from here when the alert's given. Can you arrange that?"

"Perhaps," Noren admitted. "What happens to me if I fail?"

"Nothing worse than what'll happen if we don't try it, at least not as far as the Scholars are concerned. The villagers—" The Technician frowned. "Officially I'm here to protect you from the villagers. If you're caught by them after I'm gone, you may be in trouble, especially if the story that you attacked me gets out."

69)

Noren knew only too well what trouble he'd be in. If he should be caught masquerading as a Technician, he would incur even more wrath than Kern had. Yet it was that against certain doom, and even if he lived only a short while, he might manage to convince someone who would carry on after him. The fact that he'd convinced the Technician was encouraging, if he had indeed convinced him and this too was not an elaborate trap of some kind. It seemed odd that the man did not expect to be held in suspicion merely for having visited a prisoner's cell at this hour; still, what was there to lose by trusting him? "I'll try," he decided, "if you're sure you'll be all right."

"We'll make it look good," the Technician said with apparent confidence. He regarded Noren's bruises thoughtfully. "You're going to have to rough me up a bit. Otherwise I can't pass as far as the aircar, let alone fool the Scholar Stefred."

"You mean you'd just stand there and let me hit you?"

"It's necessary, Noren. Don't worry, I won't make any noise, and I ordered the jailer not to come back into the building till I called him."

They switched clothes first, Noren marveling at the strange feel of the green stuff of which the uniform was made. Fortunately its sleeves were long enough to conceal the bruises on his arms; only those of his face would have to be hidden, and he could not show his face anyway. The hat covered the ragged cut of his hair.

"Go ahead and let loose," the Technician told him, once he'd rubbed dirt on his own arms to simulate as much bruising as possible. He braced himself against the wall and added, "Think of how you felt toward me when I first admitted what I was doing at the inn."

After a brief hesitation, Noren complied. The Scholar Stefred, he judged, would demand real evidence of a struggle. The whole business was carried out in silence; the Technician didn't shrink from it, though he'd obviously had no prior experience with blows.

"Noren," he said when it was over, "I've got to be honest. You haven't much chance to elude Stefred, not if he really wants you. And I'm pretty sure he does. I could sense it in the way he spoke."

"I know. But before he gets me maybe I can win some people over to our side."

There was frank admiration in the Technician's gaze. "I'll try, too. We're up against something a lot stronger than we are, though: stronger than you realize. The Scholars have powers you can't even imagine. I agree that it's wrong for them to keep those powers for themselves, but I'm not sure I believe your idea about there never having been a Founding. You're just as smart as they are; could *you* have discovered such powers if you and everyone else had always lived as the savages do?"

"There's got to be more to it than intelligence," Noren conceded, frowning. "I don't quite see how it happened, yet it's more reasonable than people dropping out of the sky."

The Technician drew out several small objects that were hidden in the belt he still wore beneath Noren's tunic. "Hold this," he commanded, handing Noren an ordinary tallow candle stub and lighting it with a match. "The Power Cell in the lantern is weak; I must replace it before you leave." As Noren watched in fascination, he turned out the light, opened a panel in its bottom, and inserted a little red cube in place of an identical one that he stored carefully away in his belt. Then, once the lantern was burning with even greater brilliance than before, he took the candle back and produced a featureless flat disk.

"It's the recording of your trial," he told Noren. "Destroy it when you ditch the uniform."

Noren examined the thing closely, wondering how his words could possibly be preserved in such a form. "No," he said. "No, it will be better if you give it to the Scholars;

if I'd overpowered you, I wouldn't have known enough to take it. I don't mind having them hear what I said."

"You're really not ashamed, are you . . . not even of having declared that there's no Mother Star." The young Technician's tone was troubled, though it carried no disapproval.

"I'm not," agreed Noren.

"I—I don't know what to say to you, then. I can't wish you its protection, yet—well, something's lacking. It's not enough just to learn what there *isn't;* we need to know what there *is.*"

"Let's just wish each other luck," Noren said, for though he understood the deficiency very well, his feelings about it went too deep for words. He gripped the Technician's hand, wondering if any villager had ever done such a thing before. When it was too late, the man having been securely tied and the jailer called, he realized that he did not even know his friend's name.

He held the light low when he left the cell, so that his face was in shadows, and he did not speak to the jailer, who nodded respectfully as he passed but did not question his actions. There was little chance of his being recognized; villagers did not look at the features of Technicians. To them Technicians were not men, but beings of a different order, and one was assumed to be like another. The idea of an ordinary person wearing a Technician's uniform would not enter anyone's mind.

The street was dark and silent. Noren walked rapidly through the village and headed out along the road toward Talyra's farm. He did not want to ask her help, for he knew she'd be shocked by the masquerade, but there was no one else from whom he could possibly get clothes. He'd be taking a risk; if he was caught by her family, he would be shown no mercy. He would have to reach her from a hiding place he'd used more than once in the past: the cluster of rocks on the knoll against which the farmhouse nestled. There had been an understanding between them that if a yellow pebble was tossed in between the woven mats that hung at her window, she would climb out and meet him there. She would no longer be expecting such a signal, however, and he hoped she wouldn't be too incredulous to respond.

All at once another thought hit Noren, and he stopped in the middle of the road, appalled. There was a worse risk than capture in contacting Talyra! With sickening chagrin he realized that he indeed had something to lose by trusting the Technician. Everything in the man's manner had indicated sincerity, yet if he'd misjudged . . .

He had been aware that the switching of places could be an elaborate plot, but no motive for it had occurred to him. Now he wondered. The two Technicians could be working together. The other man, who would not be going in the aircar, could be watching Talyra's house, expecting to get evidence against her; and he could have seen to it that there would be villagers there, too.

Noren could not take that chance. He was sure enough of the young Technician to gamble his own safety, but he was not willing to jeopardize Talyra's.

Yet what else was there to do? This was a spoke road; he could reach no other village except by way of the center he'd just left, and it was too late to return there, for dawn was already brightening the sky. He would have to lie low somehow until the next night. Though farms lined the road, to be seen from a distance by farmers would not endanger him; they would not approach unless faced by an emergency such as illness, since Technicians, whose ways were inscrutable, were left to their own devices. Real Technicians, however, would surely search the area. He'd have to hide in the wilderness, and he could not get to the wilderness without passing both Talyra's farm and his family's.

Despairingly, Noren trudged ahead. If there was anyone

he did not want to encounter, it was one of his brothers; yet since Talyra's house might be under observation, he must go by it without a glance. What could he do if he ever did reach another village? he wondered. He could buy clothing without challenge, perhaps—though most people's clothes were made at home, a few shops did carry garments sewn by seamstresses—but he had no money and besides, Technicians would undoubtedly be expecting such a move. The shopkeepers would be either watched or warned.

Someone was coming toward him along the road. Noren felt a chill of apprehension, but he knew he must walk calmly forward. Though in the dim light he could not make out whether it was a farmer, there was no reason to suppose that it wouldn't be, and if he kept his lantern down and gave no greeting he would be ignored. To his surprise, as the figure came closer he saw that it was a woman. For a woman to be out alone before sunrise was very odd.

And the woman did not ignore him. "Sir!" she called out clearly. "Forgive me for presuming to approach you, but I could not wait at home. My parents don't wish me to accept nurse's training."

Noren froze, overwhelmed by astonishment. It was Talyra's voice.

As she approached, he was torn between his desire to run to her and the impulse to run away. When she recognized him, she would be stunned; he must reveal himself with care, lest she become too upset to cope with the situation. Setting the lantern on the ground, he raised one hand to his face, and disguising his voice as best he could, called back, "My greetings, citizen! May I be of service to you?"

She was by this time close enough to see him, but as was normal for villagers, she noticed only the uniform. "I am pleased by your concern, sir," she replied formally. "Are you not the Technician who is coming to take me to the training center? If I've erred in addressing you, I'm most sorry."

(74

He reached for the large bundle she carried, turning from her to set it beside the lantern. "Talyra," he said quietly.

The girl let out a gasp, and Noren whirled; before she could speak, he had caught her in his arms and was holding her close to him.

As the first rays of sunlight touched the Tomorrow Mountains, gilding the uppermost ridges with gold, Noren and Talyra left the road for the shelter of a dense purplish thicket, for Noren realized that although a Technician alone would arouse no curiosity among the farmers, a Technician embracing a village girl would be a strange sight indeed. Presumably, men and women Technicians embraced in the privacy of the City; but the High Law forbade them to look upon ordinary people with love of that kind.

They sat on the ground, sinking into the spongy gray moss that grew beneath the webbed-stemmed shrubs, and kept low enough to be well concealed. At first Talyra sobbed hysterically, too overcome by Noren's miraculous appearance to care about anything else. After a short while, however, she pulled away, voicing the inevitable protest. "Noren," she exclaimed in wide-eyed horror, "to wear a Technician's clothes—it's blasphemy!"

"I'm already convicted of blasphemy, Talyra, and of heresy as well. Is this so much worse? I didn't steal the uniform; it was given to me."

Talyra dropped her head, her long dark hair hiding her face from him. "I—I'm all mixed up," she faltered miserably. "Everything you've been doing is wrong, but at the trial, I could think only of how I couldn't bear to have you punished. It was all my fault—" She began to cry again. "Why do you even speak to me, let alone kiss me? I thought you must hate me! And it's sinful—indecent—for me to be letting you touch me when you've committed such sacrilege; I hate myself both ways."

"Darling," he said gently, "you mustn't. It's *not* sinful! My arrest wasn't your fault, either; I never for a minute thought you'd report me. Don't you know why I had to say what I did? It was the only way to convince them that you're innocent."

"You—you lied? You wouldn't lie to save yourself, yet you did to protect *me?*"

"That wasn't the same kind of lying," he said gravely.

"I guess not," she agreed. "Noren, you were so brave to talk to the councilmen as you did! I—well, I understand a little, I think."

"You see now how bad it is for the Scholars to keep things from us?" he asked eagerly. "You see how they've tricked people with the Prophecy?"

"No! I know you're mistaken, and I'll never see how you can believe the things you said. But I understand that you do believe them. I understand that being honest means more to you than anything else. Oh, Noren, I'm sure the Scholars won't punish you harshly! They couldn't!"

"I'm not going to give them a chance," he declared. "Talyra, you realize that I've escaped, don't you? That if I'm recaptured, I'll be killed?"

"Killed!" She stared, incredulous. "They've never sentenced anybody to die, not even for impenitence! It's a terrible thing to escape, but I just won't believe they'd kill you for it."

"Not for escaping," he explained patiently. "For refusing to recant."

"But all heretics recant," Talyra protested. "Whether they're penitent or not, they at least retract whatever they've said."

"I'm not going to. Do you think that when I wouldn't deny the truth for your sake, I'd do so to save my life?"

"No," she said slowly. "No, I don't think you would. And the Scholars wouldn't want you to." Frowning, she went on, "I don't know how they get heretics to recant, but they surely don't ask them to lie. Your idea of the truth's twisted around, Noren, and somehow they'll make you see that. Perhaps . . . perhaps it's like the innoculations Technicians give: the needle hurts, yet without it we'd all get sick and die."

"Talyra," he demanded, "do you believe it's right for the Scholars to hurt people to make them see things their way?"

She averted her eyes. "I—I'm not sure," she confessed in a low voice. "It doesn't seem so, yet the Scholars are High Priests, and they know everything; how could they do anything wrong? You said yourself that truth's more important than comfort. Well, the Prophecy is *true*—"

Noren could see that she was genuinely unable to imagine that it might not be. "I'll put it another way," he said. "If you believe that what's done to heretics is for their good, then why didn't you denounce me? You would have called the Technicians if I'd been sick, even if it meant having me taken away to the hospital outside the City; why didn't you feel the same way about getting me cured of heresy?"

There was a brief silence. Then, baffled by a paradox she could not resolve, Talyra cried, "Because I don't want you hurt for any reason! I don't want you imprisoned! May the spirit of the Mother Star not forsake me; I want you to go free!"

"You'll help me, then?"

"I'll help you even if I'm condemned for it, Noren."

"You won't be, and you mustn't condemn yourself, either," Noren said with concern. "You must trust me, darling, as I'm trusting you. I know some things you don't, and there are Technicians who know them, too, like the one who gave me his uniform." He went on to tell her what had happened, hastily and with little detail, for he knew they hadn't much time. "You'll hear that I attacked him,"

77)

he concluded, "but it's not true; we made up that story to save him from punishment."

The idea of a Technician taking a heretic's side against the Scholars was bewildering to Talyra, but she accepted Noren's word, giving her own that she would never repeat any of what he'd disclosed. "It's not going to be easy getting clothes for you," she said thoughtfully. "Have you any idea how we're to manage it?"

"Can't you get some of your brother's old ones?" he asked, puzzled. "By this time he and your father will be working in the fields."

"But I can't go back now. Mother would be there, and she'd not let me out of her sight again. I left a note, you see, when I came away this morning."

Noren frowned. He had forgotten for the moment what Talyra had said about leaving home against her parents' wishes. "You haven't told me why you changed your mind about the training center," he muttered, deciding that to reveal the reason she'd been appointed would be needlessly cruel.

"Do you have to ask?" she replied, blushing. "Being a nurse would be much better than living with my parents forever, or working in a shop or an inn. Mother doesn't understand. She thinks I'll get married someday."

"Won't you?" he inquired painfully.

"Noren! When I broke our betrothal, you surely didn't think I'd ever marry someone *else!*"

He held out his arms and she came eagerly, as if there had never been any rift at all. The ways of girls, Noren decided, were even more mysterious than those of Scholars.

"After the trial," Talyra continued softly, "when I knew they'd take you away and I'd never see you again, I spoke to the Technician who had offered me the appointment. I asked if I could still accept, and he said yes, he'd come for me today or send his partner. I was glad because I thought that while I was being trained, I'd at least be somewhere near the City where they were keeping you. But Mother was dreadfully worried. There are those stories, you know, about people who go to the training center and then just disappear—"

Noren held her tight. "I'm worried, too," he declared. It was quite true that there were occasional unexplained disappearances from the training center. To be sure, the Technicians always told families that they must not grieve, that the person who'd vanished was not dead, but had been honored by being given special and secret work of his own choosing. And it happened rarely; still, feeling as he did about the Scholars' secrets . . .

"Are you saying you don't want me to learn as much as they'll teach me?" she asked.

He could scarcely say that, Noren realized; he'd have gone gladly to the training center himself. Talyra would make a good nurse. She wouldn't mind following the orders of Technicians, for she'd feel no resentment at not knowing all that they did. Nurses lived in every village to tend the ill and injured before the Technicians arrived, to carry out whatever treatment was prescribed, and to deliver babies; they were admired and respected by everyone.

"No, darling," he told her. "If you'll be happy as a nurse, that's what you must become."

She lay back against his shoulder. "I'll never be happy without you," she admitted. "But I would like the work, I think. I'm of age, and if I'd waited at home for the Technician, Mother couldn't have stopped me from going with him; but I thought it would be easier if I just slipped away."

"That puts your helping me in a different light," Noren said ruefully. "If you can't go home without being seen, we must forget it, for I won't have you do anything dangerous."

"Do you think I'm afraid?" Talyra demanded indignantly. "Noren, nothing matters to me but your safety!

79)

There must be some way I can get clothes for you in the village; no one even knows you've escaped yet."

There'd be no dissuading her, Noren saw. She had hesitated at first not from fear or unwillingness to defy convention, but from a real conflict of conscience; Talyra had never lacked spirit when it came to getting her own way. Having determined her course, she would hold to it.

"I could buy clothes and say they were for my brother," she suggested.

"I haven't any money."

"I have: the coins I've been given each Founding Day. And there's my great-aunt's silver wristband."

"I couldn't let you use those," Noren protested.

"They've always been yours," she said simply. "I was saving them for my dowry."

"But Talyra," he went on, "later, when they're searching for me, they would question the shopkeeper, and your brother, too. You'd be at the training center by then, and the Technicians there would make you tell them everything."

"I suppose they would," she agreed unhappily. "Whatever I do, they'll find out afterwards. Noren, there's just one way it will work; they've got to think you forced me. We've got to make up a story the way you did with the Technician."

"How could I force you even if I wanted to?"

She turned scarlet. "You're stronger than I am. You could make me swear by the Mother Star to do anything you say."

"But I wouldn't—not that way!"

"Of course you wouldn't, but people will believe just about anything of you now. After what you said about having drunk impure water, any girl would be scared to death of you. And besides, anybody who'd attack a *Technician*—"

(80

That was all too true, Noren realized. It would be assumed that he had no integrity whatsoever. Yet Talyra's alleged refusal to break an oath by the Mother Star, even one forcibly extracted, would arouse no suspicion, for her piety had been acknowledged by the village council itself.

"Could you carry it off, Talyra?" he asked dubiously. "Accusing me, I mean?"

"I could to put them off your trail," she declared. "I won't wait for the Technicians to ask; I'll go to the councilmen as soon as your escape's made known, and send them to look for you in the wrong direction. It's the same sort of lie you told about not trusting me, isn't it? And since they're convinced you don't trust me, they'll be ready to believe that you'd try to get even."

"What if they require you to swear that it's true?" he objected.

Talyra laughed. "They won't. I'll cry and carry on so that nobody will even consider doubting."

"It might work," he conceded. "Yet oh, darling, if you were caught—"

"So what? I wouldn't be convicted of heresy, only of aiding an escaped prisoner."

"You'd be punished. You'd lose your appointment to the training center, too."

The girl scrambled to her feet. "We're wasting time, Noren. I've got to hurry if I'm to buy the clothes and bring them to you before that aircar arrives at the jail."

Noren got up also. "Talyra," he said sadly, "you can't bring them to me. It's already too late. You've got to hide them where I can pick them up tonight, and then look for the Technician; because he'll probably start out to your farm as soon as the aircar leaves. Even if he hasn't been planning to, he may suspect I'm hiding there when he finds out about the switch. We can't risk his catching up with you; and besides, I may not be able to wait here."

81)

"Where would you go?" she asked, dismayed.

"Into the wilderness. I'll have to if they're hunting for me."

"The wilderness!" Talyra was horror-stricken. "That's so dangerous!"

"I'm in danger anyway."

She stared at him, beginning to take in the fact that he would always be a fugitive. "Where will you go after you get the clothes? What will become of you?"

"I don't know," he admitted frankly. "I won't pretend that I can ever come back, Talyra."

They were both aware of the likelihood of his recapture, and that it must not be mentioned; they must go on as if the escape could succeed. "Where shall I hide the clothes?" she asked, trying to keep her voice steady.

"At the schoolhouse." It would be deserted, he knew, since there was no school during harvest season; and it was on the opposite side of the village from the jail, where everyone would be gathering to see him taken away. "Put them in the hollow near the place we used to go for the afternoon break—remember?"

"I'll always remember," she whispered, caressing his bruised cheek. "Noren, it—it just wasn't meant to work out for us, was it? You couldn't ever have been happy with the life we'd have had. You're—well, you are what you are, and our loving each other wouldn't have made any difference."

"No," he said quietly. "But I love you more than I could ever love anyone else, Talyra."

"I—I'm proud. It's crazy, when I'm so sure you're wrong about things, yet I'm proud of you for being brave enough to be yourself."

He hugged her to him. "I don't feel brave when I think about not seeing you again."

"We've got to be. Let me go before I start crying." Talyra freed herself and resolutely picked up her bundle. "I know

(82

you don't want me to talk about the Mother Star," she told him, "but I'll say this anyway: may its spirit guard you. I've got to be myself, too, you see, and I couldn't let a person I love go off without a proper farewell. It's not so foolish as you think! Someday—well, maybe you'll find it's been with you all along."

Noren stood watching, his own eyes wet, until she vanished around a bend in the road, wondering in confusion how anything that meant so much to Talyra could be wholly false.

V

NOREN DID NOT RETREAT INTO THE WILDERNESS THAT DAY;
the thicket proved hiding place enough, though in order to
watch the road he couldn't avoid exposing himself to view.
Occasional farmers passed by and one or two of them
looked at him curiously, but showed no signs of suspecting
him to be anything but an ordinary Technician. There was
no reason why a Technician should not sit quietly in the
shade if he wished to, although it wasn't usual. The weather
being suffocatingly hot, he was probably envied. Those
farmers would be surprised, Noren thought ruefully, if they
knew he was obliged to rest not by the heat, but by hunger.

It was his second day without food, and he was feeling
the effects. He had not told Talyra, for there was nothing
she could have done and it would only have worried her;
but he knew that if he was to walk to the schoolhouse that
night, he must reserve his strength. That was why, after
much inner debate, he decided to risk waiting out the
day where he was. If either villagers or Technicians had

launched a full-scale search, he would have had no chance to elude them, but they apparently were convinced by Talyra's story to hunt elsewhere—either that, or they simply assumed that he would not stay in the area most likely to be combed.

That set him to thinking. He had made no plans as to what he would do once he got rid of the uniform, other than to leave the village far behind. It mattered little where he headed, for the problems of finding work and of avoiding recapture would be the same everywhere. In other localities he would not be recognized; however, since Technicians could talk not only with each other but with all villages by means of Radiophone Machines, they'd undoubtedly alert people to be on the lookout for a stranger of his description. It would be wisest to stick to farms, staying at each only long enough to earn a meal. Yet he could not travel the roads by day lest he be spotted from an aircar. He'd have to walk at night, or else go cross-country, which would be perilous at best. In his heart Noren knew that he could not move from farm to farm indefinitely. Sooner or later he would be caught.

He looked out through the clustered web of bushes toward the mountains. There? *Beyond the Tomorrow Mountains,* the Prophecy said . . . what did lie beyond? There was little point in wondering. In order to reach the mountains, he would have to go through an endless stretch of total wilderness, and while he'd learned that the water was drinkable, there would be no food. To be sure, the savages lived there, and they must eat something; but he had no way of guessing what it was. The High Law's prohibition against tasting any plant that grew in unquickened ground was not as absurd as the injunction against "impure" water, for most such plants were indeed poisonous. And a tale he'd once heard about savages eating creatures of the streams was too fantastic to be credited; Noren's stomach, empty though it was, turned over at the mere thought. The

85)

Tomorrow Mountains were tempting, but unattainable.

Moreover, his real aim was not to run but to talk with people, people who might question the Scholars' supremacy if not openly oppose it. There'd be few opportunities for that if he spent his life in hiding. And might he not last as long—perhaps longer—by using bolder tactics? The Scholars would expect him to hide. They had immeasurable power and would eventually be able to locate him, but their search would be systematic; they would begin where it was most logical for him to go. The last place they would look would be at the walls of the City itself!

Excitement rose in Noren. They'd tried to take him to the City and would therefore expect him to get as far away as possible. Yet the markets outside the walls were the one place where a stranger would be inconspicuous. The markets were unlike a village. There'd be different kinds of people there: not only traders, not only those anxious to attend the religious ceremonies, but men adventurous enough simply to want to see the fabled towers for themselves. And then too, there would perhaps be many Technicians, some of whom might listen to his ideas. His heart raced, and for the first time since his arrest he felt a surge of elation. Despite himself, he still felt drawn to the City. That was where knowledge was. If he hadn't many days of freedom left, he would take advantage of them! He would follow his original plan and go to the City not as a prisoner, but in his own time, of his own will.

An hour before noon the regular rain started, and to his amazement, Noren found that the smooth fabric of the Technician's uniform in some strange way repelled the drops. He did not get wet at all. Often enough he'd been soaked to the skin and had not minded, for the scorching sun of afternoon dried clothes quickly; but it was galling to think that more comfortable ones existed. He would discard them with regret. Fingering the lantern, he realized that he would discard that with regret, also. It was made mostly of the bonelike material and of glass, but inside the glass globe were metal parts. Metal was sacred; he, a heretic, was certainly the last person who'd be thought worthy to be in possession of any; yet he felt no more guilt than when he had drunk from the stream. He *knew* he'd committed no sin. All the High Priests in the world couldn't shake that conviction, no matter what Talyra thought. Still . . . something was missing. There were pieces that didn't quite fit. The Technician's words came back to Noren: *It's not enough just to learn what there isn't; we need to know what there is. . . .*

Holding out cupped hands, Noren let the rain fill them, thinking again how unreasonable it was to suppose that an event as natural and as predictable as sunrise could be controlled by the Scholars. Four days with rain, two without, week after week forever—one might as well believe they determined the hour of dawn! Yet in the light of his newest theory, rain puzzled him in another way, since it was obviously the source of pond and stream water, and could logically have been pronounced impure, as that was. Still, the Scholars could hardly have required people to transport enough City-purified water from village centers to keep the cisterns full, much less to carry cistern water into the grainfields. So they'd conveniently neglected to decree that rainwater was forbidden, and to explain the discrepancy had declared that they themselves made it rain. Why, he wondered, were people so gullible?

The clouds dispersed on schedule; the pungent smell of drying moss hung in the hot, thick air; the sparkling beads of moisture disappeared from the gray-green webbing that joined the stems of nearby shrubs. Slowly the afternoon dragged to its end. Noren watched the moons come up, noticing with illogical surprise that their crescents were not much fuller than on the night of the dance. That had been only three nights ago, yet it seemed a long way back.

When it was dark, he started for the village, pausing by

87)

the first bridge he crossed to assuage his thirst at a forbidden stream. His body was stiff and sore from the beating and he was also weak from hunger, but he knew he must inure himself to that; it probably wouldn't be the last time he would have to go several days without food. The light of his Power-lit lantern, reflected in the dark water, dazzled him as he bent down to drink. He still found it incredible to be carrying such an object; it was the first Machine he'd been permitted to handle since the memorable day on which he had touched the aircar that had landed at his father's farm.

He dared not walk through the village before the taverns closed, so he waited on the outskirts until a lamp burned in only one building, the radiophonist's office. That was always open in case there should be need to summon the Technicians in some emergency, though ordinary messages to and from the City were transmitted only by day. Noren strode swiftly past, but to his dismay the radiophonist himself, having caught sight of the brilliant lantern, appeared in the doorway. "Sir!" the man exclaimed. "Sir, may I beg your assistance?"

Noren froze. He was not qualified to perform any task for which a Technician's help would be asked, and what was more, if he showed his face he might well be recognized, if only by his bruises. Yet neither could he ignore the request, for that too would arouse suspicion.

"My greetings," he said evenly. "How may I be of service to you?"

"I am pleased by your concern, sir," said the man, stepping into the street. "The Radiophone Machine has stopped working. I planned to send someone to Prosperity tomorrow to report it by way of their Machine, but if you would grant me a few moments, that would not be necessary."

In panic, Noren tried to think of some legitimate excuse, but he could not. To refuse would not be appropriate behavior for a Technician; if he did so the radiophonist, who had undoubtedly seen him at one time or another, might look past the uniform to his face. Yet how could he repair a Machine of which he knew nothing?

"I will examine it," he declared resolutely, and with a sense of helpless despair entered the dimly-lighted room. There were two other men there, friends of the radiophonist on duty; any misstep could mean that an outcry would be raised, and the fact that no real Technicians could be called made it all the more certain that he, having had the unprecedented effrontery to pose as one, would be dealt with by the mob.

The Radiophone Machine rested on a small stone table in one corner. Noren had never seen it before, but he knew what it did: in some wondrous manner it transmitted the voices of faraway Technicians to whoever stood close to its grille, and vice versa. No one was permitted to touch it but the radiophonists; they alone among villagers were entrusted with the sacred task of Machine operation. A position of such prestige could be obtained only by those consecrated to it through appointment to the training center.

But though radiophonists were trained in the operation of the Radiophone Machine and in the rules governing the occasions upon which it could and could not be used, they were told nothing of its inner workings. Knowledge of that sort was, according to common belief, beyond the scope of the ordinary human mind and could be absorbed only by Scholars and Technicians. Noren did not agree, especially since he'd learned that not all Technicians had such knowledge; still he couldn't deny that he himself possessed none of it. He did not know anything about Machines except that they worked by Power, and that if Power was absent, they could no longer function.

He surveyed the Radiophone Machine thoughtfully. He must do something, he knew, and the maintenance of his disguise depended on doing it with apparent confidence. "Perhaps," he asserted boldly, "its Power Cell is dead."

"Yes, sir," replied the radiophonist. "I think, sir, that it's past due to be checked."

Encouraged, Noren recalled that the young Technician had remarked that his usual job was the checking of radiophone equipment. Very likely he would have checked this Machine had he not been taken away in the aircar. In his belt he had carried Power Cells, one of which he had inserted into the lantern, thereby causing the light to burn more brightly; could it be that the same one would make the Machine work again? It was a gamble, but if it failed he'd be no worse off than if he hesitated.

"I do not have any new Power Cells with me," he said, "but the one in my lantern may serve. I shall see." He switched off the light and carefully opened the panel in its bottom as he had seen the Technician do, withdrawing the small red cube that contained the mysterious Power. That part was easy. The problem would be to open the Radiophone Machine.

It was not reasonable, Noren decided, that a panel would be placed in its bottom; this did not look like a thing that should be turned upside down. The opening must be in the back. He grasped the Machine with trembling hands and started to turn it around, whereupon it gave forth loud crackling and hissing sounds. It took all his courage not to let go, but since the radiophonist and his friends did not draw back in terror, he concluded that these sounds must be normal.

The Machine's back did indeed have a panel, but it was evident that it could not be unlatched in the same manner as the one in the lantern. Noren cursed under his breath. If the radiophonist had watched the process of replacing Power Cells before, as he undoubtedly had, he must know perfectly well how to remove the back; yet he would not presume to advise a Technician and would be dumbfounded if his opinion were to be sought. On the other hand, he would be horrified by the sacrilege if the Machine was clumsily handled. Noticing in desperation that its sides curled over the panel whereas its top did not, Noren pressed upward and found that the entire back slid out easily. His relief faded quickly, however, when inside, amid a maze of appallingly complex devices, he saw not one Power Cell, but four.

He scowled, debating as to his next move. If there were four, then obviously four were needed; yet they appeared to be exactly alike. Would all four have died at the same time? Probably not, for if they had, that would mean their death was predictable, and "checking" would be unnecessary. He should therefore need to replace only one; but which? Was it possible to tell by looking? The Power Cell the Technician had removed from the lantern hadn't looked any different from its replacement, so perhaps it was usual to proceed by trial and error. Noren scrutinized the cube in his hand. One surface, he saw, was unlike the others in that it had a metal button in its center; he must take care to position it exactly as the Machine's old cubes were positioned.

One by one, Noren removed the Power Cells, putting his own in each successive place while the men watched reverently. Each time he held his breath; if it did not work anywhere, his ignorance would surely be exposed. But on the third try it did work. "There, sir!" exclaimed someone. "That's done it." Leaning over, Noren saw that a red light had appeared on the front of the Machine and was deeply grateful for the comment; he would not have known how to tell whether he'd succeeded.

"Thank you, sir," said the radiophonist. "It's fortunate that you passed by tonight."

"It is indeed," Noren replied, as he replaced the Machine's back panel.

"Will you not take the dead Power Cell away?" the man inquired anxiously, indicating the discarded red cube. "It cannot, of course, be left unprotected, and it would be irreverent for me to lay hands upon it."

"Certainly I shall," said Noren, suppressing a laugh, and thrust the thing casually into his pocket. "Goodnight, citizen."

He walked down the moonlit street, his now-useless lantern swinging from his hand, exhilarated by his triumph. There was nothing so awesome about Power! Surely anyone intelligent enough to be appointed a radiophonist ought to be able to replace Power Cells without the aid of a Technician . . . or was intelligence necessarily the basis upon which radiophonists were chosen?

Of course it wasn't, Noren perceived suddenly. A radiophonist's job, he saw, was not at all difficult. It demanded not skill, but willingness to follow instructions without overstepping certain prescribed bounds. Those who did the job were admired because they operated Machines, which most citizens viewed with awe and veneration; but far from being superior to others, the radiophonists were equally awed by the Power Cells. And that, no doubt, was the way the Scholars wanted them to be.

No wonder he hadn't been offered an appointment to the training center! No wonder the craftsmen and traders he knew, most of whom were much shrewder than that radiophonist, had not been appointed either! The few people who disappeared from the place must be the ones who'd shown more initiative than the Scholars had anticipated. They must be the ones who had begun to learn too much.

He had no need to worry about Talyra's safety there, he realized with relief. Talyra was intelligent, but she would not ask for information beyond what she was given; furthermore, though a nurse's work was more demanding than a radiophonist's, it in no way infringed upon the Technicians' sole right to the Power and the Machines.

At the schoolhouse all was quiet. Noren made his way cautiously around the building, glad that the moons were up and yet fearful of being observed. The spot where he and

Talyra had liked to sit was at the far edge of the school-yard, half-hidden by a clump of shrubby growth. In the hollow there he found a neat pile of things: trousers, a tunic, and between the two garments, a carrying-jug of pure water plus a knotted kerchief. The latter was heavy; as he untied it, he saw the white gleam of coins, far more coins than could have been acquired in any way but by the sale of the treasured wristband. She had given him all she had. He paused a short while, staring at the flattened moss where they had spent happy moments together, and then firmly closed the door on a part of himself that could never be regained.

Smoke rose from the chimney of a sturdily-built farm-house, and warm lamplight shone out through the dusk. The work-beast in the fodder patch raised its head as Noren approached, giving a warning bellow; he paid no attention. He could not go on without eating, and the only way to get a meal was to ask for it. Stumbling across the dusty yard, he called at the door in as firm a tone as he could muster.

The night before, after changing into the clothes Talyra had obtained for him and ditching the Technician's things in the depths of a pond, he had gone on until dawn, forcing himself despite his hunger to cover as much distance as he could. He'd passed straight through Prosperity, afraid that if he waited there to buy food, someone would remember him from his recent trip in pursuit of the trader. When morning came, he'd ventured to get breakfast at the first farm he had reached; but though he'd offered to pay, the farmer's wife had been surly and had given him only a stale chunk of bread. Noren had taken it to a depleted clay pit nearby, where he'd gulped it down ravenously and then, too exhausted to try another place, had slept through the day's heat, sheltered by sedges that grew out of coarse purple moss. Now it was evening again, and if he could not get supper, he would be unable to walk much farther.

He had no choice but to make the attempt, dangerous though it might prove.

The matting of the door before him was pulled back and a motherly-looking woman exclaimed, "Lew! Lew, come here!" Noren found himself being propelled inside by a stout, brawny man who studied him briefly, then indicated a chair by the lamp. The room was thick with the dizzying odor of stewing fowl. Noren sat down. Nine or ten small children stared with interest, and he realized that his bruises as well as his presence would demand comment, though the only explanation he could think of was at best a flimsy one.

He forced the fear out of his voice. "I—I've been delayed," he told them. "I was to meet my cousin in Prosperity and help him take a load to the City markets, only I left the road to rest and—well, slipped into a quarry. He'll wait in the next village till tomorrow, and I'm sure I can catch up, but I'm awfully hungry. I can pay—"

"You don't need to," said the woman cordially. "I've fixed plenty; we'll just set another place."

"Thanks, I'd appreciate that."

"Cistern's out back, if you want to wash up," the woman said, surveying him. She fingered her apron. "Why, you're just a boy! The City's a long way off—"

"Not too far for a young fellow his age," her husband Lew interrupted. "I went to the City markets once, the year I finished school; right before we were married. It's really a sight. And the music—you never heard anything like that music they have at the Benison." He smiled, remembering. "Inspiring, it is."

No doubt, thought Noren, the Scholars could arrange inspiration with the same efficiency they employed in arranging everything else. He had heard often of the Benison, a ceremony held early each morning, before the Gates, to open the markets for the day's business; but it hadn't occurred to him that to avoid attracting notice he would have to attend. The idea dismayed him, for the crowd would be smaller than on holidays, and he did not believe that he could bring himself to kneel, as one must in the immediate presence of Scholars.

Lew grinned at him. "You're having a real adventure, I'll bet. Does it come up to your hopes, being on your own?"

"I guess so."

"We've got supper almost on," the woman put in. "Dorie, you take him out to the cistern."

One of the younger boys tagged along, and both children appraised Noren curiously as he splashed water over his bruised face and arms, then filled his stoppered carrying-jug. "I don't think I'd like an adventure," commented Dorie.

"I would," retorted her little brother promptly. "The City's where the Technicians live. Have you ever talked to a Technician, mister?"

"Yes."

"That's what I want to be when I grow up."

"Silly!" cried Dorie. "People don't grow up to be Technicians."

"But I want to run a Machine."

Noren looked at the small boy, who was as yet too young to know that wanting was not the same as getting, and his heart ached. This child, he sensed, was someone who would care. *You could grow up to run a Machine, or even to build one,* he thought, *and you wouldn't need the title of Technician, either.*

Would Lew and his wife listen to reason? Would they agree that their sons and daughters had a right to the knowledge that could give them Machines, and more? Maybe he should risk telling them; it might be his only chance. Suppose he never reached the City?

In the big kitchen, the woman was ladling hot stew into brown pottery bowls. Noren closed his eyes, leaning against the stone doorway; hunger was making him giddy. For an instant he was back in his own mother's kitchen, at home. Was he a fool to have given up everything that mattered to other people for the sake of a truth that would lead him ultimately to death?

The girl Dorie clutched at his hand. "What's the matter?"

"Nothing—nothing's the matter."

"Yes, there is." With the quick intuition of childhood she announced, "You're *afraid*."

"No—"

"You shouldn't be," the child continued. "The Prophecy says the spirit of the Mother Star protects everybody, and as long as we believe in it nothing can hurt us."

"Does it?"

"Don't you *know?* Mother, he—"

"Yes, of course I do!" Noren said hastily. " *'It is our life's bulwark; and so long as we believe in it, no force can destroy us, though the heavens themselves be consumed.'* " So long as we believe in it. It was his misfortune, maybe, to believe in something a good deal less comforting.

They stood behind the wicker benches while the woman lit the table lamp and began the familiar words in a calm, unhurried voice: " *'Let us rejoice in the bounty of the land . . . from the Mother Star came the heritage that has blessed it . . .'* " With effort, Noren kept his voice steady and clear. These people would not understand his heresy. If he were to speak out, there would be more danger of harm to them than to him, he perceived; they would be lost without their faith. Perhaps the Scholars' greatest cruelty was in the way they deluded the good, kind people who were hoping in vain for the fulfillment of a false promise.

He tried to eat slowly, without revealing the urgency of his hunger, and to talk as a carefree traveler rather than an imperiled fugitive. "Your youngest son is a bright lad," he remarked to the mother, wondering if the spark he'd

(96

seen in the boy had been noticed by the parents.

"He is an adopted child," replied the woman proudly. "So is the littlest girl."

"My congratulations," said Noren, smiling at the youngsters. "They are fine children." It was a strange fact, he thought, that adopted children so often seemed brighter than most, as if the circumstances of their birth had been particularly fortunate to offset whatever tragedy had resulted in their becoming Wards of the City. There were many such babies—they were practically always adopted in infancy—and it was a mark of honor to have one, for it was well known that the women Technicians who were their official guardians placed them only with worthy families who would love them and give them good care. One wondered where they all came from, since although every village's foundlings became Wards of the City, there seemed to be more than could be accounted for in that way; it occurred suddenly to Noren that the Technicians' own orphans might be included. No one was permitted to know the parentage of those who had become Wards when too young to remember.

He scrutinized the little boy more closely. Could this child, who thought that ordinary people could become Technicians, possibly have been born as one? He had love in abundance; he seemed happy; yet had he somehow been deprived of his birthright? But that was nonsense, Noren realized with chagrin. It was no more unfair for him than for his foster brothers and sisters; knowledge was the birthright not only of Technicians, but of everyone.

"You must stay the night with us," said Lew. "We've an extra bed in our sons' room."

Noren shook his head. The thought of sleeping in a bed was tempting, but he could not accept; not only would it delay him, but to shelter him might somehow put this family in danger. "That's kind of you," he said regretfully, "but if I'm not in the next village by sunrise I might miss my cousin again. I'd best stay at the inn there."

The whole family walked out to the road with him after the meal. "Thanks for the supper," he told the woman. "You're surely a good cook."

She smiled and squeezed his hand. "May the spirit of the Mother Star be with you," she said.

"And with you," Noren answered, half-wishing he could mean more by the words than a courteous response to hospitality. He turned rapidly and started up the curving road, toward the top of the hill.

Noren stopped at many farms after that, for breakfast or for supper, but rarely more than once a day. Some families were cordial, as Lew's had been; others were less so and demanded payment. When possible he asked for work before offering money, for he knew he must save as many of Talyra's coins as he could to use at the markets, where there would be no farms and he would have to buy food from shopkeepers. That meant that he got little sleep, since he traveled by night, but working in someone's fields was safer than sleeping in them. It was increasingly hard to find hiding places, for the closer he got to the City, the fewer patches of uncleared land he found.

He passed through villages only in darkness. It amazed him that he encountered no Technicians searching for him, nor even heard rumors from the farmers of such a search; and as the days went by the tension in him grew. If the Scholar Stefred wanted him caught, why wasn't a more intensive effort being made?

At last he could endure it no longer and decided to risk a deliberate inquiry. The people he ate with that day were friendly, but did not seem particular devout; the subject, Noren felt, could safely be raised.

"I hear they're on the lookout for an escaped heretic," he said casually.

"Oh?" the farmer replied. "I was in to the center only

yesterday, and nobody said a word about that."

"It was a trader who told me," Noren asserted. "Perhaps the man's not thought to be near here; traders pick up news from all over."

"I can't understand why anybody would get himself convicted of heresy," the wife declared.

"Some people just don't believe everything in the Prophecy, I guess," said Noren in a noncommittal tone.

"No doubt, but why do they admit it when they know what's bound to happen? It's all words anyway; is that worth suffering for?"

"Heretics must think so. Or else they think that the High Law's not what it should be, and that if they could get people to agree with them things could be changed."

"Rubbish," said the man. "The High Law is as it is, and the best way for a man to live comfortably is to follow it and keep his mouth shut."

"Once," Noren said slowly, "I heard a heretic say that he cared more for truth than for comfort."

"Goodness!" exclaimed the wife. "A nice boy like you shouldn't be talking to heretics. You could get yourself in trouble."

"He said it in public," answered Noren with a straight face. "It was at his trial."

"What happened to him?" she inquired.

"He was convicted and locked up to be turned over to the Scholars. Do you think he deserved it?"

"Frankly, I don't," the man admitted. "Live and let live, I say; I don't hold with punishing a man for what he thinks. But you'd not catch me talking that way in the village." His eyes narrowed with sudden suspicion. "You wouldn't repeat it, would you?"

"No," Noren assured him, "I wouldn't."

It was apparent that his escape had not been publicized; perhaps Talyra had not even needed to use the story they'd concocted. If the inhabitants of villages along the road hadn't been alterted to watch for him, Noren concluded, it could only be that the Scholars were hoping he'd feel falsely secure and would grow careless. Their strategy was more subtle than he'd anticipated, which was all the more reason for him to move with caution.

Yet he could not resist sounding out more farmers as to their opinions. The first one's view seemed predominant; though there were some sincerely devout people, and others who took out a dislike of the Scholars' supremacy on anybody who dared oppose it, the majority of those he met couldn't have cared less whether the Prophecy was true or the High Law justified. Like his own father, they were interested only in practical affairs. Noren soon found that he could safely make comments bordering on heresy as long as he saw such people in the privacy of their homes, but he guessed that in a crowd they would be quick to clamor for his condemnation.

Would those he met at the City markets be any different? Noren wondered. If they weren't, he had no chance whatsoever to arouse opposition to the High Law; he must face that fact realistically. And what action could be taken even if he did succeed in convincing people? He had never gotten that far in his plans; he'd merely felt—and still felt, despite everything—that refusing to believe lies was in itself an act of importance.

During his none-too-frequent intervals of sleep he dreamed a lot. There were the old recurring nightmares of the City, now immediate and concrete: he would find himself bound hand and foot, facing the Scholar Stefred, who towered over him in a dark cavern filled with terrifying Machines; and he would wake trembling, telling himself that he could elude capture forever, yet knowing better. But there were also other dreams in which he was not afraid, but instead was on the verge of meeting secret, inexpressible things that he approached with joy—things concerning the ultimate, forbidden knowledge that was hidden behind the City's walls. Always, to his frustration, he woke just as he was about to learn the answers. On those occasions he could scarcely wait for dusk before starting off, and he drove himself to walk faster and faster through the night, knowing that it was foolish, yet seeing no real reason to resist his growing compulsion. The City and its mysteries had become a goal both feared and longed for; but the longing outweighed the fear.

It became harder and harder to locate spots where he could rest. Farms were small and crowded close together near the City, while villages were comparatively large; almost all the wild plants had been cut. Then too, there were no streams. Long, straight conduits stretched off into the distance from sandy beds that were thereafter dry, and the work-beasts were watered in unnaturally-shallow ponds. At first that puzzled Noren, but before long he figured it out: the water was being channelled into the City itself, purified, and then sent out through the clay aqueducts that paralleled the main roads, from which pipes branched off to fill the huge village cisterns where people drew what they needed to supplement what was collected from rain. Fortunately he had the carrying-jug; he'd been replenishing it at farms in any case, since he might have aroused suspicion had he stopped for a meal without requesting water.

The day came when at first light Noren could see nothing around him but flat fields—newly-planted grainfields, the season zone being the same as Prosperity's—without a tinge of purple anywhere, nor yet of gray-green apart from fodder. There were a good many houses, but he'd had plenty to eat the previous evening and he never stopped for breakfast unless his shelter was already chosen, for he felt it was dangerous to walk far after sunrise. This time he had no choice; he must keep going.

The sky to his left was yellow. One of the moons, it was hard to tell which, traced a thin white curve above a silhouetted barn. Overhead a few fading stars displayed a faint, determined sparkle. Where was the Mother Star supposed to appear, anyway: in one of the constellations, or in some unnatural place like the zenith? Noren couldn't recall that the Prophecy told, and since whoever had written it had gone to so much trouble to manufacture details like the exact date, they might at least have mentioned where to look. Not that that wasn't a silly question to waste thought on when there were so many true enigmas, like what stars *were,* for instance—real stars! Having walked for countless hours under them, Noren had often stared upward in bafflement, wondering whether even the Scholars possessed knowledge of that sort.

The sun bulged over the horizon, blinding Noren momentarily, and in the same instant he heard an ominous sound. An aircar was floating toward him above the field! With the new-risen sun behind it, it was hard to see; but a long, dark shadow preceded it, and it was headed directly for him.

Noren did not have time to consider the situation; he reacted instinctively. Without stopping to think that if by any chance the men in the aircar weren't hunting for him, it would be unwise to attract their attention by an attempt to evade them, he threw himself headlong into the ditch beside the road. As he fell, a sharp rock stabbed into his knee, dazing him with pain, and he lay helpless while the aircar hovered and dropped lower.

Incredibly, it did not land. The Technicians saw him; Noren was sure of that, for as he turned onto his back their faces were clear, but to his astonishment the aircar rose abruptly and drifted off in the direction of the City. Bewildered, he tried to climb out of the ditch—only to find that the injured knee would not support his weight.

VI

FOR SOME TIME NOREN REMAINED IN THE DITCH, AT A LOSS to know what to do. He could go no farther alone. Once the worst of the pain subsided, he realized that he would be able to walk with the aid of a strong bandage; but the fabric of his tunic was too coarse to tear, and in any case, he could not climb. Moreover, the Technicians would undoubtedly be back for him. Though those particular ones apparently hadn't known that he was an escaped heretic, they would surely report what they had seen, for it was not normal for a villager to run from Technicians; and they would then be told that a fugitive was being sought.

As the sun rose higher, he propped himself against the stony bank and prepared to hail the first passer-by. As close to the City as he was, the road would be heavily traveled. He had no choice but to trust to luck in being found by someone who would help him without asking too many questions.

Luck was with him: a trader's sledge appeared before

anybody else came by, and the trader was bound for the markets. He was a lean, brisk man who answered Noren's shout with cheerful alacrity. "I fell, and I can't walk till my knee's bandaged, I guess," Noren told him ruefully, "but I can drive. I'll spell you if you'll take me." Something in the man's manner warned him that it would be best not to mention his coins unless he had to.

"I'll do that," the trader declared. "I'd like to drive straight through tonight so's to get there by mid-morning." He boosted Noren to the seat and, yanking the reins, cursed casually at the work-beast.

After so many days and nights of effort, it was a relief to sit back and let himself be carried along. Also, he was less conspicuous, for on this road sledges and strings of work-beasts outnumbered people on foot. That would compensate, Noren hoped, for the peril of going through village centers in broad daylight. It was his first good look at the region's centers, which, like the local farms, had quite a few buildings of sun-dried brick instead of stone; clay must be more plentiful than at home, where all that could be found was purified by Machine for the making of pipe and pottery.

The sledge jarred, and a fowl squawked noisily; Noren twisted around. There were hens in back, in wicker crates. Did hens sense that they were on the way to the butcher? Of course hens weren't very bright, but then, there were times when brightness was a questionable advantage. He sucked in deep breaths, trying to dispel the fogginess from his mind; it was hard to keep his eyes open. He found himself wondering how long it had been since he had left his own village.

And then a new question worked its way into his thoughts: just how did the Scholars . . . kill a person? The rumors gave no hint. All the people he'd ever heard of —aside from the few who'd been hanged or who'd been victims of accidents, rare illnesses or murder—had died of old age. How Technicians died no one knew; and as for the Scholars themselves, it was generally supposed that they didn't, though that was probably untrue.

Throughout the long, hot day the work-beast plodded steadily forward, resting only during the pre-noon downpour. When the rain stopped, Noren took over the driving, but the dazed, lethargic feeling stayed with him. The trader was not a talkative man and for that Noren was glad, since between his drowsiness and the persistent ache in his knee it was all he could do to keep a firm grip on the reins. He ought to be more afraid, he thought. He ought to be watching with alarm for the inevitable approach of another aircar, but it all seemed too unreal to matter.

At sundown they halted again by a pond, where the work-beast was allowed to drink, and shared bread washed down with ale from a jug that had been stashed under the seat. The trader drank considerably more of this than Noren, and as a result drove only a short while after they started again; soon he was snoring in the back of the sledge, leaving Noren to keep the work-beast moving. The road was well-lighted, for all three major moons were at full phase and even Little Moon seemed to shine with extraordinary brilliance. *The time when the Mother Star itself shall blaze as bright as Little Moon,* he thought wistfully: if there could indeed be such a time—a time when some immutable power would bring about the downfall of the Scholars and the fulfillment of all their empty promises —how different the world would be! *The ancient knowledge shall be free to all people . . .* why ancient? Noren wondered. Why had the Scholars who wrote the Prophecy used that particular word? It was almost as if there'd been a source of knowledge that had preceded them.

Long before he reached it, Noren could see the lights of the City. The whole valley seemed to glimmer. There were dozen of lights, white and yellow and green, swarming around a shining beacon that made him feel that if the

Scholars wished, they could place the Mother Star in the sky themselves. He had known that the City was lit by Power, but he had not dreamed that there could be so much Power in the world at one time. He drew rein, overcome by emotions he could scarcely interpret. The moment he'd been anticipating was at hand: the end of his search was in sight, for better or for worse, and he looked upon it less with terror than with eagerness.

When dawn came, the trader roused himself and clambered back onto the seat to resume driving. Noren relinquished the job thankfully; the sights before him were too wondrous to claim anything less than his full attention. He was almost there. Ahead, the scalloped walls of the City stood tall behind a conglomeration of ordinary stone and brick buildings and the long, low wattle structures of the markets. As he watched, the rising sun illuminated the immense silvery barrier and the incredible spires behind it, shooting back dazzling streaks not merely from their widely-spaced windows, but from the entire surface of each tower.

Noren stared, spellbound. There, in those soaring towers, was hidden all the knowledge he sought. Was it possible that other travelers could see them without feeling the unbearable desire they aroused in him? Surely even Talyra, who must have come days ago to the training center, could not have remained unstirred!

The trader thrust the reins back into Noren's hands momentarily and peeled off his outer tunic. "Going to swelter again," he remarked matter-of-factly. "Say, is this your first trip to the markets?"

"Yes."

"Quite a sight, huh?" The man waved a casual hand toward the spectacle that in Noren had evoked near-reverence. "You know, someday villages'll be like that. Ordinary folks'll have all the stuff the Technicians've got, Machines of their own and everything."

Abruptly, Noren's head cleared. This man might be persuaded; at any rate, it could well be his last opportunity to try. "Do you believe in the Prophecy?" he asked directly.

His companion swore. "What d'you mean, do I believe it? I'm no fool heretic."

"I mean do you think it's right for us to wait all that time to have what the Technicians have? To be kept from knowing all there is to know? Knowledge isn't property; it should be free! We could have Machines right away, for instance, if ''

The man studied Noren intently. "We couldn't understand stuff like that," he said. "Someday folks'll be smarter than us, and then—"

"Technicians are men like other men, and so arc Scholars! *They* understand, and we could, too, if we weren't afraid."

"Say, you better be careful. They way you talk, you could get yourself into a mess." He leaned over and spat into the street.

"Yes," admitted Noren levelly. "But if enough of us talked about it—well, maybe we could make something happen."

The trader turned, grabbing Noren's wrist with tense, calloused fingers. "You mean that? You don't like being bossed by Technicians that think they know everything; you don't fall for a bunch of phony stories about Mother Stars and sacred Laws, maybe?"

"You know they're not true, too!"

"Sure, I know. What's fair about them that live inside the walls having stuff the ones outside ain't got?"

"That's exactly what I mean! If there was only some way we could—"

Speculatively, the man asked, "Ever hear what happens to people that think your way once the Scholars get hold of 'em?"

Noren nodded slowly. The trader said nothing more, but took the reins and continued on in silence. Before long they drew to a halt in front of a wattle-and-daub shed. "This is where I unload," he announced. "Stick with me, and I'll introduce you to some pals of mine." He tied the work-beast and went around to the back of the sledge, lifting out one of the crates of cackling fowl and disappearing with it into the building.

Excitement exploded in Noren. At last, someone who shared his beliefs! And it had been implied that he would meet others who shared them! There was, of course, a possibility that the trader would betray him, perhaps even try to claim a reward for doing so; but since the Technicians must already have a good idea of his whereabouts, the risk seemed worth taking. Anyway, he had no choice but to wait, for he could go nowhere without something to bandage his knee.

When the unloading was finished, the man drove on to another section of the markets. Noren surveyed the long rows of open stalls with interest. Here the traders from many villages met to bring produce from the farms, which the Technicians paid well for, and to purchase fine craftwork as well as the less common herbs, yeast, and the many commodities—glass, cloth, paper, writing styluses and the like—that came from the City alone, where they were made by Machines. Strangely enough, however, the place seemed nearly deserted. "There aren't a lot of peor le around," he observed, puzzled. "Is it always like this?"

"Most everyone's in the plaza," the trader said shortly. "A heretic's going to recant this morning, and they'll all be there to see the show. We will, too, soon's I can get you a bandage."

The sledge lurched ahead, its runners grating on sand already marred by countless tracks. Near the stable where they left it was a fabric stall, and Noren, in producing the money for a stout strip of cut cloth, could not avoid displaying his entire kerchief full of smooth white coins. The trader eyed them, but made no comment; he simply went ahead and wrapped Noren's leg tightly until it was stiffened by many layers of bandaging. When it was finished, Noren stood clumsily, his knee hurting fiercely as he shifted his weight, and hobbled along without objection. The last thing he wanted was to watch some other heretic being forced to go through the degrading ceremony to which he himself had sworn never to submit, but his companion seemed insistent, and the man was his only link to people who might prove kindred spirits.

They reached the plaza late, for the stabling of the workbeast had taken time and Noren was unable to walk fast; the ceremony was already in progress. Little of it could be heard, since they stood at the outer fringes of a vast, muttering crowd, so far back that to Noren's relief he was not made conspicuous by his failure to kneel. Though the majority of the spectators had done so, others like themselves had abandoned propriety for the sake of getting a good view.

The plaza faced a stretch of unobstructed City wall, in the center of which were the tall, majestic Gates. In front of them a white-paved platform surmounted a wide flight of steps. The backdrop of glittering towers, rising so high above the walls that Noren had to tip his head to glimpse their tops, was awesome, but he could devote little thought to it; his attention was focused on the occupants of the platform. They were Scholars. He knew they were because of the brilliant blue robes they wore, robes he'd seen in the paintings that adorned the village hall and schoolhouse: longer than women's skirts, but less full, with flowing sleeves that in the case of the center Priest were trimmed with bands of white. A number of Technicians were also present, and between them knelt the prisoner.

He faced the Scholars, his profile to the assembled people, with his hands bound behind him. His gray penitent's garments looked filthy; if his captors had any decency at all, he could at least have been given new ones!

But there was no reason to suppose that they were that humane, Noren thought in sick despair. How could anyone who'd opposed them be so contemptible as to buy his life with obeisance?

This man had been convicted of heresy, which meant that he once had believed at least some things contrary to the Prophecy or the High Law. Yet he knelt there, unabashedly declaring that he acknowledged the Book of the Prophecy to be "true in its entirety" and retracting "all criticisms" that he might ever have made of anything! Either he was the lowest sort of coward or . . . or they had done something awful to him, something past any stretch of the imagination. Though no signs of injury were apparent, Scholars might well have more subtle means of inflicting pain.

Shuddering, Noren watched with growing contempt both for the High Priests and for their victim. He was not close enough to see faces, but the man's bearing was shameless. He spoke with seeming conviction rather than with reluctance. The Scholars were silent, impassive, accepting this submission as if it were no more than their just due. What had they done to change someone who'd once defied them into a consenting tool of their authority?

They will never change me, Noren promised himself grimly. *No matter what they do or what they threaten, I will not deny the truth; I will not become like that man; I will not recant!*

There was an atmosphere in the crowd that he did not like; it was akin to the temper of the people in the village who'd taunted him at the time of his own arrest. Only the presence of the Scholars, he guessed, prevented it from erupting into something uglier. The animosity was directed not toward them, but toward the heretic. And Noren could not help sharing it. He could not help feeling more scorn than pity: not, as with the majority, because of the prisoner's heresy, but because he had sold out.

"We missed the best part," the trader remarked cryptically during a pause in the ceremony. He had, Noren noticed, been talking to a friend who'd approached him some time back. "All that's left now is the sentencing, and that's always the same. Come on."

"Where?" questioned Noren.

"A bunch of us are getting together to eat," the man answered in his brusque, decisive way. "I'm taking you along; but by the Mother Star, you'll be sorry if you've lied to me."

The place to which the trader's friend took them was a ramshackle shed behind one of the market buildings. It was dark and dingy and smelled like a stable; in fact it probably had been a stable at one time. "Sometimes we sleep here when we haven't the price of a room at an inn," the trader said. "You can stay if you like, only don't repeat what you hear."

"I won't," promised Noren, with mounting excitement at this clear indication of the men's sentiments. It amazed him that heresy could be spoken aloud at any sort of gathering. But, he reflected, the Technicians weren't empowered to arrest anyone who hadn't been convicted in a civil trial, and though the people who lived permanently at the markets had a village government of sorts, they probably did not go out of their way to watch travelers.

The earlier arrivals had brought food and ale, which they proceeded to share informally. There were five or six of them, an ill-assorted lot, most of them men Noren would never have suspected of caring for the things that mattered; he had to remind himself that if they disbelieved the Prophecy and risked open criticism of the High Law, they must care. And it was evident that they did take such risks, for though the trader vouched for him, he himself was eyed with hostile suspicion.

A big, rough man clutched Noren's shoulders in a viselike grip. "What did you think of that weakling?" he demanded, in obvious reference to the heretic whose recantation they had all observed.

"He sold out," Noren declared.

"And you wouldn't?"

"No!"

The man released him. "You sound as if you mean it," he conceded. "They all do before they're caught, of course; but you've as much backbone as any. He did, too, once— used to be a friend of ours." He grinned unpleasantly. "Well, he got what he had coming, and don't think we didn't give him our share."

"Are you trying to scare me?" said Noren, covering his confusion with a laugh.

"Just making sure you know what you've gotten into," the big man said. "Lots of farm boys don't."

"I know, all right," Noren assured him. He wondered what these men would think if they knew he had already been tried and convicted; for some reason he couldn't explain, he felt that it would be unwise to tell them yet.

He sat silent, eating food he scarcely tasted and listening to the discussion of the others with elation that was tinged, somehow, by an uneasiness he did not understand. He didn't need to convince this group, for its members were saying just what he'd despaired of ever getting across to anyone! They hated the Scholars; they considered the Prophecy a fraud; and above all, they resented the exclusive rights of the Technicians. There was a great deal of talk, much of it lewd, on all these topics; and not until it had gone on for some time did Noren see what disturbed him about it.

There was nothing these men did believe in. They spoke of Power and Machines, but never of knowledge; and not once had anyone mentioned truth. Nor had they any plan for improving matters. To be sure, Noren had no plan himself; but he had always supposed that if this many heretics ever got together, their first move would be to form one. "Mightn't there be some way we could change things?" he ventured during a lull in the conversation.

One of the men gave a bitter laugh. "Change things, he says! Why, there's nothing we or anybody else can do against Scholars."

"All you traders ever do is talk," protested a younger man. "We should rebel openly, that's what we should do."

"And get arrested for it? What would that buy us?"

"I've told you before, the Scholars will have to deal with us in public. There'll be none of this nonsense about civil trials then! They'll show their hand, and people will begin to see them for what they really are."

"I haven't noticed *you* doing any rebelling."

"It won't work unless a lot of us take action at the same time."

"It won't work anyway."

"It might!" Noren argued. "If enough people would oppose the High Law—"

"Aw, people won't listen," said the trader. "Guys that quote the Prophecy at you every time you start to talk to 'em—they don't deserve no Machines anyhow. It's men like us should be getting that stuff."

"Knowledge and Machines should be for everyone!"

"Even the ones too dumb to care? What for? You and I, now— Well, no use talking about it. There aren't enough smart guys in the world. I heard once the Scholars have a way to blow the whole City up into clouds. Burn every last thing, all at once, see, so's the Technicians'd have nothing left better'n what the villagers got. If we could grab hold of *that*—"

"Destroy the City?" Noren was shocked. "That wouldn't be right; it wouldn't do any good at all. What we want is to have more Cities, Cities for everybody."

"We can't," said the young man with frightening intensity. "The Scholars and Technicians will be too powerful as long as anything of theirs remains. We can't have the kind of world we want without destroying this one; it's corrupt, evil."

"The High Law is," agreed Noren. "But that's no reason to smash the good along with the bad. If we did that, some knowledge might be lost."

"We want no part of the Scholars' knowledge!"

"Knowledge—truth—is' the most important thing there is," Noren maintained. "The only trouble is that the Scholars are keeping it all to themselves when we should have it, too."

"You're right," put in another trader. "Why destroy what we could use? If we once got inside the City, we could take it over, maybe, and get rid of the Scholars. People would kneel to *us* for a change."

"I don't want anybody kneeling to me," said Noren, not bothering to point out that taking over the City was manifestly impossible. "No man should ever kneel to another. It'd be just as wrong for us to have that kind of power as for the Scholars to have it."

"I'd say it was our turn," someone asserted, and others muttered agreement.

In desperation Noren switched tactics. "The Technicians wouldn't obey us," he said.

"Them?" The young man laughed. "We'd kill them in any case. That's something we can start on right now."

Aghast, Noren exclaimed, "You're speaking of murder!"

"I didn't take you for the squeamish type."

"I'm no murderer," Noren declared. "And anyway, some of the Technicians are on our side."

The whole group turned on him with renewed hostility. "Where'd you get a stupid idea like that? All Technicians are our enemies."

"That's not true—" Noren broke off, helpless, for he might imperil the one who'd helped him if he told about his arrest and escape; it was becoming more and more apparent that these men were not the kind he was looking for. "I mean—well, they'd be on our side if we could talk to them, because the Scholars are hiding knowledge from them, too." In contrast to his hopes, he had seen few Technicians around the markets; there would be little opportunity for persuasion, yet they were still potential allies. Certainly they weren't to blame for a Prophecy by which they themselves were deceived or a High Law in which they had no voice.

"Look," the trader told him roughly, "you'd better get this straight. We don't trust no Technicians! If we get a chance, we'll kill as many as we can; they've been on top too long as it is."

"Killing people's wrong," insisted Noren.

"Since when are Technicians people?"

Noren stared, horrified. There was no real difference between these rebels and the villagers he'd known all his life! One kind thought Technicians were more than human; the other, less; neither had any true concern for the right of each man to be judged on his own merits.

Yet on second thought he saw that there was indeed a difference. His present companions were worse. They were even worse than the Scholars, who at least did not murder and destroy. There was a legend, he recalled, that told of how at the time of the Founding, before the Prophecy had been made known, an evil magician—whose name was unspeakable—had tried to rule the world by force; and of how he had been vanquished by the Scholar's establishment of the High Law, which forbade such rule. It was likely that they'd started that legend themselves to mask the Law's real intent; still, overthrowing them would hardly solve the world's problems if men like these were to seize power instead!

"We don't trust nobody that talks to Technicians, either," announced the big man in an ominous tone. "How do we know you're not a starcursed spy?"

"You'll have to take my word," said Noren heatedly. "I'm as much against the High Law as any of you, but I'll not go along with your ideas for what to do about it."

At that moment somebody glanced through the open door of the shed and cried, "Technicians! Outside, watching—"

"He must've brought them here; none ever came before."

Cold with dismay, Noren realized that they were right. He very probably had been followed, and instead of arresting him immediately, the Technicians were gathering evidence against his companions. He should have known that his presence would expose them to danger! Though they couldn't be seized directly, a trap could be arranged, as it had been for him; and little as he liked their talk, he had no desire to see them condemned for it. They had not, after all, actually done anything, nor were they ever likely to. They were powerless against the City, and if they tried to murder any Technicians, the villagers would deal with them in short order.

"By the Mother Star, he'll not leave here in one piece," growled the big man. They converged on Noren; then, abruptly, the light from the doorway was cut off by the Technicians' silhouetted figures. It was the last thing he saw.

When he came to, it was night, and he was lying on the dirt floor of the now-abandoned shed. He sat up, rubbing new bruises and realizing that only the entrance of the Technicians had saved him from worse. Why hadn't he been arrested? They must have known his identity; why else would they have followed him? It didn't make sense! Or perhaps . . . yes, perhaps they'd been unwilling to lay hands on him in the presence of the others. The men, being heretics unlikely to take their word, wouldn't have believed Technicians had authority to touch him, since it was unheard of for someone already in their custody to escape;

it would have looked as if they themselves were disobeying the High Law.

Noren reached into the inner pocket of his tunic, knowing even before he did so that Talyra's coins were gone. He had no chance to make converts, for he was friendless, without money to live on, and there could be little doubt that his recapture was at best only a few hours away.

As the night waned, Noren wandered aimlessly; though his knee throbbed painfully under the bandage, he was able to limp, and some inner urge would not allow him to keep still. It was not merely an urge to evade capture. Rather, he was irresistibly drawn to a place where the great towers, the central one topped with its blazing beacon, were in full view.

Dawn found him back at the plaza. In front of him the City walls thrust up, solid and forbidding against the pale morning sky. He noticed that their surface was not straight, but curved, and wondered why they had been built that way. There were so many inexplicable things about the City, so many things that he longed desperately to understand.

At the lowest corner of the broad flight of steps leading to the Gates, he slumped wearily. What next? Arrest was imminent; he could neither buy food nor, because of his bad knee, could he work for it; and what hope was there of achieving anything if the only people who recognized the High Law's fallacies wanted either to destroy all that was good in the world or to set themselves up in the Scholars' place?

An aircar, sunlight catching its rotors, hovered briefly and dropped out of sight behind the high barrier. On either side of the steps, produce was being loaded into boxlike caverns in the walls; several Technicians were supervising. Noren eyed them nervously, then turned his back and sat on the bottom step, looking out toward the market stalls that lined the opposite side of the square. A crowd of people was again gathering. All at once music, loud and heart-stirring, burst from somewhere behind the Gates and reverberated through the plaza. It swelled in volume until Noren felt as if he might burst also; it was like nothing he had ever heard, and it made him want to sing or to shout or even to cry.

It faded; the crowd hushed. Above him the huge Gates parted and a blue-robed Scholar appeared, flanked by four Technicians. Immediately the people in the plaza fell to their knees.

Startled, Noren remembered too late the Benison that preceded the daily opening of the markets. The Scholar would read from the Book of the Prophecy. He had no desire to stay, but he would only attract attention to himself if he moved, for everyone was waiting, motionless, eyes raised toward the sky in sober respect. Yet he would *not* kneel! If he was reprimanded, he decided, he could state quite honestly that the injury to his knee made it impossible.

He turned toward the Gates and lifted his eyes with the rest. A trace of breeze fluttered the sleeves of the Scholar's robe as he opened the book. His voice, mysteriously amplified, floated past Noren, on out to the edge of the plaza with undiminished clarity.

" *Let us rejoice in the bounty of the land! For the land is good, and from the Mother Star came the heritage that has blessed it; the land has given us life—*' "

The knowledge they were hiding could give people a better life, thought Noren bitterly.

" *Those who have brought forth life from the land are rich—*' "

But not as rich as those who had access to the Power and the Machines.

" *For through the land's taming shall our strength grow,*

that we may be ready to receive the ancient knowledge—' "

No doubt, when the predicted date arrived, people would be told they weren't ready; the Mother Star would hide its face in shame! Noren scowled. He knew the words well and in fact had read the entire book many times, having been taught his letters from it as a child, but he had not spotted that loophole before. Whoever had inserted it had planned carefully.

" ' *. . And the people shall multiply across the face of the earth, and at no time shall the spirit of the Mother Star die in the hearts of men.' "*

All the families, Noren reflected—all the good, sincere people who recited those words every time they sat down to eat—they'd been tricked by the Scholars into putting their trust in something false! Talyra trusted it implicitly, and she too was the victim of cold-blooded deception. . . . Glaring at the High Priest who stood above him, he was abruptly overpowered by the hot anger that had been building up in him for years. He could no longer contain it. What do *you* believe, Scholar? he raged. What is it that lets you stand up there and exhort people to attach their natural faith in goodness to what you know is a figment of somebody's imagination?

He looked back at the mass of rapt faces. Those people would never turn against the Scholars. There was no conceivable way he could make them listen, nothing he could do that would be even a small step toward changing the world into the sort of place the Prophecy described. And he was almost too weary to care. He almost wished the Technicians would arrest him and get it over with

The spired towers glistened overhead, dazzling his vision. All mysteries were sealed away there . . . and he had a right to share those mysteries! Yet neither he nor anybody else would ever be granted that right. The idea of its depending on the appearance of a mythical Mother Star was too firmly entrenched. *The spirit of this Star shall*

119)

abide forever: there was a certain degree of truth in that declaration. By the success of their deceits, the Scholars had *made* it true.

People wouldn't oppose the High Law on being told that the Prophecy wasn't authentic because that would be acting not so much against bad leaders as against their own beliefs. The real trouble, Noren saw suddenly, was that most people had no reason to think the Scholars were bad. As High Priests, they did not interfere with ordinary villagers' lives. Yet if someone were to commit an act of overt defiance, wouldn't they have to interfere? Wouldn't they be forced to silence him immediately, without waiting for the formality of a civil trial?

Noren clenched wet fingers, an idea forming out of his desperation. They were going to kill him sometime. Why not in front of the whole Benison assemblage? Why not in a way that would provide the people who revered them with proof, real proof, of their underlying ruthlessness?

His heart raced. The Scholar was reading the last page of the Prophecy; within seconds after he closed the book, the music might surge up again. There wasn't time to deliberate. Noren rose from the step and moved forward.

" '. . . *Through the time of waiting we will follow the Law*—' " As those words were reached he was part way up the flight, above the crowd; heedlesss of the pain in his knee, Noren found himself climbing without stumbling. He marshaled every bit of strength he could collect, throwing it all into his voice.

"No! We will *not* follow the High Law; it is evil! It's wrong for a few men to create a Law above village law and keep all the knowledge for themselves!" He glanced upward over his shoulder; the Technicians had left the Gates and were coming down toward him, unhurriedly and without any show of emotion. "There should be Machines for everyone, Power for everyone, and knowledge should be free!"

His words resounded hollowly from the walls behind him. Stunned silence pervaded the crowd; what would have been greeted with wrath on a less formal occasion evoked only shock when it came as an interruption of a ceremony like the Benison. "The Prophecy—is—a—fake!" Noren shouted. "It's a *fake!* There is no Mother Star!"

Something jolted him, thrusting him forward onto his injured knee, and its pain cut through him like the jab of a knife. The Technicians hadn't yet reached him; it was as if he had been assailed by some invisible force from within. Noren crumpled, his agony eclipsed by the growing numbness of his body. Just before the music overrode all other sound, he heard a gasp from the crowd and a woman's cry, "Blasphemer! See, the Star has struck him!" whereupon he realized that in the minds of the people he had been struck down not by the Scholar's order, but by supernatural intervention.

His eyes blurred; the incomprehensible thing they'd done seemed to have immobilized him. He tried to grip the edge of the step above, but his fingers would not move; they were frozen, somehow. None of his muscles would act. It occurred to him that this was very likely a natural part of dying.

The music exploded into the air, vibrating through his head. Hazily Noren was aware of the greenish shapes of the Technicians as they lifted him and carried him through the Gates, into the City itself.

VII

NOREN REGAINED CONSCIOUSNESS IN A TINY ROOM, WITH-
out doors or windows but dimly lit by Power. It did not
look like a jail cell: the walls were of a pale, clear green
that was rather pleasant; the floor was covered with thick
padding; and the couch on which he lay was smooth and
soft. Moreover, everything was very clean. Even his garments were clean, for they were new ones, made of ordinary fabric but beige, not brown, and styled exactly like
Technicians' clothing.

How had he arrived in this place? he wondered, getting
to his feet. He had no recollection of anything else in the
City. Strangely enough, his exhaustion was entirely gone
and his arms and legs seemed to work normally; the pain
in his knee had disappeared along with the bandage.
Yet if he'd slept long, he should feel hungry, and he did
not. What had happened? They'd lifted him from the
steps . . .

He pressed his hand to his mouth, a surge of nausea

rising in company with an overpowering sense of failure and of fear. His impulsive attempt to expose the Scholars' ruthlessness had not done any good; he was to be killed in secret after all. His death would be wasted: worse than wasted, for they'd managed to turn his words to their advantage by creating the impression that they'd had no hand in his falling, that the Mother Star itself had punished him.

He should have foreseen, Noren thought despairingly, that they would not kill him before making an effort toward getting his recantation.

Why hadn't he realized that? he asked himself in perplexity. Had he dreaded their unimaginable ways of coercion so much that he'd wished for immediate death . . . or had he actually *wanted* to be caught?

With honest self-appraisal, he saw that he had indeed wanted it. He had wanted to enter the City on any terms whatsoever! Furthermore, he'd known underneath that there was only one way left in which he could defy the Scholars: by confronting them and proving to them that not all heretics could be subjugated.

All right, he thought grimly. He was in their hands and totally helpless, but there would be certain compensations, compensations of which he'd been inwardly aware, and that gave him an edge of sorts. The circumstances of his recapture had been of his choosing, not theirs, and he was the stronger for it. It was impossible to guess how long it would be before they killed him, but he had little doubt that horrible things would be done during the interim. They would try to make him recant. He must not attempt to imagine how, for if he did, fear might sap his new-found strength; he must simply take the things as they came.

An opening appeared in the wall where a door, made of the same solid green material instead of matting, was swinging back. Two Technicians stood there; Noren straightened and, at their command, stepped into the corridor without protest.

He had hoped that he might see something of the City during his remaining days of life, but the room to which he was brought was as featureless as the hall leading to it. It was quite large, again lighted by Power, again with softly colored walls and floor. At one end was a dais upon which three Scholars sat at a curved table. They wore the usual blue robes, and their faces were indistinct; Noren had the impression that he might as well be facing a row of Machines. Certainly these men showed no more feeling.

"Aren't you going to kneel?" asked one of the Technicians, who, oddly, had not done so themselves.

"I am not," replied Noren. He stood at the foot of the dais, his arms folded.

Nobody tried to force the issue; the Technicians left without restraining him in any way, and as yet none of the Scholars had spoken. He stood in silence for a long time before he realized that they were measuring his nerve.

Watching their faces, he saw that the apparent lack of feeling was deliberate, a mask. It was presumably meant to frighten him. But beneath the mask they were alert, intelligent men, men with whom a real argument might be held. At the trial he hadn't been able to argue with his judges; they'd simply labeled his statements as heresy and let it go at that. Though the Scholars might do the same, they would be capable of going further if they chose. They could not believe the Prophecy as the councilmen did. While they wouldn't admit that in public, mightn't they to a person who was going to die anyway? If he could convince them that he would never be coerced into recanting, he might at least have the satisfaction of hearing them concede that his theories were correct.

He had nothing to lose by trying, Noren decided. Taking the initiative, he began, "You must have been surprised when I gave you the chance to arrest me."

"Not at all," replied one of the Scholars. "We could

have arrested you at any time since you left your village; we had you under constant surveillance. But it was more to our purpose to let you come to us."

Noren suppressed the dismay he felt. That must be a lie, for surely they couldn't have anticipated what he himself had not consciously intended! "You're wrong if you think I did it because I considered myself beaten," he declared.

"We don't. But you have learned that you cannot win support for your theories. You've also learned other things that you don't yet recognize. Frankly, Noren, we're glad you robbed that Technician of his uniform. Though we didn't plan it, your temporary escape will benefit us in the end."

"Mainly I've learned that I don't care what you do to me," asserted Noren, torn between relief that the Technician's story had been accepted and consternation over the untroubled confidence of these men. "I spoke at the Denison not only to tell others the truth, but to show them how far you'll go to hide it; I thought you might kill me then."

"It's not going to be that easy." The Scholar frowned. "Just what do you mean by 'the truth'?"

"What you call heresy. I understand it, so there's no point in pretending I'm as naive as most people. I know all about the Prophecy."

"You don't know nearly as much as you think you do," commented the Scholar dryly.

"Don't you think a villager can be smart enough to figure it out?"

"I don't think you have the background to figure it out."

"You mean because I was brought up to believe in the Mother Star, I should believe in it. But I don't. I'm admitting that I don't, that I know the whole Prophecy's a fake, a trick to make people content with having men like you keep all the knowledge for yourselves—"

A second Scholar broke in sharply, "You're mistaken.

The Prophecy's statements about the Mother Star are true. Everything you've been taught is true, except for a few exaggerated legends."

"Don't bother to say that, not with me."

"Why should you doubt it?"

"Because it's not logical or possible; magical things like new stars and people coming out of the sky don't happen, and they never will. If there were to be a new star, you couldn't know ahead of time, and anyway, even if you could, it would have nothing to do with your suddenly getting generous with the Power and the Machines!"

The Scholar's reply was delayed slightly, and when it came it carried an aura of flat finality rather than of anger. "What you're saying is false according to the Book of the Prophecy. You will suffer for holding such ideas. And you are wrong."

"The Book of the Prophecy is not sacred; you Scholars wrote it yourselves, the way *you* wanted it," insisted Noren, trying to match the man's cool assurance. "You can do anything you like with me, regardless of my ideas, as you can with anyone. I have no choice about what happens."

"You had a choice between accepting what you were told and living out your life peacefully, or deciding to do your own thinking," the first Scholar said slowly. "Now you have a choice between admitting the error of your opinions without further ado, or admitting it later, after certain experiences that will persuade you to cooperate."

"I'll stick to my opinions," Noren declared. He hoped his voice sounded louder than it seemed to.

"The consequences of independent thought can be less inviting than you realize."

Noren didn't answer. After a short wait, the men proceeded to play back the recording of his trial. He remained silent and impassive as he listened; to hear his own words repeated was strange, but not dreadful. He did not regret the statements he'd made. At the finish, when he was asked if there were any that he wished to modify, he declined without hesitation.

The third Scholar, the one in the center, hadn't said anything; he had simply watched, and yet had somehow given the impression that he was the most formidable of them all. Finally, in a soft but commanding voice, he spoke. "I must warn you, Noren," he said levelly, "that if you persist in your defiance, the consequences will be grave and irrevocable. You have no conception of the things that can happen to you here. This is your last chance to obtain our mercy."

"I don't want your mercy," said Noren angrily.

"Why not?"

"Because I'm not your inferior. To accept mercy would be the same as kneeling to you."

One of the other Scholars turned. "The boy is bold enough, Stefred," he remarked. "Will you let such boldness pass?"

Noren's skin prickled. So this was the Scholar Stefred, the dreaded Chief Inquisitor who had given the young Technician his instructions. No heretic, it was said, could resist Stefred's methods.

"In time," Stefred said confidently, "this boy will kneel to me in public and retract everything he has ever said against the Prophecy and the High Law. Until then let him speak as he likes. I am interested in what he has to say." To Noren he continued, "We have a number of questions to ask you. Will you swear by the Mother Star to answer them truthfully?"

"I'll take no such oath, since we both know it to be a farce."

"You are frank, at least. Can I assume that you'll be equally frank in response to the other questions?"

Noren looked him in the eye. "I have nothing to hide," he said. "It's you who are hiding information; you, not I, have cause to fear the truth."

"Very well." Stefred leaned back, nodding to his associates to begin the questioning.

It went on for a long time. Noren answered candidly, having no desire to conceal anything aside from the details of his escape, which fortunately were not touched upon; and at first the game was not too disagreeable. The Scholars, instead of trying to extract heretical admissions, soon turned to opposite tactics: they tried to trap him into statements that could be construed as partial recantation. He refused to be trapped, and matching wits with them proved rather exhilarating.

After some hours, however, he was trembling with fatigue. The same questions had been repeated not once, but many times. Quite a few of them were foolish ones having nothing at all to do with the subject at hand; questions about his childhood, his family, his private thoughts about things entirely unrelated to the Prophecy or the High Law. . . .

"No more of this," he declared at last, fearing that at any moment he might collapse. They had not told him he must stand throughout the inquisition, but there were no chairs in the room and to sit on the floor seemed akin to kneeling. "There is nothing more to say; I've told you the whole truth."

"We cannot be sure you have. Besides, there were a few questions to which you gave no responses at all."

"Some things," protested Noren indignantly, "are none of your business!"

"Everything is our business in an inquiry of this kind."

The details of his feelings toward girls, about which all too much interest had been expressed, could have no possible bearing upon heresy, Noren felt. Surprisingly, they had not mentioned Talyra specifically or asked anything that could conceivably be related to her having helped in his escape, though he'd dreaded it constantly, knowing that if they did he would have to lie, since to remain silent might cast suspicion upon her. The questions he'd resented had been of a different sort. Most of them seemed stupid, for if Scholars knew anything at all about human nature, they could easily have guessed the answers; on second thought, however, it occurred to him that their aim might merely have been to catch him in an obvious falsehood.

"I will not answer anything else," he announced.

"You will," Stefred assured him, rising. Stefred himself had taken little part in the questioning, but he had listened with avid attention, hoping, no doubt, to detect some small inconsistency in Noren's responses. Now he touched a button on the table before him, summoning the Technicians. "We are specialists in the study of people's minds, Noren," he said, "and when someone does not tell us all we need to know, we have a way of compelling him to do so. You will find this frightening, but if you are sincere in your desire to be honest, you have nothing to dread from it."

The Technicians brought not a chair, but a low, padded bench on which they required Noren to lie. He complied without struggle; resistance was useless, he knew, and he was so tired that he scarcely minded. The needle that was stuck into his arm did frighten him, but not until a few minutes later did he become really terrified.

The thing that frightened him was the realization that he was speaking, speaking rapidly, yet without full conscious control.

Noren never knew exactly what he said under the influence of the drug. He knew only that it was Stefred who questioned him and that he was unable to hold anything back. He talked on and on for hours, yet the hours went quickly; he could not judge the time. He could not see anything but the blue-robed blur of the Scholar who bent over him, and who, surprisingly, spoke with a gentleness that had no cruel undertones. Hazily, he realized that the questioning was retracing all the same ground that had been covered before: his beliefs, his desires, his fears . . . and above all, his reasons for what he had done. Why had he become a heretic? Why did he hate Scholars? Did he want to kill them, and if not, why not? Did he want to seize power for himself?

They had asked that last question constantly right from the beginning, disguised in different forms. It must be impossible, Noren had decided, for Scholars to conceive of anyone's not wanting power! They must think all heretics were trying to replace them. No wonder they cared so much about getting public recantations.

While drugged he could not reason that out, but he was aware that the point was being examined again from every possible angle. Then, eventually, he ceased to be aware of anything at all.

Later—perhaps a day later, perhaps more—he awoke in the small green room where he'd originally regained consciousness. Immediately terror engulfed him. What had he done? Had he spoken of Talyra or the Technician, or denied the things he had sworn to himself he'd never deny? Had they somehow *changed* him?

No, he realized. He was still himself. He was still sure that they could not force him to recant. If it were that simple—if they could do it merely by sticking a needle into somebody's arm—they would not bother with all the preliminaries.

The Technicians brought him food: good food, though he had little appetite for it. Then he was taken back to the large room to confront the same three Scholars. Again, he remained standing. He was no longer tired, he found, and his mind was absolutely clear. To his astonishment, his spirits were high. So far he had triumphed over these men; they weren't nearly so powerful as they pretended to be.

"We are satisfied that you have not lied to us," he was told. "It is impossible for anyone to lie while under the drug. A man can keep back information if he's determined to, but if you'd been concealing any we'd wanted from you, we would have known."

Relief lifted Noren's spirits still further. His worst fear had been that he might have been made either to betray those who had helped him escape, or to say something he did not believe; but if he'd done so they would surely boast of their success.

"We have learned a great deal about you," Stefred said. "We've learned, for instance, that you really want the knowledge we have here in the City. You long desperately for it."

"I've never denied that," Noren agreed. "Knowledge is the right of everyone; it should be available to all. Of course I want it."

"You want it not only because it's been kept from you, but for itself."

"Yes, I do."

Stefred eyed him thoughtfully. "Like everything else, knowledge has its price," he said. "Would you be willing to pay the price, Noren?"

On the verge of assent, Noren felt a vague sense of alarm. He'd already demonstrated that he was willing to pay with his life; what more could they ask? "That would depend on what it was," he said cautiously.

"In this case, it involves an ordeal that you would find quite difficult."

"No ordeal would be too difficult if it led to the truth you're hiding," declared Noren, with a sudden, irrational hope that they might actually decide to enlighten him.

"If you recant voluntarily," Stefred announced, "you will be given access to more knowledge than you can absorb in a lifetime."

Noren recoiled, stunned first by disappointment and then by his own stupidity in not having spotted the trap. That they could obtain recantations by bribery when threats had failed hadn't occurred to him, yet it was all too logical.

"Think before you answer," Stefred went on. "I know you're tempted. I know you well enough to be sure that it's a more painful temptation than the first offer you were made. Think: is your pride in your ability to hold out worth more to you than knowledge?"

Noren's head swam. Put that way, his determination to hold out seemed arrogant foolishness, a contradiction of everything he had said about what he was seeking. Yet there was a flaw; there had to be. That was not the way it should be put.

He raised his eyes. "Knowledge is worthless apart from truth. It's the truth I really value, but if I recanted, I'd be lying. Truth belongs to everybody; to recant would be to accept your right to keep it from the other villagers."

"That's your final word?"

"Yes."

Stefred did not seem disappointed; as a matter of fact he looked quite pleased. It was probable, Noren thought dejectedly, that they'd known all along that the bribe would be refused. If they'd analyzed his mind as well as they said they had, they must have known. They must also have known that the memory of this lost chance would keep on hurting right up to the end.

"Perhaps you're better off," said one of the other Scholars. "Knowledge can be frightening, after all; sometimes people are better off without knowing everything. Sometimes they're aware of that underneath."

It was a skilled twist of the knife; Noren caught his angry reply just in time, realizing that to defend himself against the implicit accusation would be beneath his dignity. "Perhaps," he agreed, "especially since I have no reason to think you'd have kept your word in any case. Where do we go from here?"

"You know, I suppose, that we've hardly begun."

"I know," Noren replied grimly. They would not raise the subject of killing him yet, he felt, not while he was strong enough to laugh at them.

"Whatever you may think to the contrary," Stefred stated, "you are going to be compelled to recant. Your recantation will be wholly sincere and will be obtained by a means that you'll be powerless to resist. I shall not describe the procedure in advance; I'll merely say that it's beyond your present comprehension and that I judge you to be more vulnerable to it than average. You have until tomorrow morning to think that over."

The ultimatum was more unnerving than Noren had imagined it could be. He stood silent, utterly dismayed, while without another word the three Scholars left the room; then, blindly, he followed as the Technicians escorted him back to his own quarters. There he collapsed on the couch, unsure of his ability to endure the hours of delay and thankful that no one was present to observe his lapse of self-control. *More* vulnerable than average? Stefred must have been lying, bluffing; surely he'd not displayed any vulnerability.

But the Scholar's eyes had not been veiled as for a bluff, and he had spoken with the force of total conviction.

When morning came, Noren was led through a maze of passageways and finally, after a puzzling wait in a small cubicle within which he felt an odd sense of motion, he found himself thrust through a tall door that, although also solid, had slid aside to admit him. There was light, brilliant daylight streaming through a window; Noren glanced out and drew a quick breath. The glistening towers were no longer above him, but stood directly opposite. He was high above the City walls! He looked down, seeing that they were merely the outer faces of a ring of domed structures. The huge silver circles dazzled him as he gazed across them to the busy markets and the grainfields beyond. This was what Technicians must see when they traveled through the air.

Reluctantly, Noren turned his attention to his surroundings. His guards had withdrawn, and at first he thought himself alone; but as he stepped further into the room, he saw that someone was seated behind a large desk made of some shiny white substance. Because the man was dressed in clothes similar to the ones Noren himself wore, it was a moment before he recognized the Scholar Stefred.

"Sit down, Noren," Stefred said, indicating a not-uncomfortable looking chair next to his own.

"I'd rather stand," replied Noren defiantly.

"As you wish. But we'll be spending a good deal of time together." Stefred's voice wasn't angry; it didn't even seem stern. Noren stood motionless, nonplused. The room was not the sort of place he had thought he'd be taken to; there was nothing particularly ominous about it. To be sure, he noticed a number of Machines that were incomprehensible to him, but he also noticed inviting shelves of books. One of the books lay open atop a pile of papers, as if hastily set aside. Did Scholars spend the time between ceremonies in rooms like this, unrobed, reading books as he himself might do if he had the chance? Though he'd denied their superiority, he had not pictured them as human in just that way.

Stefred leaned forward. "I believe you've been honest with us," he said. "I believe that when you say truth is more important to you than anything else, you mean it. We are now about to see whether you have what it takes to live up to what you claim."

Noren was silent. Would he? he thought, fighting for composure. He'd made up his mind that he would, no matter how much whatever they did to him might hurt; but suppose they really had a form of pressure against which he'd be powerless?

"You have courage," Stefred remarked, almost with

warmth. "I shall challenge it; aren't you curious as to how?"

"I've got a pretty good idea," Noren said evenly.

"Really? You've heard all sorts of ghastly stories, haven't you, about the goings on here in the City—things that no one can describe, no one can even imagine?"

"They're part of the sham. If you believe me, you know you won't get anywhere by more talk, so you've no recourse but to put me to torture. There's no mystery about that."

"Does the prospect frighten you?"

"No," said Noren staunchly, hoping his knees wouldn't give way.

"That's the first lie you've told," the Scholar observed. He hesitated, giving Noren an appraising look. "I'll be frank with you, Noren. If I thought I had a chance of getting your recantation in that way, I could not proceed without trying it; there are some good reasons why we don't resort to the method I'm about to use with a person who can be made to cooperate through any other means. Fortunately, I already know you well enough to be sure that torture wouldn't work."

Astonished, Noren barely suppressed his breath of relief. This was undoubtedly another trap; still the admission restored not only his hopes, but his wavering self-esteem. Perhaps they had no mysterious means of defeating him after all, and he would *not* give in from mere fear of them!

Stefred regarded him soberly. "You're surprised. You weren't sure in your own mind, were you? You believed you could stand up under it, but you weren't absolutely sure." Keeping his voice level, he continued, "That's something one seldom knows about oneself, but we Scholars are usually able to tell. You see, we're interested not only in what people do, but in why they do it; and once we've determined why a heretic is holding out, we can judge what sort of persuasion he's susceptible to. In your case

135)

I am certain that physical discomfort, however severe, would have no effect. What I'm going to do is rather more complicated, and as I've said, it's undertaken only as a last resort."

They stared at each other, Noren resolving that he would not be the first to drop his eyes. There was something strange in Stefred's manner; though the words were cold, Noren sensed none of the calculated coldness he had felt during the inquisition. *Why, he admires me!* he realized suddenly. *This Scholar needs to break me, but underneath he admires me for standing up to him. He acknowledges me as a true opponent.* The thought was heartening; on the strength of it, he managed a forced smile.

Stefred returned it, his own smile looking surprisingly genuine. "You're wondering what can possibly be worse than the pain to which you'd steeled yourself. Tell me, what makes you think it's going to be?"

Caught off guard, Noren could only stammer, "Why—why—"

"You haven't an answer. You've got plenty of intelligence, but you haven't yet learned to make full use of it. You question a great many things that other people accept, but still, inside yourself, you're holding to premises for which you have no valid grounds. That's one of the ways in which you're vulnerable, Noren. I'm not going to treat you like a helpless victim; I shall fight on your own terms: the terms you chose when you stood before us and claimed intellectual equality as your birthright."

"I claimed the right to knowledge. There's no equality as long as it's hidden from me."

"True. You will be armed with what you need. But first, let's dispose of some of those false premises. Number one: we never said that you were our inferior, or for that matter, that any other villager was. Because many of *them* told you so, you assumed it was our idea. It wasn't."

Noren scowled, stricken by confusion. This was scarcely

the kind of attack he'd been anticipating. "Number two," the Scholar went on, "we never threatened you with torture. We never threatened you at all. We merely told you that we could compel you to recant, and you assumed that we had no better weapon than fear. Like many of your other assumptions, that's wrong. Some of what I do to you will be terrifying, but you won't be swayed by that; when in the end you recant, you'll do so of your own free will, because your innate honesty will leave you no choice."

"No," Noren insisted, "I'll never go back on what I believe."

"That's a very dogmatic statement, and it's unworthy of you. If you cling to it, you'll be going back on the key point in your defense: the assertion that you care more for truth than for comfort." Rising, Stefred fixed penetrating gray eyes on Noren. "The next few days aren't going to be comfortable; truth, when it conflicts with your personal opinions, is not easy to confront. Yet you maintained over and over again that you wanted to know the truth. All right. Your wish is hereby granted. My weapon is not like anything you ever expected, Noren. I'm simply going to give you what you asked for."

Noren shook his head. "You tried to bribe me before; I haven't changed my mind."

"This isn't a bribe. There are no strings attached, and you aren't being offered a choice. You've already passed the point of no return."

"There must be a catch," protested Noren skeptically. "As you yourself told me, there's a price for knowledge."

"Of course there is," Stefred agreed. "In the first place, once you've become privy to the secrets I'm about to reveal, you will be confined to the City for the rest of your life."

That, thought Noren, was unlikely to be long. "It would have happened anyway," he said. "No heretic has ever left the City."

"Not often, but there's a small chance when a person's repentance comes early. For an enlightened heretic, however, there is no release; our secrets must stay within these walls. And there are other consequences. You're in deeper waters than you realize; before I'm through with you, you're going to be shown things—unpleasant things—that even the Technicians don't know." The Scholar approached Noren, his tone carrying more force, yet at the same time more feeling. "Did you demand truth for its own sake, or merely to prove yourself right? Do you value it enough to take its consequences without protest?"

"I do," Noren declared, "if you can convince me that what you tell me is really true. I won't accept empty words." With chagrin, he saw that he had made a concession by admitting the possibility that Stefred might not lie; yet somehow he couldn't help feeling that this man was not like most Scholars. In any case, he could scarcely have answered otherwise.

Stefred sighed. "You'll receive more than words," he informed Noren, "and the consequences will be grimmer than you suppose. I warn you that a day will come when you'll be willing to give up everything you care most for in order to escape them."

Did they think he didn't know they were going to kill him? Noren wondered. Just because they'd never threatened to, did they think him naive? Aloud he said, "I made my choice long ago. I'll have no complaints as to where it leads."

"You're mistaken. I'm willing to bet that when the time is ripe you will stand here in this very room and give me all sorts of arguments as to why you should be let off."

Deliberately and with effort, Noren laughed. "I see what you're trying to do. If you could make me refuse your offer now, under these terms, it'd be the same as making me say that I don't really care about truth after all."

"You're very perceptive," the Scholar acknowledged.

"However, as I explained, it's less an offer than a judgment. Hard as it may be for you to credit, you've convinced me that you do have the right to the facts about the Prophecy, which as you've guessed are not quite the same as the official interpretation. They are not the same as your interpretation, either; but then, your information has been very limited. It will be limited no longer, Noren. You've won what you wanted." With a strange note of sympathy he added, "I only hope you'll never be sorry that you did."

VIII

NOREN SAT IN THE CHAIR STEFRED OFFERED HIM AND
waited with a mixture of excitement and resignation, aware
that he'd been maneuvered into a position in which, for
the time being, he had no choice but to play along. The
Scholars' tactics were diabolically clever. He could not
tell whether he would actually be given the truth or whether
there'd be further attempts to deceive him, and if he was
taken in by deception they would triumph; yet were he to
resist truth when it was offered, they would achieve a final
and ironic victory.

His spine tingled. To learn the real secrets—the underlying secrets that were kept not only from the villagers but
from the Technicians—would be worth all he'd gone
through. Perhaps Stefred was sincere; after all, what harm
could it do the Scholars to enlighten him before he died?
They might even see an advantage to it, for if the truth
was as unpleasant as Stefred had intimated, they might
think it a fitting punishment; but in that case the triumph

would be his! Suddenly Noren recalled the remark that had been made during his inquisition: *Knowledge can be frightening . . . sometimes people are better off without knowing everything.* He was indeed being challenged, he decided. They were daring him to back up his conviction that it was always preferable to know.

He watched Stefred's movements curiously, seeing that the Scholar was handling a small Machine of some sort. Then, abruptly and without warning, the room was plunged into total darkness; the bright day of the City had somehow turned to moonless night. There was a penetrating humming sound. Noren clenched his icy fingers and tried to gulp down panic. He counted the seconds.

When he reached forty, a dazzling, fiery sphere burst into being in front of him. It dimmed slightly, so that he was able to look at it without blinking, yet at the same time it grew, tendrils of cold flame trailing out from its edges. It was about to envelop him, Noren felt. He wanted to hold his head up, but he could not bear the sight for more than a few moments; he closed his eyes and crumpled in the chair, biting his lip to keep himself from screaming.

The room turned black again, and Stefred's hand touched his shoulder. "We'll try again," the Scholar said, not unkindly. "We'll keep trying until you can watch it through, because you will soon be required not merely to watch, but to understand."

Noren drew himself erect and concentrated on understanding. The fire reappeared, larger and brighter than before; and this time, though his mouth was dry and his heart thumped as if it would burst, his eyes stayed open.

"Do you know what this is, Noren?" Stefred's voice went on.

"It—it looks like the sun, but there's no heat."

"Yes. But it's not our sun. And it's only a picture; this is a picture of a star, up close. Star, sun—they're the same thing."

"But the stars are much smaller," Noren protested.

"They look smaller because they are far away."

That was reasonable. But then how could the Scholars get pictures of them up close? How could they get such pictures in any case, pictures that moved, pictures that looked *real?* "Is this sun one of the stars we see in the constellations, then?" he asked.

"You have never seen this particular sun. It is the Mother Star."

Noren controlled his gasp of astonishment and did not reply.

"You've been told in school, haven't you, that the world is round and that it circles the sun?" the Scholar continued. "Well, there are many worlds, Noren; unnumbered worlds, circling other suns, the stars." The image was instantaneously extinguished and another took its place: a greenish globe, splotched with irregular areas of white and blue and brown. "Here you're looking at such a world. A whole earth; an earth with fields and streams and mountains—and Cities, hundreds of Cities, many of them larger and grander than you could possibly imagine."

As Noren watched, he saw the world come alive; the globe faded and it was as though he were flying over the land, and then he seemed to be walking through the streets of the Cities themselves. There were people dressed in exotic clothing like none he had ever seen; there were wide, deep streams with little houses floating on them; and once there was a vast expanse of blue water stretching all the way to the horizon. Even stranger, there were towering plants with dark green foliage and brown stems thicker than a man's arm! There were also other things that he could not begin to identify. He couldn't absorb the barest scrap of what he was seeing, and yet it filled him with an agonizing, irresistible longing to be part of it and comprehend it.

But it was gone. There was only the shining globe again,

receding into the distance.

He knew then what Stefred's strategy must be. This glimpse of the forbidden, ultimate secrets was designed to tempt him past endurance; though not a bribe in itself, it was the prelude to a proposition that he would find very hard to stand out against. All the same, he could not regret having had the glimpse.

"Haven't you any questions, Noren?" Stefred asked.

He had so many questions that he would not have known where to begin even if he had wished to reveal his craving for further knowledge; again, he resolved to remain silent. But Stefred, apparently, was not through tantalizing him. "I'll give you some of the answers anyway," he said.

When Noren didn't respond, the Scholar went right on. "A great many years ago," he began, "the world you saw had so many Cities and was so crowded that people were dying because they could not get enough food. There was no land left to grow more food. The Technicians of that world were able to travel to other worlds that circled the same sun, but on some of them they found only rock and ice, and some had no solid ground at all. The rest—five that were quite similar to the home world—were quickly filled up. They couldn't raise enough food there, either."

Despite himself Noren burst out, "How could they go from one world to another?"

"There is a way. They eventually came to use what was called a starship, a ship that enabled them to visit not only the worlds of their own sun, but those of far-off stars. Look." A shape grew out of darkness: a Machine, massive and cylindrical, a glistening thing that somehow resembled the towers of the City. "It is propelled by Power. Inside there is space for hundreds of people to live and work; and in starships like this, Noren, our ancestors arrived at the time of the Founding."

No, thought Noren desperately. It couldn't be; the Founding was only a myth. . . .

"They came upon this world only after years of searching. A new discovery had made it possible for them to reach other suns in less time than it had once taken them to circle their own, but there were few stars of the right type near theirs, and not all worlds are places where men can live. Some are barren; some are too hot or too cold, or have air that is poisonous; some are occupied by other forms of life. This was the first suitable one they found."

Again, Noren saw living scenes take form in front of him: first the interior of the starship, and then a smaller ship coming down out of the sky and the people getting out of it. In the background were the familiar yellow ridges of the Tomorrow Mountains.

After a long pause, the room grew light once more and the picture disappeared.

The Scholar smiled quizzically. "Well?"

Noren met his eyes. "Even if I were to accept these pictures—if I were to believe in the Founding, and concede that people came out of the sky instead of having once been savages as I guessed—I still couldn't believe in the Mother Star."

"But you have seen it. It is the sun of the world you were shown; it is, as the Prophecy says, our source."

"If that's so, how is it that we can't see it in the sky?"

"It is too far away."

"Will it come closer?"

"No. What will happen is as yet beyond your comprehension—"

Triumphantly Noren broke in, "If it's not coming closer, then how can you tell us it will someday appear? Nothing can change the fact that you've created the Prophecy as an excuse to keep what's here in the City away from people!"

Stefred returned to his desk, pausing thoughtfully. "Nothing can change that," he admitted. "Nevertheless, the entire Prophecy is true; you will accept it and revere it."

"I will not. These things—these pictures—should be for everyone; what right have you not to share them? If our ancestors all came together in a ship, what right have you to hide the knowledge that came with them?"

"You will concede us that right."

"To buy more enlightenment for myself? If you think so, you've underestimated me," Noren persisted.

"I doubt it," Stefred said. "If anything, I've over-estimated you. As I told you, at present you have no option in regard to your enlightenment; it is going to proceed whether you like it or not, and it's quite possible that you won't. The next phase is considerably more painful."

"Oh," Noren said resignedly, "so you're threatening me after all."

The Scholar shook his head. "We don't want it to be painful for you, Noren. Parts of it will be; truth often is. But the pain won't be the sort you've anticipated, and I will not subject you to any that can be avoided."

"Which is another way of saying that if somebody won't go along with you, it's 'unavoidable' for you to punish him. Naturally you don't want to; you'd be much happier if we all agreed without making trouble—"

"Actually," Stefred interrupted with a strangely un-readable look, "we're delighted whenever a person proves willing to do his own thinking."

"Just so you can demonstrate your power over him?" Noren found, to his amazement, that he was disappointed; for some reason he had begun to think better of Stefred.

Quietly the Scholar replied, "You are not ready to understand why. I can't ask you to trust me because I'm aware that you have no basis for trust, but all the same, I hope you'll remember what I'm going to say to you." He leaned forward again, and his tone carried no trace of cruelty or deception. "You are about to undergo some very difficult and frightening experiences. During the course of them you'll learn a great deal that you've been longing to know, but you will suffer in the process. That can't be prevented. We Scholars have suffered in the same way. It is not punishment, but an inherent part of the truth you've chosen to seek out. You see, Noren, such truth involves not merely facts, but feelings. Some of the feelings aren't pleasant, but if you really mean the things you've been insisting—the things about its being better to know first hand than to believe because you're told you should—then you won't mind experiencing them."

Noren stared. The sympathy in Stefred's manner seemed too warm to be faked. "Are these experiences designed to make me believe the Prophecy?" he asked suspiciously.

"They are designed to show you the origin of the Prophecy. If you emerge from them believing, it will be because you've accepted the proofs; what a man believes is not subject to force."

"You're not talking as you did during my inquisition," Noren observed, bewildered.

"I am not," the Scholar agreed, "but in neither case have I lied." He smiled. "You have a quick mind. You've spotted an inconsistency between my ultimatum to you and the statement I just made; you think you have me trapped. Think deeper! If you understand your own system of values, you'll see that no inconsistency exists."

But it did, Noren thought. The bald assertion that his recantation would be sincere and that it would be obtained through means he'd be powerless to resist surely couldn't be reconciled with an admission that beliefs could not be forced; that is, it couldn't unless . . .

Unless real proof could be presented. If they could *prove* the Prophecy, he'd be unable to resist them. He was indeed vulnerable in that sense, for to ignore proof would be a violation not of their principles, but of his own.

(146

He had never suspected that they might have proof. He'd given no thought to such a possibility; he'd feared only that they might torture him or, more recently, that they would practice some ingenious form of deception. And wasn't that still a danger? Wasn't it conceivable that they could make false proofs seem real? How, thought Noren in anguish, was he ever to judge?

"I've at last cracked your armor," Stefred was saying. "For the first time you doubt your convictions, and it hurts. You're beginning to realize that if by some remote chance we are right and you are wrong, it is going to hurt a great deal."

The man's analysis was all too accurate. Noren reflected ruefully. The idea of finding himself wrong was more upsetting than all the earlier warnings; Stefred had gained the upper hand.

"But consider this, Noren," the Scholar continued seriously. "You wouldn't be capable of feeling such hurts if you lacked the ability to evaluate what you're shown. You'd either label all the proofs offered you fakes, or, if we had some way of forcing them on you, you would accept them without question; in neither case would you feel distress. The fact that you do—that you're willing to open your mind to it—is evidence that your regard for the truth is reliable."

Noren looked up, seeing his antagonist with new respect. Why hadn't Stefred used his advantage? He was certainly shrewd enough to have done so, for he had uncanny knowledge of what went on in people's thoughts; yet he'd strengthened the defense he must destroy. He'd spoken as if truth were important to him, too!

Meeting the Scholar's gaze straightforwardly, Noren said, "I'm not afraid to be wrong about the Prophecy, sir. I won't deny it, if it's proven, but what difference will that make? I still won't recant, because recanting means more than accepting the Prophecy; it means accepting your right to keep things away from people. I won't acknowledge that no matter what you prove about the Mother Star."

Stefred showed no sign of disapproval; in fact he looked almost as if he'd received the answer he wanted. But his reply was impassive. "You'll be amazed at what you can be brought to do," he said dryly, touching a button at the corner of his desk.

The door of the room slid open, and the two Technicians reappeared. Noren's stomach contracted. All at once his fear rushed back, more debilitating than ever before. *He's playing with me,* he thought in despair. *He encourages me only to prolong the pleasure of breaking my spirit.* At Stefred's nod, Noren felt his arms gripped firmly; then he was being taken down a ramp and along a narrow, solid-walled corridor in which there was no apparent opening.

They ordered him to sit in a heavy, padded chair with a weird-looking leather headrest and an appalling assortment of unfathomable apparatus attached to it. Noren obeyed, seeing no use in resistance. He was tilted backward so that he was half-reclining. The cramped little room was windowless; light came, somehow, from the ceiling, dimly illuminating a panel of dials and switches on the opposite wall. One of the Technicians moved a lever at the top of the panel, causing a small red light to glow.

Resolutely, Noren told himself that they must not see his terror, and from somewhere he got courage to relax his muscles while they fastened various bands and wires to his head. He realized that this Machine would do something mysterious and overwhelming to him, and he was filled with foreboding; the interview with Stefred had left him deeply shaken. Yet part of him wanted desperately to believe Stefred. The Scholar had said the things he'd said as if he meant them, and some of them were things no one else—not even Talyra—had been willing to admit.

Thinking of Talyra, Noren felt a surge of sadness. He would never see her again. And what had he achieved? He had convinced only one person; he had not made the faintest dent in the Scholars' aura of power; and he would die in the end, no matter how bravely he bore this ordeal. Why, he wondered, wasn't he sorry? Why was he still so determined never to give in even if some of his theories proved mistaken?

A young woman entered, dismissing the Technicians, whom she evidently outranked although she wore no Scholar's robe. She carried a syringe; taking Noren's arm, she wiped it with a chilling, pungent solution. Her eyes avoided him, but there was pity in them as she plunged down on the needle.

The sting was intense, but brief; he felt a flash of heat spreading through his veins. It was not unduly unpleasant in itself. He lost awareness of touch and seemed to be falling through miles of emptiness, though he could see the unyielding walls and the woman standing before the control board, her hand on a switch below a winking yellow bulb. Then the room was black, and colored suns were expanding somewhere in his mind: not pictures, but images totally independent of sight. His eyes would no longer open, but he heard the switch close with a resounding metallic click.

He expected pain, but it did not come.

Instead, he was in the starship. He recognized it immediately and was perplexed over the sudden transference; then in the next moment he was conscious of the fact that he was not himself any longer. No . . . he was himself, but he was someone else too, simultaneously. The other person's thoughts and knowledge came naturally into his mind as if they were his own.

He was a Scholar. He stood at the round window of the ship—a viewport, it was called—and looked out at the earth, the other earth, the world of many cities. He could not see them from where he watched, but he knew what they were like; he knew countless things about them that had never been in the pictures. He knew the people, also, for they were his own people; he was a Scholar not of his world, but of theirs. And in that world a Scholar had no rank, no secrets. It was all as it should be: knowledge was free to everyone. The part of him that was Noren rejoiced. It *could* be that way, it was not a foolish idea! That was how it had been meant to be all along.

But his rejoicing did not last, for somewhere, buried deep inside him, lay knowledge so terrible that he dared not bring it forth consciously. It had nothing to do with High Priests or their secrets. It concerned something more basic than that, some horror too vast for contemplation. The Scholar could deal with such thoughts; Noren realized that it was he, as himself, who lacked courage to let them surface. He must find the courage, he knew. He must not shrink from any knowledge that was available to him.

Deliberately, he suppressed his own identity, allowing the feelings of the Scholar to surge into his mind. He looked out at the green globe beneath him and thought of the people . . . millions upon millions of people, the people not only of this world but of its neighboring ones: their lives, their achievements, their hopes; their harrowing struggle to create a civilization in which everyone had equal rights to power and machines and wisdom; their audacious dream of interstellar expansion . . .

And he knew that the people were going to die. All of them.

It was not because they couldn't get enough food. That problem could have been solved. Though of the fifteen planets in the solar system, the six fertile ones were fully settled, already one world of a distant star was being explored; there would someday have been many more. But there was a far worse problem that he and his fellow-

Scholars had discovered very recently, and it had no solution.

He, the Scholar, was counted among the wisest of his
people, and everyone agreed that if he could not save them,
no one else could. Nevertheless he had consulted all the
other Scholars in all the cities of the Six Worlds, hoping
that someone would prove wiser than himself. No one had.
The tragedy that was about to strike was beyond the scope of
human wisdom to prevent. It would take place soon, and
instantaneously; there was no possible way to stop it. All
that mankind had accomplished in the thousands of years
since the first civilization had grown out of savagery was
going to be wiped out, all, that is, but the knowledge preserved in the computers aboard the starship and its sister
ships of the fleet. With sorrow he accepted the fact that
there was *nothing* he could do: nothing but to stand at
the viewport and passively observe what was going to
happen.

Men approached him. "It's nearly time," said someone.

Noren nodded. "Take us out," he replied curtly, as if
accustomed to command.

There was a peculiar sensation, not so much of motion
as of dislocation. The green globe disappeared. After a
little while the other men returned. "We are well beyond
the solar system," one of them said. "Ten minutes to zero,
sir." He added hesitantly, "Will you—watch?"

"I must." Noren was not quite sure why he must; he
certainly did not want to. Even as the Scholar, he was
afraid. Yet for some reason he felt a responsibility to do
it. He could not save the Six Worlds, but he might perhaps save the people of the new and far-off research station, a handful of people who, with the fleet's passengers,
would soon be the sole survivors of the entire human race.
His plan for saving them was vague and very desperate.
Somehow observation of the disaster would contribute
to that plan.

"Maximum filters," he ordered. The glass in the viewport darkened. He could no longer see the stars. He could not even see the sun, which at this distance was no brighter than a large star in any case.

But it soon would be.

I'm dreaming, thought Noren in panic. *It's like other nightmares; before anything dreadful happens I'll wake up.* . . . One did not feel nameless terror like this except in nightmares. One certainly did not become someone else, someone whose thoughts were beyond understanding.

His eyes were fixed on the center of the viewport; his companions had dissolved, as people do in dreams. The ship too was dissolving. Before him, a pinprick of light began to grow.

It grew as it had in the picture, but it was not harmless now, not cold; it expanded into a swollen mass of incandescence, a blinding, pulsating sphere of pure light and intolerable heat, and though his flesh was not burned, he felt the pain of burning. He had doubted when told that the picture showed the Mother Star. He could not doubt now, for he knew that this star was unlike others: surely normal stars did not explode like this, engulfing their worlds, turning them not merely to ash, but to vapor! There was a word for such stars, drawn from the mind of the Scholar, and the word was *nova.*

Passage of time had no meaning. Even before the nova's light had become visible, the worlds circling that star had ceased to exist, and their people with them; yet the blazing brilliance of it would endure. It would someday reach far galaxies. The Scholar, perhaps, had watched in silence; but Noren was so overpowered by it that he could not hold back his screams.

When he awoke, Stefred was beside him. They were in the little room with the Machine, but the woman had gone and the apparatus no longer touched his body. He lay back in the reclining chair, sweating.

"Do you understand what happened to you?" Stefred asked quietly. His tone was concerned, compassionate; Noren turned to him with an instinctive, unreasoned conviction that the compassion was real.

"I—I was dreaming, I guess," Noren replied dazedly. "Those pictures you showed me must have brought it on. It was sort of a nightmare; did I cry out, or anything?" He averted his face, mortified at the thought that he might have done so.

"It wasn't an ordinary dream," Stefred told him. "You see, Noren, when there's need we can make people dream what we want them to."

Noren drew back, stunned less by surprise than by his own near-surrender. Once again they'd tried to weaken him through terror, and this time they'd come all too close to succeeding. Furthermore, if they'd done it once, they could do it over and over; no wonder they'd been so confident of their ability to break him without physical torture! "I do see," he said hopelessly. "You think I'll give in rather than go through worse nightmares."

Stefred's hand closed reassuringly on his. "You have it twisted. I think you'll consent to go through them, because dreams of this kind aren't mere nightmares; they are true. What happens in them once did happen; they will teach you much that would otherwise remain beyond your grasp."

Horrified, Noren whispered, "You mean it—it really was like that? The sun grew so big that it burned up its worlds . . . and all the people died?"

"Yes," Stefred admitted with sorrow. "I know how it feels to watch; I've dreamed the same dream myself. All Scholars have."

Noren frowned. It had never occurred to him that Scholars, despite their privileges, might undergo ordeals of their own. "Then you're not expecting to break me this way," he reflected. "Is this done to all heretics?"

"Just to those who will not be satisfied with anything less. Truth, Noren, can be quite terrible. Not everyone can face it. I'm exposing you to this only because you convinced me that you could."

For a long time Noren thought. He was not sure just how he knew that the dream was indeed true; it was partly that the feelings of the person he'd become had been real feelings, separate from his own terror—and partly that he could sense Stefred's sincerity. There was a subtle difference in the Scholar's manner that made plain that in earlier interviews, his emotions had been deliberately concealed.

Slowly Noren declared, "I—I believe you, sir. I believe that by keeping such secrets from the villagers and Technicians you're trying to be kind. But I don't think that's right. I don't think people need to be protected from the truth. Even when it does hurt, it's—well, it's how things *are*."

"I agree with you," the Scholar said gravely. "In this case, however, the issue's not that simple. There's still a lot you don't know. Are you willing to dream again, Noren?"

"Do I have a choice? You said before that I didn't have."

"Your choice at that point had already been made. But you've had complete freedom to choose from the very beginning; the Technicians at the inn, for instance, couldn't have induced you to speak as you did if you hadn't wanted to. We don't control people. We don't even try. You would not be here if you hadn't chosen to seek knowledge that wasn't available elsewhere."

"I haven't been fully informed about what I was choosing, though," Noren protested.

"No one ever is; information's a matter of degree. And as you become better informed, the decisions get harder."

Stefred paused and then asked again, "How about the dream?"

"It's . . . nightmarish?"

"Yes. It's even more so than the first, but as you say, it's how things are."

"Then I guess I can't stop now. I don't want to stop."

"I thought not." The approval in Stefred's voice was unmistakable. He prepared a syringe, continuing calmly, "I'm going to give you something to make you sleep, and for many hours you'll sleep peacefully; you must have rest and nourishment, which you'll receive from injections, to regain your strength. After that you will find yourself back in the starship. What you hear and what you feel won't be faked; like the witnessing of the nova, it was recorded long ago from the memories of the First Scholar. He was a real person, and he actually experienced it. For him it wasn't a dream from which he could wake up."

"Why did he make himself watch the sun explode?"

"So that he could relive it in his mind later, while a Machine recorded his thoughts. He knew that we of the future could learn more from dreams than from words or pictures."

"But then why didn't I realize that while I was dreaming?"

"You cannot have access to his whole mind," explained Stefred. "The dream's content is limited both by what's in the recording and by your own reactions. Since you retain your personal identity, most of what you meet is strange to you; it can't all be comprehended at once."

"I didn't know what was going to happen at first," Noren reflected. "The First Scholar must have known all the time, but I had to—reach for it."

"Yes. The further you reach, the more you'll learn; but it takes courage." Stefred hesitated, then added, "The First Scholar had a great deal; you can draw on that as well

155)

as on his knowledge, and you'll need to. You will share his feelings fully, Noren, because it so happens that you are very much like him. He was older and wiser, but essentially he believed what you believe."

Then he must have been a heretic! Noren thought. No—no, in his world such beliefs hadn't been considered heretical. They'd been approved, and Stefred's respect for the man was clear. Incredulously he asked, "Are you—a Scholar—telling me that my heresy isn't wrong?"

"I can't tell you what's wrong and what's right. That's a decision every person must make for himself, though you may find it helpful to know how the First Scholar made his."

"I must be still dreaming," Noren murmured. "Everything's turned around."

"Not really. You are looking at sides you haven't seen before."

"But . . . some of what you've said supports *my* side, sir! Why should you side with someone who opposes you, someone who's got to be silenced?" Was it possible, thought Noren wonderingly, that there were secret opponents of the system among the Scholars themselves?

Smiling enigmatically, Stefred answered, "I've always been on your side. I couldn't let you know until I was sure of where you stood; but from now on I have nothing to lose by it, and everything to gain."

(*156*

IX

HE WAS THE FIRST SCHOLAR AGAIN. HE WAS ABOARD THE starship, but he no longer looked out through its viewports; instead, he sat at a large white table with a group of people, some men, some women. He knew them all, but their faces were dim and their names didn't matter. The only thing that mattered was the topic under discussion, which lay so heavily upon him that everything else was blurred.

"The colony will not survive," said someone.

"It must survive," declared Noren. "It is all that is left of mankind."

"Of course it must," another agreed. "Haven't we made every provision for its survival? Why else did we throw all our worlds' energies into the preparation of this fleet as soon as we learned that the sun would nova?"

"To put it bluntly," replied the first man, "we did so because there was nothing else to do. We had to keep busy at *something*. There were less than six weeks; we could not build new starships, we could merely recall and re-equip those we had. We've saved ourselves, only a few hundred of us. Our generation will live. The next will die."

"You speak as if our goal were self-preservation!" protested Noren angrily. "You forget that we were chosen by lot from among the best-qualified scientists of the Six Worlds, and that we were sent not for our sake, but for the colony's. The technicians at the existing research station don't have enough scientific knowledge to establish a permanent settlement; ours is needed."

"It may be needed, but it will prove useless. The research station is utterly dependent upon the arrival of a supply ship every five weeks. People can't live there without supplies; the environment of the planet is just too alien. Why, the soil itself is poisonous and has to be treated each season before it will produce edible crops, not to mention the fact that ground and surface water contains enough of the same poison to cause chromosome damage. If the water purification plant ever stops functioning, all future babies will be mutant idiots!"

"And purifying water on a larger scale won't be simple," added someone else, "even if we succeed in controlling the weather so that the need can be partially met by rain. We equipped the fleet as best we could, but the machines we have won't serve an expanding population, and since the planet has no useable metals, we can't manufacture more. The only hope is to synthesize metal, yet without proper research facilities we couldn't achieve that if we worked for several lifetimes."

"Yes," admitted Noren, frowning. "Yes, I know." He, the First Scholar, did know; and the knowledge had weighed on his mind ever since he'd been informed that he had been chosen to lead the final expedition. It had torn him inwardly, obsessed him so that he'd been barely able to sleep or to eat or even to talk with his wife. It was an insoluble dilemma: the planned colony could *not* survive, and yet it *must*.

Most of his companions had refused to recognize the hard truth, and that was understandable. More than thirty billion people—the entire population of the Six Worlds—had been doomed by the nova; it was too cruel a thing that the descendants of the few who'd escape would also be doomed. The facts, however, were indisputable: only one planet with a breatheable atmosphere had been found during the limited interstellar exploration accomplished in the short time since the invention of the stardrive, and that one did not have the natural resources needed to support human beings. It was the world of a metal-poor star, and what little metal it had once, aside from that chemically unsuitable for fabrication of machines, had apparently been extracted in past ages by miners from some other solar system who had depleted it and gone on. Their origin was unknown; no contact had ever been made with another intelligent race; to continue the search for a better planet was impossible without a source of nuclear fuel and concentrated food. In any case, the fleet's ships would have to be dismantled to provide an adequate life-support system for the colony. They carried more equipment than people, since an opposite policy would have been self-defeating; still the equipment could not last forever, and without it, humanity would face extinction.

So far he had not tried to destroy anyone's illusions. The morale of the Six Worlds had been raised during those last terrible weeks by the thought of the expedition that was to save one small remnant of mankind, and, within the starships' computers, the entire store of mankind's knowledge. He'd known that if the real situation were to be grasped, the expedition's members might give up in despair. They must not give up! They must proceed as if survival was possible, so that somehow, a solution might be found.

159)

But now the Six Worlds were gone; the fleet was enroute to the new planet, and because the starships were not limited by the speed of light, they would get there very soon. A decision had to be made, a decision so appalling that Noren was unable to grasp its nature, however deeply he reached into his mind. The First Scholar did not want to think about the decision. To do so brought him pain, yet the people around the table must accept the fact that their mission was going to fail unless they made some drastic change in the plans formed by the Six Worlds' now-non-existent government.

"It would be different," he said to them, "if the planet could support an independent colony. But it can't. No one ever expected people to live there without supply ships. Though foods can be raised if the soil is enriched and treated and the seed irradiated, without metal no industry can be established, so even the machines for inactivating native poisons must be imported. It's been assumed that tools and machines could easily be sent; the whole concept of expansion to worlds with insufficient resources was based on that assumption."

"With the food shortage at home so crucial, it seemed better to send equipment and bring back grain than to wait for the discovery of worlds that could become self-sufficient," they agreed.

"But we've got to be self-sufficient now!" insisted one of the men. "Are you telling us we're stuck with a world we can't develop?"

Noren nodded gravely. "The old techniques, the ones that worked in our home solar system, won't do," he stated, not understanding half of what he, as the First Scholar, was saying. "We don't have enough equipment, and we don't have the means to build it. We have problems that never occurred on the Six Worlds: problems like the poison that permeates the soil, ground water and native vegetation; the need for irradiation of our grainseed to kill fungi;

(160

and above all, the lack of metallic elements suitable for industrial use. I believe those problems can be solved. But they can't be solved quickly; we must find a way to synthesize useable metals through nuclear fusion of other elements, and with inadequate facilities that will require generations of research. There is no shortcut. Moreover, if mankind is to survive, the population must be built up during those generations. We're far too few to maintain the technology necessary for the support of such research, or to produce enough descendants with creative minds."

"How can the population be built up when we must ration our tools and machines merely to supply the population that already exists?"

"There's no easy answer," Noren admitted. "We can't save the human race unless the population grows, yet it can't grow without the equipment only technology can provide—"

"Why can't it?" a woman interrupted. "For thousands of years people lived on our mother world without any technology at all, and the population grew very rapidly."

"Our race evolved on the mother world. The environment wasn't alien. People could survive in the wilderness; they could eat the native plants, and they could kill and eat animals. The water didn't have to be purified. The trace elements essential to our form of life didn't have to be added to the ground, nor all wastes recycled to prevent loss of those elements. There weren't lethal diseases against which no one had natural immunity."

"And our forebears weren't used to the comforts of civilization as we are," another woman added.

"We're going to have to do without comforts," retorted somebody grimly.

"Yes. But it's not as simple as that." Noren sighed. From the First Scholar's mind came the realization that these people were all scientists, all highly educated and very intelligent, whose background was in itself blinding them to what a lack of such background would imply. "Just suppose we did learn to live the way primitive peoples once lived," he said wearily. "Forget about luxuries like prefabricated shelters, powered transportation, communication networks, lighting, farm machinery, imported tools, clothing and medicines: all the things that colonists would normally have. Assume only that cropland was initially fertilized with the chemicals we've brought and treated each season to inactivate the native poison, that the grainseed was irradiated, that weather was controlled to provide enough rain for the crops, that a water purification plant of sufficient capacity to supplement rain catchment was built, and that provision was made for recycling of wastes. Of course, we must also assume nuclear power to maintain these essentials, and we must assume that vaccines for the local diseases could be developed before the drug supplies gave out. Under those conditions, do you think our descendants could last indefinitely?"

"Why not?" several men began confidently; but the faces of others grew thoughtful. "No," said one of the women in a low voice. "No, it wouldn't work. As long as we were alive, we could keep things going. Maybe we could teach our children enough so that they could. But our grandchildren, born into a non-industrialized world—"

"They wouldn't understand," another conceded. "The machines would be magic to them; they wouldn't be able to fix them if they broke down, much less find a way to synthesize the metal needed to supply an increasing population. They'd have to be nuclear scientists for that, and the people of primitive agricultural societies just can't be educated as nuclear scientists. They haven't the background, and what's more, they don't *care*. People care about things that seem relevant to the life they know."

"No community can be primitive and technological at the same time," someone else declared, "unless it's importing what its people can't make. Civilization and technology go hand in hand. We're going to be stranded on a planet where advanced technology is required if humanity's merely to stay alive—that is, if it's to stay human and not fall prey to the chromosome damage that would reduce its intelligence to the animal level. If our grandchildren lose that technology, they'll have no chance to start over from scratch; and they will lose it if they revert to primitive ways."

"Lose knowledge?" protested a young man skeptically. "The knowledge will be there in the computers; it will be preserved forever."

"The knowledge will not be in the computers," said Noren, "after the power plant breaks down."

For a moment nobody spoke; they sat horror-stricken, stunned by a fact so obvious that they did not see how it had been overlooked. They'd grown up believing that the memory of a computer was more eternal than the shape of the land, for on the Six Worlds there had been no shortage of power; the information stored in the computers had remained there until the final holocaust. But they knew, of course, that a computer's memory consisted of electrical impulses, and that one instant of power failure would be enough to wipe it out.

"We've been in a state of shock," Noren said. "Six weeks ago we learned that thirty billion people were about to die; it's hardly surprising if we failed to think rationally. But we must do so now—"

"All this talk is meaningless," a man broke in abruptly. "It doesn't matter how long the equipment lasts; it would make no difference if we had enough to supply endless generations. There won't be endless generations. Our wives are experienced scientists, too old to bear many children, and the people at the research station will begin to die when they hear about the nova."

"That's crazy," objected another. "Why should they?"

"What happened on the Six Worlds?"

"All right, there was panic. Some people went mad, some killed themselves. But that was different; they were going to die anyway, and they were afraid."

"The members of this expedition were chosen from the Interplanetary Association of Scientists," the man reminded him. "Medical and psychological screening tests were given to eligible couples, the same tests administered to those previously sent. Of the ones who passed, all had an equal chance in the lottery; yet some of them committed suicide even before the lots were drawn."

"I didn't know that!" several people exclaimed in dismay. Noren was silent; the First Scholar had known, but he had tried to forget.

"It was kept quiet," the man said. "But the fact is that most people who've grown up with the idea that they're part of an advanced culture with thirty billion citizens just can't live with the knowledge that it's gone."

"We're living with it," someone pointed out.

"That means nothing, since if we were among those who couldn't, we wouldn't be here."

"There might be another explanation for those suicides," someone else suggested. "They might have sacrificed themselves to give others a greater chance in the lottery."

"A few, maybe. Not very many." In a tone of unshakable certainty the man asserted, "Emotionally, the research station workers belong to the Six Worlds, not to the new world; they signed up for short tours of duty and never planned to settle there. They have no children, for they're waiting to start their families when they get home. They've been getting news from home on every supply ship. When they hear that all civilized planets have been destroyed—that mankind has been wiped out except at that one alien base—their spirit will be fatally crushed. They not may kill themselves, but they won't carry on the human race, either."

"They'll not have much choice once the drug they've

been using wears off. Besides, pioneers have always managed in the past."

"These people didn't choose to be pioneers. They weren't reared in the kind of society pioneers come from; the Six Worlds' was so complex that they never developed any independence, and they had no desire to break away. Right now they're probably scared to death because the regular ship's late! Oh, they'll have babies in time—but a lot of those babies will be subhuman mutants because when the people learn the truth, their hope will die, and they'll stop bothering to avoid unpurified water."

"You're mistaken," Noren contended. "Surely it will work the other way; they'll know that they've got to be more careful than ever, that everything in the future depends on them."

"I wish I could agree. But they'll also know that there isn't likely to be much future, and not everyone has your courage, sir."

Noren did not feel very courageous; as the First Scholar he was tired and despondent, and he knew that a dreadful decision was soon to be made. "In any case," he said slowly, "we seem more or less agreed that the colony is in grave peril one way or another, and that if we can't come up with a solution, there's little hope for it."

"There is no solution. The colony will die, and humanity with it; and when the power goes off, humanity's knowledge will be lost."

"Is—is this all . . . futile, then?" a woman faltered. "Have we launched this expedition for nothing? I won't believe there's no way to save mankind!"

The time had come, Noren realized, to speak of his plan: the desperate, horrifying plan he did not wish to think of. "There may be one," he found himself saying, "if we dare to use it—"

Across the room from him a door burst open. A man

stood there, a man who quavered, "Sir, we've illness aboard! Three people are stricken!"

Noren jumped to his feet. "Illness? That's impossible; we all had medical examinations and everything on this ship was sterilized."

"It hasn't been diagnosed yet." With still greater distress the man added, "One of those ill is your wife, sir."

Noren's heart lurched; the room swirled around him and then began to dissolve. He found himself transported to another, after the manner of dreams. For a brief instant he knew he was dreaming, but he was quickly engulfed once more by the emotions of the First Scholar.

He stood by a bed upon which a woman was lying. She had long, dark hair, like Talyra's, but he could not see her face. Only her voice came to him, the voice of the woman he loved.

"What use is there going on?" she demanded feebly. "Who are we, a mere scattering of people in a fleet of ships bound through emptiness to an alien world, to say that the human race is worth preserving? There is *nothing left*, darling! Don't you understand? Everything's gone; there's nothing to look back to any more."

"I understand," he told her, forcing the words through trembling lips. "I watched! I saw it, you did not—and I say that there is a reason to go on! If we don't, the colony has no chance at all."

"Why should it have? That world was never meant for man. Man wasn't meant to outlast the sun. We should have died when the others did."

He knelt beside her, holding her close to him. "Think of those who came before us," he insisted. "Think of all the labor, all the suffering of the generations past—"

"I am thinking of it! I'm thinking it will be better not to start that again; what end did it serve?"

"None, if we give up now. We have a responsibility."

(166

"To whom? To the thirty billion dead?" She began to cry hysterically.

He felt tears on his own face. "Dearest," he murmured, "dearest, we can't know. We can't see what end we serve; we know only that there's no one but us to keep up the struggle."

"I—I *can't*," she sobbed. "I can't, knowing what I do."

"You've known for weeks, as we all have. Nothing has changed."

"It has! Before, it was theory; we were told it would happen, but it wasn't real. Now all the worlds are consumed. The universe is empty—empty! No one can live knowing that! The people on that planet will die when they find out, as I am dying now."

"You're not dying," he said soothingly. "The doctors will cure you, and you'll feel differently when you're well. Trust me, dearest. I won't let you die."

"You don't understand," she whispered. "Darling, there's no cure. I . . . couldn't face it . . . I took some pills."

"Talyra!" he cried out. The sights and sounds of the dream were fading; he was aware only of the girl, who had gone limp in his arms. Somewhere in the background he could hear voices, faint and far away: "An overdose . . . three people so far . . . if it's affecting *us* this way, we who knew beforehand and bore the knowledge, those who didn't know are bound to be crushed by it."

He looked down at his wife's colorless face, and it was Talyra's face; Talyra's eyes looked up at him, and she was not dying, but already dead. He wept, and the voices receded further into the distance. "The others may give up too, when they hear."

"No!" Noren exclaimed, his own voice as remote and unreal as the others. "They will not hear; I now see that we mustn't tell them. If we don't, they'll have no way of knowing, for the new world is so many light-years away that the nova will not be visible there for generations."

Noren awoke wrenched by sobs, deep, silent sobs over which he had no control. Talyra . . . he'd been holding her in his arms and she was dead, dead because civilization was gone and mankind was gone and it was futile to go on trying. The whole human race was going to die out.

At the sight of his surroundings, he came abruptly to himself. Talyra wasn't dead. It had been the wife of the First Scholar who had died. Moreover, the human race had somehow lasted after all. Why had it, when its doom had seemed so sure?

Stefred stood in a corner of the little room, his back turned. Noren sat up; his feet touched the floor and found it solid, though in the wrong place, somehow. "Why didn't things happen as the people of the fleet expected?" he asked.

"Do you think there was a real danger?" Stefred replied, his voice giving no clue as to what he himself thought.

"There must have been," Noren said positively. "Even though the nova was kept secret—which I'm still not sure was right—there didn't seem to be any way around the other problems."

"The First Scholar found a way," said Stefred, coming to Noren's side. "If he hadn't, none of us would be here."

"It was something frightening, something he felt awful about," Noren recalled. "He—he had the idea, but I just couldn't get hold of it."

"His plan was not in this particular recording," Stefred told him. "It's hard when you reach for a thought that won't come; but Noren, many of the First Scholar's thoughts are too complex for anyone who knows little of the Six Worlds. They can't be made available until a person's ready to understand their significance."

"There are other dreams, aren't there?"

"Yes. But they keep getting rougher. You need not go

on unless you choose to."

"I want to go on, sir." Noren took deep breaths, steadying himself, and then burst out, "Why did she have Talyra's face?"

"A dream is more than a recording," Stefred explained gently. "Each person experiences it differently, depending on what he brings to it. The recording contains no sounds, no pictures, but only thoughts; and when you as the First Scholar thought of the woman you loved, her face came not from his memory, but from yours."

"Will it work that way with other things?"

"It may." Stefred looked at him with sympathy. "Perhaps you've wondered, Noren, why it was necessary for me to give you drugs during your inquisition; perhaps you felt it an indignity. I had no choice. It wasn't that I suspected you of lying, but merely that I had to know more about what's buried deep in your mind than you could have told me while you were fully conscious. There is an element of risk in these dreams, for with some people they can stir memories better left untouched, and I don't want you to be harmed."

He spoke as if he cared, Noren noticed with wonder. Why should he care whether a heretic was harmed or not?

Another thought hit him, an appalling thought. "Sir, I— I've drunk impure water! I didn't believe before—"

"How often, Noren?" asked Stefred gravely.

"Five or six times, maybe."

"Don't worry about it. The damage is done only if you drink more than that."

Noren sighed with relief before he recalled that he was not going to live long enough to father children in any event. Somehow, despite his grim prospects, he had stopped thinking of what lay ahead. He even found Stefred's prediction that he wouldn't mind sharing the feelings of the First Scholar to be quite true. "What . . . became of him?" he faltered, as Stefred took his arm for another injection.

"You must experience it in order to understand. We'll proceed now; you're taking this well, and I see no reason to delay."

After that Noren lost track of time. He was never fed, but neither was he hungry; they controlled all bodily needs with injections as they controlled sleep. He was not plunged directly into the dreams without sedation as he had been the first time when, Stefred admitted, they had been making one last attempt to see if he could be panicked into capitulation. Since then they'd attached no apparatus to his head until he was unconscious. During his periods of awareness they questioned him searchingly as to his impressions; he was required to think the experiences through. Then he would sleep again, and dream again.

Someone was always with him when he awoke: usually Stefred, but occasionally the young woman who operated the Dream Machine. She was a Scholar, he was sure, for she knew what was in the dreams and discussed them. He no longer saw any Technicians; that seemed strange until it occurred to him that it was feared that he, who disapproved of secrets, might give some away.

At first he was puzzled because the woman Scholar wore no robe; but since Stefred rarely wore his either, he concluded that the robes, which he'd learned were mere outer garments that covered ordinary clothes, were put on primarily when it was necessary to impress someone. In themselves, Scholars looked just like anybody else. Noren had once thought them ageless, as did all villagers, but the woman seemed very little older than he was; and when he stopped to think about it, he realized that within the City there must be other young ones, even children. How did they feel about things? he wondered. Were they, too, frightened when they were first made to dream?

He was still frightened; he grew cold with apprehension every time he was given an injection, for being the First Scholar was not at all enjoyable; yet he wanted to keep dreaming. Stefred would grant him respite if he asked,

Noren knew, but he couldn't do that. It was not just a matter of pride. It was more a matter of an unquenchable desire to know all that had happened, however dreadful those happenings might have been.

He understood, of course, that dreams were proving certain aspects of the Prophecy; that had become evident when he'd absorbed the truth about the Mother Star. Gradually, Noren became aware that they were also proving something else. This awareness was painful, but the pain of giving up long-cherished theories was overshadowed by the First Scholar's suffering, which he found bearable only because of his knowledge that others—including the young woman —had borne it and had survived. If they could, so could he! After all, the First Scholar himself had borne it, and as Stefred had pointed out, for him it hadn't been a dream from which he could wake up.

But the First Scholar had not survived. Somehow, without being told, Noren knew that the final dream would end with the First Scholar's death.

He was back in the room with the white table, again surrounded by the members of his staff, and this time he knew he must present the plan. He must make them accept it, though he was well aware that they would not like it any better than he did himself.

"It's easy enough not to tell the research station people about the nova," someone was saying, "but it'll be a good deal harder to explain why no more supply ships are going to arrive."

"We won't explain," said Noren.

"But sir, we can't hide *that!* We mustn't even try to, because if we do, they'll wear out the equipment too fast. There's got to be rationing."

"There's got to be more than rationing. People must learn to do without any offworld equipment at all in their daily lives."

"That's impossible. We know they can't survive that

way, at least not as human beings. If they drink unpurified water too often, the next generation will have subhuman intelligence."

"They can survive as long as somebody treats the soil, irradiates the seed, provides rain through weather control, purifies additional water, and vaccinates them against disease."

"Who's going to do that after we die?"

"Our successors."

The man at his left frowned. "We've been over all this. I thought it was agreed that our successors will lose their technology if they live in a primitive fashion."

"They will," Noren replied. "So the only answer is that they must not live in a primitive fashion. To develop the viewpoint they'll need to carry on our research, they must live in a city where technology is preserved: a walled city within which the power plant and the computers and all the essential equipment can be kept safe for posterity."

"That contradicts what you just proposed about learning to do without such equipment in everyday life," objected another man. "And besides, when the population expands, there won't be enough to go around."

"Within the city very little expansion will be possible."

"We need population growth," a woman protested. "You said so yourself only yesterday."

"For the world as a whole, yes. And outside the city we'll have it; a primitive agricultural society will expand there even more rapidly than the ancient ones, which knew nothing of medicine."

Everybody stared at him, suddenly grasping the implications of what he was saying. Their eyes were large with dismay; though their faces were indistinct, the eyes seemed huge. "You're suggesting a *caste system?*"

Noren paused; to the First Scholar, the thought of some people being allowed to live in a manner that others weren't permitted to share was serious heresy indeed. "Yes," he heard himself declare. "There is no other way."

There was a cold, shocked silence. "I think you're right, sir," one of the men finally conceded. "It could work; those in the city could act as custodians of the equipment and the knowledge, and at the same time they could do the research that would someday enable machines to be manufactured through synthesization of suitable metals. That would solve everything. It's a brilliant idea, but it has one insurmountable flaw: we can never get the majority to accept it."

"We certainly can't," others agreed. "People won't vote for a scheme that puts some in a city with all the equipment while the rest are left outside with none. They wouldn't even if they were aware of the emergency, let alone if we keep the nova secret."

"I know," Noren admitted painfully. "There is no possibility whatsoever of establishing such a system by vote."

"Then we'd better not even propose it. It would be tragic to let them vote down their only chance of survival."

"I'm glad you see that," he replied gravely. "I thought I'd have to argue more."

The faces were blank, for no one yet perceived his meaning. Noren was just beginning to perceive it himself, dipping deep into the First Scholar's memories in his efforts to understand. The government of the Six Worlds had been wholly democratic, he realized. For countless years no dictator had imposed his will on any of those worlds' people; the very concept of tyranny had all but died out; that he should suggest that they seize power was beyond his companions' comprehension.

Noren felt as if he were split in two: he was still the First Scholar, and he shared the First Scholar's misery; yet at the same time he was enough himself to see that the terrible, radical plan was simply that the Scholars should control the City and its contents without giving the villagers a voice in the matter. And to these Scholars, *that* was heresy! It was the worst heresy any of them had ever heard.

But it was a different sort of heresy from his own. The First Scholar did not believe that his plan was right; he did not believe that the world ought to be as he was trying to make it. He hated his own words even as he said them. Yet he knew that he must say them, for he was describing the one way in which mankind could be saved from extinction.

"There will be no violence," he continued. "We will simply build the city and bar the research station people from entering. They know as much as we do about how to utilize what natural resources there are; they can manage very well if we treat enough cropland, establish weather control and a supplementary water system, and provide them with seed and fertile eggs from our cargo. They are not armed, so they cannot resist us—"

The blank faces came alive with emotion: shock, horror, anger. "You're not serious! Impose this by *force?* We'd be setting ourselves up as dictators—"

"The people will remain free," Noren declared. "They will govern themselves; we'll assume no power over individuals, nor will we interfere in local affairs. We will control only the offworld equipment and the knowledge that would otherwise be lost."

Voices assailed him. "Control *knowledge?*" they cried, aghast. "You are taking us back to the Dark Ages! If there is anything that should never be controlled, it's the right of the people to know."

"Yes, a Dark Age," he admitted, "a Dark Age through which our knowledge will be preserved and passed from generation to generation in secret, while the people forget what they once knew. They must forget the Six Worlds; all memory of that vanished civilization must be wiped out so that a new and lasting culture can grow. Otherwise they cannot bear the loss, and there can be no second chance."

(*174*

He realized with despair that he was arguing against everything he had ever believed, everything he had cared about; yet he could not help himself. And Noren knew that this feeling was not his alone, but was also the First Scholar's, for to him, as to all his companions, the most sacred thing in life had been the free pursuit of truth.

"He is not himself," someone murmured. "The death of his wife has unbalanced his mind."

"His wife was right," the man opposite him said in an ominous tone. "If it's come to this, we should have died with the others."

Grief overwhelmed Noren: grief for his wife, for the Six Worlds, for the ordeals now confronting the survivors. "This plan has been in my mind ever since I assumed leadership of this expedition," he said quietly. "I shall bear full responsibility for it; I shall not put it to a vote even here among ourselves. Thirty billion people who are now dead charged me with the task of ensuring that something would outlast them. I must fulfill that mandate by the only means open to me."

"You are insane," asserted the man angrily. "We of the Six Worlds managed to abolish totalitarianism after centuries of oppression and strife; it was the greatest achievement of our civilization. It would be a poor memorial to those who died if the thing to outlast them was a renewal of that evil."

"There will be no totalitarianism. As I said, the people will have self-government."

"You advocate forced stratification of society! That's evil, too."

"It is an evil," Noren answered wretchedly, "but in our present situation it's a necessary one." He was appalled to hear such words from his own lips.

"Aren't you aware that nearly every dictatorship that ever came into power termed itself a necessary evil?"

"Yes, I am," said Noren, astonished by the things of

which the First Scholar had been aware. "But by 'necessary' they meant something quite different from what I mean. They meant necessary to whatever they happened to value higher than human freedom."

"There is nothing of higher value!"

"True. And we're not going to abridge anyone's freedom, nor yet the freedom of the new world's society to develop in its own fashion. We'll merely be withholding things that cannot last long in any case if we fail to act." He hesitated; the plan was complex, and there were parts that could not yet be revealed even to his companions, parts that—as Noren—were beyond reach. There were also justifications so foreign to his past experience that they slid by hazily in the dream. . . .

". . . We must choose between imposing a stratified culture and allowing the human race to die out," he found himself continuing. "Such a choice never arose before. It never could have arisen on the Six Worlds. But we face it now; have we really a choice at all?"

"Yes!" cried his antagonist with rising fury. "I'd prefer to die than to become a dictator."

"So would I," agreed Noren in anguish, "so would I. But I would not prefer to let mankind perish, so I'll stake my life on the rightness of this course. I shall carry through the plan. If you want to stop me, you will have to kill me."

The man stood up. He had grown taller, it seemed; and though his features were still dim, he had become more real, more individual. "If I have to, I'll do it," he said. "I will kill us all, if need be! I'll blow this ship to space dust before I'll allow it to be used as an instrument of despotism."

Noren could no longer see any of the rest, for this opponent loomed too large in the dream; but he could hear their voices. "Perhaps we will all lose our sanity . . . perhaps suicides weren't the worst we had to fear . . . perhaps it's true that no one can endure to outlive the Six

Worlds! Our two best leaders have become madmen."

In the man's eyes there was indeed madness; he looked at Noren with fanatical contempt, and then, abruptly, he turned and ran.

The white table disappeared, and Noren found that he too was running, running down a long bright tunnel toward a thing that the First Scholar knew to be the starship's control board. He was dizzy with terror; his breath was torn from him in agonized gasps, for he was too old a man to run easily.

The antagonist whom he pursued stood before an array of switches, levers and flashing lights. "I mean what I say!" he shouted. "I will disable the safety circuits and put on enough power to blow this ship."

There was no time for argument, no time to wait for other men to come; Noren knew that before they could reach him, the starship would be vaporized. If he had been younger and stronger he could have fought the man and overpowered him, but as the First Scholar he was not. The First Scholar had no alternative. He saw that some of the lights had gone out and he saw hands thrust into an opening in the control board, entangled in bare-ended wires; he raised his arm to touch a single switch.

A flash of blue fire nearly blinded him. Noren shrank back, releasing the switch, and the man's form crumpled, fell; there was the stench of charred flesh. He stared down in horror. *I've killed a man!* he thought dazedly. *I said there would be no violence, yet already I've killed by my own hand. . . .*

Others by this time had crowded around. He lifted his head, willing himself to assume the bearing of a leader. They would follow him, he knew; they would go along with the plan. But if this was how it had begun, where was it going to end?

X

GRADUALLY, THROUGH MANY DREAMS, NOREN EXPERI-
enced it all: the building of the City; the unloading of the
starships; and the nonviolent but rather ruthless way in
which the research station people were transformed into
villagers who, given the minimum essential technological
aid, could fend for themselves in the wilderness of an alien
world. But it wasn't easy. The First Scholar suffered in-
tensely throughout, and as Stefred had predicted, Noren
shared the agony fully.

Many of his sensations were pure nightmare. Because
he was still partly himself, the impressions were often in-
coherent; he was experiencing mental reactions to events
rather than events themselves, and though he could call on
the First Scholar's knowledge, the facts that came into his
mind were hard to interpret. Even the feelings were sometimes diffuse, chaotic ones that he could not put into words.

At first, during his periods of wakefulness, he found it
hard to believe that keeping the secret of the nova had

really been necessary. Surely few if any villagers would have gone so far as to kill themselves! Some of the men in the dreams shared this opinion. "Human beings have instincts that enable them to survive and adapt under almost any conditions," they insisted. "We owe these people the truth! Though some may not prove able to take it, the majority will."

"You're missing the point," others replied. "Of course they could survive physically, but their morale would be destroyed; suicide's just an extreme expression of the feeling almost everyone would share. And instinct wouldn't help in this case. To remain human here, we've got to *defy* instinct. People's instinct tells them that water that tastes pure is safe; it's mere training that stops them from drinking it. The shock of knowing about the nova would strip away their protective training, at least temporarily; and if they turned to instinct—the instinct that would let them drink the water and perhaps even adapt to a diet of native plants, as we expect to adapt the embryonic animals we've brought for beasts of burden—their children would suffer irrevocable brain damage. They'd survive, all right, but at the expense of generations yet unborn."

The First Scholar understood that. He knew that no evil was worse than extinction of the human race, and though dissidents reminded him that at certain points in the Six Worlds' history similar arguments had been invalidated, he knew such an analogy was false. There'd once been a time when his ancestors had claimed that abridging people's rights in order to prevent overpopulation of the mother world was essential to survival, but it had not been essential at all. On the contrary, voluntary reduction of the birth rate had worked very well, for if the mother world hadn't become overpopulated to some degree, interstellar travel would never have been developed—and in that case, nobody would have escaped the nova.

This was different, for this was a matter not of how

future humans would handle their problems, but of the terrible possibility that the next generation would be sub-human. Such a risk couldn't be taken. Moreover, he began to see other reasons why keeping the secret was important to the success of his plan.

He had known from the beginning that all offworld equipment would have to be preserved within the City if the colony was to last long enough for scientists to learn how to synthesize metallic elements suitable for the manufacture of machines. There were a number of reasons for this. In the first place, if that irreplaceable equipment fell into the hands of people unqualified to use and maintain it, it couldn't be kept operative; and while the research station workers were qualified, their descendants wouldn't be. Besides, recycling of worn metal parts, and indeed of all offworld materials, was going to be necessary over the years, and if such materials were allowed outside the City, some would be lost. Some would be lost simply by being stored outside air-conditioned buildings, since the planet's atmosphere was corrosive to the metals of which certain machines were built. And of course, once the population began to expand, there would not be enough tools and machines to go around; then people would start fighting over them. The colony was too small and weak to withstand much fighting.

But above all, the First Scholar knew that the existing equipment could not go on working forever even if it was carefully safeguarded, nor would it serve an expanding population forever; there would come a time when more *had* to be manufactured if survival was to continue. The supply of metallic trace elements for initial enrichment of cropland would also run out. Synthesization of metal had to be achieved by then, and that was utterly dependent not only on the education of future scientists, but on maintenance of research facilities and on preservation of the computers containing the Six Worlds' knowledge. Those things would be possible only within the City; the City would need all the offworld equipment merely to function.

Depriving the people outside the City of that equipment, however, would be a terrible shock to them. The even greater shock of knowing about the nova might be too much not simply because they had strong ties to the Six Worlds, but because if they knew, they'd be aware that there was nothing they could personally do to improve their situation. They couldn't face such frustration without being united by some immediate aim; he had realized that when he formed the plan, and had wondered what aim he could give them. By keeping the secret he solved that problem.

To Noren's dismay, he solved it by making them hate him.

Initially, the research station consisted of one large opaque dome in which people had been living and working, plus smaller ones containing power and water purification plants; Noren, as the First Scholar, looked down on them from the shuttlecraft in which he and some of the other Founders were descending, finding himself aware that such domes were standard equipment aboard all starships. They were easy to erect: an immense bubble was inflated, then sprayed with a substance that hardened to an impervious shell. The Outer City was to be composed of all the bubbles carried by the fleet.

As soon as the shuttlecraft landed, the captain, by radio, called a meeting in the existing dome; and when all the research station's people were inside, awaiting the newcomers' appearance, its doors were locked. They stayed locked—permanently sealed, in fact—during the days it took for the remaining passengers of the fleet to land and to build the huge circle of adjoining domes that formed the City's outer boundary. Those imprisoned in the original dome were unharmed, but outraged and bewildered; they had no idea what was going on. They could not look out,

181)

and no one spoke to them. Then, once the City was fully enclosed, a new exit was cut in the outside of their dome, and they saw that they were at liberty to leave. Unsuspecting, they did so, taking nothing but the clothes they wore and whatever articles they had in their pockets; it never occurred to them that they'd be unable to get back in. At the moment their fighting spirit was aroused, and all they wanted was their freedom. To find themselves in the wilderness, outside a vast ring of domes that had not been there previously, was so astonishing that at first they didn't understand the significance of what had happened. They encountered no people; they seemed to be free. And so they were. Nobody ever employed force against them again, but there was no way for them to enter the City.

The nucleus of the first village had already been prepared by the Founders: a large water cistern connected by pipe to the City, surrounded by enough cleared and treated land to support the existing population. There was also one stone building containing irradiated grain seed, the fertilized eggs of fowl with hens to incubate them, and enough concentrated rations to last until the first harvest. Inside that building were posted the rules of the game: the research station workers were to raise a larger crop than their previous experimental ones; they would receive no tools and no help except for essential medical supplies, which they could request by radiophone; purified water— for irrigating the fields as well as for drinking—would be supplied continuously, but no further food. No reason whatsoever was given for these instructions.

Though the people were stunned, they were not despairing. The only explanation they could think of was that they were the subjects of some fantastic psychological experiment, and they decided to play along, thinking that it would be an interesting challenge for which they'd eventually be well rewarded. They were all intelligent, highly-trained men and women who were ingenious enough to apply their technical knowledge to the fashioning of tools from stone; some, in fact, began to have fun, for on their home worlds camping out had been considered a pleasure.

Meanwhile, the Founders within the City were working even harder and having considerably less fun. All of the equipment had to be brought down from orbit, meaning endless shuttlecraft trips; and after that some of the stripped starships, which were not designed to travel through the atmosphere, were dismantled and brought down piece by piece. These starships were reassembled inside the enclosure to become the City's towers. They were built of a special material that could not be reshaped by any means available on the planet, and all material was, of course, precious; the only solution was to make them into living quarters. It was a truly awesome task. The Scholars, unused to manual labor, worked to the point of exhaustion, and their knowledge of the tragedy and of the evils to come did not help.

All this time no villager had seen or heard any of the Founders; they were figures of great mystery. The people were not afraid of them. They assumed that the Six Worlds had decided to establish a major colony, and that while it was being built, the psychological effects of close contact with the alien environment were being evaluated; they were sure the experiment would not extend past harvest day. When the day arrived, they were weary of the game; still they felt satisfaction with what they'd accomplished, and they'd developed a strong sense of community. With pride they reported their success on the radiophone. And at that point, the First Scholar faced his most heartbreaking ordeal.

He knew that the people would not be willing to continue the "experiment" indefinitely. Furthermore, it was necessary for them to create permanent things: homes to replace the simple overhead shelters they'd constructed; gristmills to grind their grain; all the necessities of an ongoing life, including primitive clothing when their durable and easily-washed synthetic garments wore out. It was necessary for them to realize that the antifertility drug was going to wear off and that they would someday have to provide for children. Most important of all, it was time for irradiation of the seed and retreatment of the soil, which required go-betweens to ensure that the equipment would remain under the City's control. He longed to offer sympathy and encouragement, but there was none he could give. Instead, he must play the role of a dictator; he must assume the blame for their severance from home to conceal the fact that home had ceased to exist.

He spoke personally on the radiophone: the first voice that had been heard over it. He announced that he had established himself as absolute ruler of the planet, that his followers had successfully overpowered the crew of every supply ship that had arrived since, and that the Six Worlds, dismayed by the consistent and unexplained loss of ships, had written off this solar system and concentrated on exploring elsewhere. The people outside the City would be allowed to live only because they were needed to raise food. A token percentage of the harvest was to be delivered the next day to the gates; if it was not, the water supply would be cut off. By his manner as well as the words themselves, he deliberately made himself out to be insane.

At first the villagers laughed. Did the experiment's designer suppose that a season of living in the Stone Age would reduce citizens of the Six Worlds to a state where they'd swallow a ridiculous story like *that?* They didn't become frightened until two days later when the water supply was indeed cut off. Even then, they held out till the last moment; they knew how much unpurified water they could safely drink. But they were young couples who expected to have families someday when they got home, and—except for a few who eventually fled to the mountains where their offspring became savages—they did not take foolish chances. Since the planet's natural climate was dry and weather control hadn't yet been established, there might be no rain for weeks. Realizing that they could not wait, they capitulated and delivered the grain.

Noren was puzzled because although there were as yet no Technicians in the City, none of the Founders were allowed to risk disclosure of the secret by going out to treat the land. Someone would have to do it. He soon recalled, however, that the original villagers had been born as Technicians; they themselves knew how to operate the Machines. The process whereby they obtained those Machines and were forced to return them was shrouded in mystery, and he perceived that for some reason it was not in the recordings of the First Scholar's memories. When he asked Stefred about it during one of his conscious interludes, he was told only that the problem had been handled in a way beyond his present comprehension, a way that had made the villagers angry and afraid, but had brought harm to no one. Lying there, waiting for the drug-induced sleep that would send him into the next dream, Noren wondered if he ought to take Stefred's word for such a thing. Instinctively, he felt that Stefred would not lie to him; still, the Scholars were admittedly trying to win him to their side. . . . And then he realized that it did not matter whether he trusted Stefred. He trusted the First Scholar! Having shared the First Scholar's feelings, he knew with absolute certainty that the man could not have made plans that would hurt anybody.

But the villagers hadn't known it. To them, the First Scholar was a tyrant, a madman; as the dreams continued, their hatred of him flourished and the bonds of their community strengthened. Slowly, Noren began to see that by hating him, people were adjusting to their new way of life much better than they would have if they'd known his true motives. They still had hope of getting rid of the "dictator" and regaining the things of which they'd been deprived. To be sure, the lack of shuttlecraft traffic had become all too evident; there could be no doubt that the Six Worlds had abandoned the planet, and the towers that began to rise within the City seemed a clear indication that no starships remained in orbit. There was thus no conceivable means of communicating with home, since only starships could travel faster than light. They resigned themselves to their fate, knowing that even if they should succeed in overthrowing the "madman" and getting control of the City, they must make do with the world they had; still, hating him gave them the strength to keep struggling. In their hearts they cherished a hope of rescue. If they'd known the Six Worlds were gone, they would have had no hope at all.

As the First Scholar, Noren knew that once the struggle became easier, the hate would become dangerous. The First Scholar foresaw things he did not like to think about. Noren tried reaching for them and, without knowing why, was badly frightened; thereafter he resolved to take one step at a time.

Village life, he learned, was harder than in his own era. For instance, there were no work-beasts; the fleet had carried animal embryos, since the planet had no large native animals, but the job of developing them through successive mutations to the point where they could eat native plants wouldn't be completed for years, and there wasn't enough grain to feed more than were kept in the laboratory. To be sure, the original villagers lived close together and had no need to travel, but gathering stones for building wasn't easy when sledges had to be pulled by men. They thought at first they might make devices called "wheels", which they were used to, but soon found that since wheels made of softstone would not turn properly and wore away quickly from friction, these were less efficient than runners. That was a blow, for the wheel seemed somehow symbolic of civilization. Then too, there were no City goods at the beginning, aside from the cloth given in exchange for grain and wild fibers delivered to the gates. The Founders had brought machines to produce the City goods that would be needed, but it took time to find the right raw materials.

The villagers assumed that the Scholars were living in luxury, but that was far from the case. Actually they too were undergoing severe hardships. In the dreams Noren was almost always hungry. Before his escape from the village, he hadn't known what it meant to be hungry, and neither, it seemed, had the Founders; but the first harvests were not large, and the Scholars bought only the barest minimum to supplement the dwindling store of concentrated foods carried aboard the fleet, leaving most of the grain for the villagers. Within the City strict rationing was practiced, not only with food but with all supplies—especially anything made of metal—and the First Scholar felt called upon to set an example by following the rules more strictly than anyone else. He and his companions considered themselves stewards, custodians; they were preserving the City's equipment not for their own benefit but for that of future generations. They could not afford any waste.

Yet despite these handicaps they continued to work unceasingly, and their work wasn't simple. Top priority, after the enlargement of the power and water purification plants, was given to the guardianship of knowledge. The starships' computers were installed with extreme care at the heart of the City, in the first tower to be erected. Those computers' memory encompassed all the past achievements of mankind, and was vital to the research work that in turn was vital to the ultimate survival of the colony. But the knowledge had wider significance. Like the equipment, it was held in trust; and to the Scholars, that trust was sacred.

But future villagers would have to do without such knowledge; to children born and reared in a society shaped by the world's scant resources, it would seem irrelevant, meaningless. Since that could not be prevented, it was best that the break come soon, for only thus could men lose their dependence on the culture of the Six Worlds. For the time being, therefore, no books were provided. It was to be a Dark Age indeed; though the First Scholar knew that after a while books could be restored, his heart ached for the people of generations to come, whose education would remain limited. From time to time, when he felt especially depressed and discouraged, he tried to think of some way to give those people an abiding hope. In the recesses of his mind an idea glimmered, but always it eluded his grasp.

Dream followed dream. The plan was working. Technological capability was being preserved where mastery of the alien environment demanded it, but people were learning to do without technology in their daily lives. They were turning to the land; despite its lacks, it was a good land, a spacious land, and it was giving them something more basic than anything shut away in the City. They were creating a culture of their own. Though that culture would be unavoidably static, their children would thrive.

He had not deprived anyone of personal freedom, Noren perceived, nor had he robbed people of the right to develop their own kind of society. The limitations were imposed by the world itself, and not by him. He'd merely withheld the material things that could not have endured had he not guarded them.

Yet he had also withheld the truth, he reflected in anguish. To violate the right to truth was evil. Not everyone cared about knowledge as he did, yet for those few who did care, he must provide an avenue. . . .

But there's still no avenue, thought Noren, waking. *We're still barred from knowledge!* And then he realized that that wasn't true. The avenue existed; wasn't he experiencing the dreams?

There came a moment—he was not sure whether he was awake at the time—when Stefred's eyes looked into his and Stefred's voice repeated softly, over and over, "You must not be afraid, Noren. What you face now will be frightening, but you must not give in to fear. . . ." And the voice stayed with him until he was so much the First Scholar that he no longer had any knowledge of whose voice it had been.

He was standing at the entrance of a tower, the tall central one called the Hall of Scholars, which like the others opened into the courtyard of the Inner City. With the part of his mind that was still Noren, he realized that there had not been so many towers when last he dreamed; and looking into the First Scholar's memories, he found that years had passed. He was older and more weary. He was also more unhappy, though indeed he could not recall anything that had ever brought the First Scholar happiness.

Except perhaps one thing. He had been happy that the colony had been saved. And now, he knew, it was once again endangered, although the danger was one he'd anticipated and had arranged to deal with.

As always, he was surrounded by people, people whose faces weren't clear in the dreams and whose voices sounded alike. "We will not deceive you, sir," they said. "The situation is bad. You have been burned in effigy in the village squares, and this morning there's a mob assembling before the gates! The villagers will not accept our supremacy much longer; soon they'll be killing the Technicians who represent us."

Noren found he could reach no information about these Technicians' origin; there was a gap he couldn't fill. "But they can't live without the Technicians!" he heard someone object. "They know that!"

"Yes, but people don't always act reasonably, not when they're filled with hate," he replied. He had made the villagers hate him in order to unite them, to arouse their hopes and their will to strive; but the need for that was past. If they started killing Technicians, all that had been done would have been for nothing. The Technicians would have to fight back; some people would defend them, and the villagers would fight among themselves; whoever won, the colony would be fatally weakened, for it was still very small. The City was impregnable to attack. Within it, equipment and knowledge could be preserved; but what good were those things if the people themselves failed to survive?

The City's people couldn't survive without the farmers, and the farmers couldn't survive without the Technicians' aid. When hate prevented them from accepting aid, the hate must be discharged; he had realized that since the very beginning, and had made plans, plans kept secret even from his closest friends. "If I were no longer dictator," he said slowly, "their hatred would subside."

"They would merely transfer it to your successor."

"Suppose I had no successor, suppose Scholars stopped pretending to be tyrants and became—well, High Priests? Suppose we were viewed as figures of mystery and awe instead of as ordinary men who've seized power? By now enough's been forgotten for us to achieve that, for the emigrant generation is growing old; the native-born villagers hate me without knowing why. To them, stories of the Six Worlds seem mere legends." With sorrow, he thought of the grief this was causing the older people, who had tried hard to pass on their heritage to a generation that neither understood nor cared. Most of the native-born were truly content with village life, and for that their elders hated him most of all.

"High Priests?" echoed his companions. "Priests of what? Surely you would not establish a false religion!"

(*190*

At their tone, he wondered if perhaps they thought him senile; he was, after all, a very old man who had outlived his time for leadership. Yet they had always supported him. He had not ruled as an autocrat; the other Founders had had equal voice in the decisions; still they had honored him and followed his advice.

"No," he assured them gravely. "Not a false religion, but a real one." He looked back on the years he had pondered it. This part of the design, too, had been in his mind for a long, long time, though he had told no one.

Most of the new world's people had no formal religion, for by and large neither the research station workers nor the scientists of the fleet had been strong adherents of the Six Worlds' traditional faiths. Now, however, their children and grandchildren were developing the kind of culture where a central religion would be needed and would be bound to flourish. It would be needed to sustain people's hope. It would be needed to make them follow rules of survival they could not fully comprehend, rules previously enforced by the elders: not using stream water or letting untreated clay come into contact with food or drink; delivering the grainseed to be irradiated; having respect for machines; all the things for which their daily lives offered no rational explanation. There were other reasons Noren couldn't grasp. But above all, it would be needed to keep the Scholars from becoming dictators in fact rather than as a mere pretense; he, the First Scholar, was sure of that.

"If we don't give people symbols for the truths we cannot express openly," he explained, "in time they'll fall prey to superstition. Their descendants may worship idols or practice barbaric rites of some sort. They won't look toward a changing future, since the inadequate resources of this planet permit them to make no progress; so they won't be prepared for the renaissance the completion of our research will bring. What's more, once the elder generation dies, we alone can ensure that the taboos essential to survival are observed, and if we're not to employ any force, we can do it only by gaining the villagers' respect."

"That's all very well to say," his fellow-Scholars protested, "but not so simple to accomplish! We can't win people's allegiance by proclaiming ourselves High Priests, and even if we could, we wouldn't want such a role. It would be worse than the deceit we began with. What you suggest is impossible."

"There'll be no more deceit," he promised, feeling a strange elation mixed with his sadness. "Trust me in this; haven't I achieved things that were thought impossible before?"

They spoke warmly to him, nodding. "You have, sir. Without you we'd have failed long ago; who else could have founded a system like this without terror, without bloodshed?"

"It must remain without bloodshed," he declared grimly, "which it will not do if the villagers are in a mood to kill Technicians." Noren knew inwardly that he had reached a decision, but he dared not probe deeply for it; it was one of the First Scholar's more frightening ideas. He let the words come to him without thought. "I will address the people," he stated.

"Very well, sir. We will prepare the radiophone."

"I will address them in person from the platform outside the gates."

"Have you lost your senses? Those people are violent, sir! We could not protect you even if we had weapons, and we have only a few tranquilizing guns."

"If you have any idea of abdicating, sir," one of the men added, "it won't work. The people will not be placated while you live."

He did not answer, since that was something he already knew and did not wish to discuss. Instead, he walked rapidly across the courtyard and into the exit dome's wide

(192

corridor, his companions following. "Please, sir—" they begged.

Turning to them, he said softly, "Did we do right, my friends? Was all this justified, as we believed, or were those who died aboard the starship wiser after all?"

"We did the only thing we could have done. The people are freer than they know, and someday there will be no more secrets. Someday there will be many cities, unlimited resources, education for everyone. This world will be like the mother world; someday we may even need spaceships again!"

They were the words he wanted to hear; he hoped they had not been said merely to humor an old man. Reaching the gates, he spoke solemnly to the others. "I have never asked you for unquestioning obedience," he said. "I do so now—" There was a break in his train of thought; Noren perceived that the First Scholar had given instructions that were inaccessible to him. "I must go out alone," he found himself concluding.

"Alone!" they cried, horror-stricken, but he ignored them. The next thing he knew the gates were open and he had stepped through; he was on a white-paved platform, and before him was the crowd. There was a roaring in his ears, and it was more than the outraged tumult of the people. It was the roar of his own fear.

The crowd was murderous. He raised his hand, hoping for silence in which to speak, but it had small effect. The villagers in that crowd did not want to hear anything from the hated, almost legendary "dictator"; upon recognizing his voice, they wanted only to kill him. For a few moments, stunned by his unprecedented appearance, they made no move; but their disbelief did not last long. They started up the steps, brandishing makeshift weapons—not only stones, but sharp stone knives—and though there was a newly-erected barrier at the top to keep people back, those weapons could be thrown over. Noren's terror was more intense than any he had ever experienced. *I'm dreaming,* he thought in cold panic, *and I'll wake up . . . before they can touch me I'll wake up. . . .*

But he saw that he would not wake up. He was frozen in the dream: the blinding sunlight, the shouts of the faceless mob, the almost tangible hatred that assailed him— those would last until he died. His only recourse was to reach deep into the mind of the First Scholar, drawing out courage, for the First Scholar was stronger than he.

And the First Scholar had known what would happen.

He had known, Noren realized, from the time he'd first formulated his plan; and he had done this deliberately. The knife that struck him down was no surprise. It was not even unwelcome, for though he wanted to live, he knew that only his death could reconcile these people to the Scholars' supremacy. By this means alone could he prepare them for the new kind of leadership that must follow.

He fell, yet was still conscious; and the people went on hurling things while his blood spread onto the white pavement and he writhed under the pain of the blows. The pain was worse than he had expected. He had not really anticipated pain; he'd thought he would die quickly, the target of many knives. After he fell, however, most of the weapons that came over the barrier missed their mark, and within moments his friends pulled him back through the gates. Noren could not hear what they said. He felt himself dropping into a pit of silence and darkness, aware only of how much wounds could hurt before killing.

Then, desperately, he was fighting his way to the surface. He'd forgotten something; he had acted too soon! He should not have gone out while there was one thing left undone.

Time had passed. He lay on a couch, and people bent over him. "The knives were poisoned," they said gently. "It's a poison native to this planet; we can do no more than ease the pain." Someone held out a syringe.

Noren's own memories engulfed him, more powerful than the superimposed emotions of the dream. A native contact poison . . . it was thus his mother had died . . . she had felt such pain as this while he, a helpless boy, looked on. He wanted only escape—whether to wakefulness or death did not matter—but a voice within him kept repeating, *You must not give in to fear.* . . . By tremendous effort he reached once more for the thoughts of the First Scholar.

"No," he protested. "No opiates; did we not agree to save what we have for injured villagers? Besides, there is a job I have not finished."

"Tell us," urged the others. "We will finish it for you, just as we'll carry out the instructions you've left for completing your plan. You must rest now."

"I'm dying!" he cried in anger. "Do you think I don't know I'm dying? What need have I of rest when I'm to get more than enough after tonight? Bring me the thought recording equipment; I have not yet recorded all I wish to."

"You would not have us record your death!" they exclaimed.

"I would have you record what I must think out before my death, since I haven't the strength to write it, or even to speak. It's there in my mind, but I've never been able to frame it as it should be—" He fell back against the pillows, exhausted, the pain overwhelming him. "I'm a scientist, not a poet," he whispered. "If I were a poet, I could find words."

"He's raving," said the voices. "We must give him sedation."

Noren struggled to rise. "No!" he cried again. "Do what I ask of you, but hurry—"

They obeyed, but he sensed their concern. "If he should die while he was recording, it would be dangerous; a dreamer could die, too."

Hearing that, Noren felt renewed terror, but he was detached from it, for the First Scholar was dominant in him now. The recording equipment was attached to his head, and his mind went momentarily blank; then all at once the detachment increased. Dimly, as Noren, he realized that he had never before dreamed anything that had been recorded while it happened; all the rest—even the episode just past, which must have been spliced into sequence—had come from the First Scholar's memories. This was different. This was real, immediate, and he knew that he *was* dying.

But he was no longer so afraid.

"It—is—evil, what we've done," he gasped. "To—to keep knowledge . . . from the people . . . is not right—"

"We know it's not right," his companions assured him. "We've always known; but if we had not done it, mankind would have perished."

"Yes, it was . . . necessary. But it will not be necessary forever. They hate us now—"

"They wouldn't hate you if they were aware of what you've given," a woman broke in sorrowfully. "They would honor you, as we do." She began to cry.

A burst of strength came into him; he must make them see, or they would not know how to use this last recording. "You don't understand," he said, mustering his waning resources. "They *should* hate us! They should keep on hating us, or at least the system we've imposed—but they won't. They will forget their birthright. When they forget the Six Worlds, as they must if they're to survive, they will forget that what we hold here in the City belongs to them. Then their hatred will fade."

"But you've sacrificed your life to achieve that!"

"Yes. Hate was destroying them." He paused; he was in no shape to explain the paradox coherently, yet he *must* make them see. "They must accept this system, still they shouldn't come to like it too much; and they may, since it will never be oppressive. That's the biggest danger in it! Benevolent controls are the most dangerous kind because the people forget what is theirs. We must not allow that to happen. Their hatred will fade, but their desire for what we hold in trust must never fade. We must tell them—"

"We can't," the others reminded. "Record more memories if you wish; tell all that you long to tell before you die; but you must know, sir, that nothing can be given to the people until our research succeeds."

"Not from my memories, no; we must keep the secret as long as our stewardship is required. But we must give the villagers a promise. They must be told that our control of the City is temporary."

"How could we tell them that without saying why? And even if we could, they would not believe us."

"They will believe," he declared. "If it's done right, they . . . will . . . believe. . . ."

He could not do it right. He was too weak; there was too much pain; and besides, he was not a poet. "If I had a gift for poetry, I could do it as I've wanted to—"

"He speaks of poetry again," the voices said. "His mind is going. We had better remove the recording contacts before he dies."

"Please, please," Noren begged, "give me the time I have left to think out what I cannot say! Someday, someone will make a book of it; the people are not quite ready yet in any case. But when all who came from the Six Worlds are gone, their descendants will need a promise—"

They conceded to his wish; he was an old man whom they loved, and he was dying. Noren had not guessed how it would feel to die. It seemed as if one ought to be afraid, but the First Scholar was not afraid. He was only weak and tired, and of course, he was in pain. If he had let them stop the pain his mind would not be clear to think, and he must think; he must not give in until this task was done.

The people must have a promise! They must not be content with a Dark Age; they must hope for something more: machines, cities, free access to knowledge—they must want them, and they must not be allowed to forget that they wanted them. Furthermore, they must not forget the spirit that had once driven men out from their mother world— and eventually, from their mother star itself—toward something that must one day be sought again. That spirit must stay with them if the human race was to have another chance. They must believe in it without knowing that mankind needed another chance; they must do so until such time as their foothold was strong and their own culture well established.

He must give them the promise and the belief.

The mother star . . . the sun that had given men life . . . it would be visible someday, but by then, no one save the Scholars would understand what it meant. Yet they must understand! They must realize that it meant something very important! And perhaps—yes, almost surely—that would be time enough. If it was not, mankind was doomed, for the equipment could scarcely last longer; so wouldn't it be justifiable to gamble? *Symbols for the truths we cannot express openly,* he'd said to his friends, but though he had left them a plan formed in the dark nights of many years, the symbols themselves had eluded him. Now, in his last hour, the central one became clear. . . .

The First Scholar had the idea and the purpose, and groped for words; but Noren already knew them. *"There shall come a time of great exultation, when the doors of the universe shall be thrown open and every man shall rejoice. And at that time, when the Mother Star appears in the sky, the ancient knowledge shall be free to all people, and shall be spread forth over the whole earth. And Cities shall rise beyond the Tomorrow Mountains, and shall have Power, and Machines; and the Scholars will no longer be their guardians. For the Mother Star is our source and our destiny, the wellspring of our heritage; and the spirit of this Star shall abide forever in our hearts, and in those of our children, and our children's children, even unto countless generations. It is our guide and protector, without which we could not survive; it is our life's bulwark. And so long as we believe in it, no force can destroy us, though the heavens themselves be consumed! Through the time of waiting we will follow the Law; but its mysteries will be made plain when the Star appears, and the sons of men will find their own wisdom and choose their own Law."*

For the first time he found comfort in those words. To the First Scholar, the thought behind them was a solace he had ached for during all the years of sorrow past. The tragedy had been surmounted. His work was finished; he could let go and sink into death, for the fierce, lethal explosion of the Mother Star had been made a symbol not of futility, but of hope.

The people crowded round, but he could not see them; he was too close to death. He was too weary, too crushed by the burden of leadership; too sick at the thought that mankind could survive only so long as he withheld from them that which was rightfully theirs. He'd done enough; why wouldn't they let him die in peace?

They would not. They called him by name, urgently: "Noren! Noren!" Over and over they called until he opened his eyes and found that it was Stefred who was bending over him—Stefred and other men and women, all of whom seemed genuinely concerned for his life.

"I was . . . dying," Noren whispered. "I was *really* dying!"

"Yes," Stefred admitted. "The last dream is dangerous, and the more closely a person has shared the feelings of the First Scholar, the more dangerous it is. You would have died when he did if we hadn't been here to rouse you."

Why had they bothered? Noren wondered. They were going to kill him anyway. And yet of course they couldn't let him die while they were still hoping he'd recant.

"You would have died in spite of us," Stefred went on, "if you had not been brave enough to live. I knew that beforehand; I had to make the decision to let the last dream begin. I knew during our first interview that someday the decision would be mine. Do you envy me my job, Noren?"

That was when Noren looked into Stefred's face and knew, with chagrin, astonishment, and a kind of awe, that they were not going to kill him. There had never been any intention of killing him. Whether he recanted or not had nothing whatsoever to do with it.

The other Scholars had silently left the room. "Stefred," Noren said haltingly, "The rumors . . . were false. I—I don't believe you've ever killed anyone. I don't believe you could."

"I'm glad to hear it," Stefred declared. "I knew, of course, what you've been assuming, but I hoped I could win your trust without bringing it up."

"You weren't trying to scare me into recanting?"

"At the beginning, yes. If you'd been susceptible, the truth would not have been shared with you."

"I—I guess I see," Noren said slowly. "You don't like the system any better than I do, but it's—necessary. You have to make people respect it. If somebody cares enough to give up his life, though, he earns the right to know *why*."

"It's something like that. As you know, the Founders didn't want to keep knowledge from people; they made provision for it to be given to anyone who values it highly enough."

"More knowledge than was in the dreams?"

"Yes."

"You've never lied to me," Noren mused. "When you said that if I recanted voluntarily I'd be given access to more than I could absorb in a lifetime, you meant it, didn't you?"

The Scholar was silent. It didn't add up, Noren realized. He'd been right to refuse the bribe; he was sure he had been, and even at the time it had been evident that Stefred was pleased by his refusal. "They just wouldn't have arranged it like that," he reflected aloud.

"How would they, then?"

"There are different sorts of knowledge," Noren said thoughtfully. "If I'd accepted the offer, I might have been told things Technicians know, but not the secret—not what's in the dreams. And now, well, now I can go on learning whatever else happens. Recantation isn't a condition."

"That's right. Still, you have problems ahead of you; there'll be difficult ones even if you do recant."

Noren shivered, knowing Stefred's warning that the consequences of truth would seem terrible must also have been sincere; but he was too overwhelmed to worry about it. He lay back, still weak and shaken by the death he had so nearly shared. "Why," he asked softly, "weren't people ever told that the First Scholar wrote the Prophecy? They look up to Scholars now; they would honor him even without understanding what he really did."

"They'd go beyond that," replied Stefred, "and it was his wish that the facts about him never be revealed. To be worshiped was the last thing he wanted; it's not what any of us want, though it happens. We try to remain as anonymous as we can."

That was true, thought Noren in surprise. They had never demanded obeisance; they had never claimed to be innately superior; they had never declared that to speak against them was blasphemy. All those ideas—the ones that weren't mentioned in the Prophecy—had been originated not by the Scholars, but by the villagers themselves. The First Scholar deserved every honor short of worship, but people wouldn't have stopped there. He had been a martyr; when their hatred faded, they'd have built statues of him and pronounced it heresy not to bow down.

Unjust though it seemed, it was better that he was remembered only in legend: the distorted legend about the evil magician who'd tried to rule by force and who had been vanquished by the proclamation of the High Law. He would be glad that forced rule was still thought evil.

"There's something I must explain," Stefred went on. "The First Scholar did not write the Prophecy, at least not the words. The idea was his, but the Book of the Prophecy itself was written later by a man who experienced that last dream many times."

"But the words were in the dream," protested Noren.

"No," Stefred said. "They are not in the recording, Noren; you supplied them yourself."

"If I did, if I put the idea and the words together, then—" Noren drew breath, suddenly taking in the implications of what he was about to say. "Then inside I must have known that they—fit."

"That the symbols are an accurate expression of the idea, yes. All words are symbols. These, being familiar to you, came naturally into your mind. They are figurative words, poetic words, and as such have more power than the scientific ones the First Scholar knew weren't suited to his purpose."

"I could say them and not be lying," Noren declared wonderingly. "The Prophecy is true!"

"You could; you passed that hurdle without even making an effort. The real question is whether you *should.*" Stefred looked down at Noren, his eyes filled with compassion and warmth, adding, "Remember that long ago you conceded that you would accept the Prophecy if I could prove it, and you were well aware that recanting means far more."

XI

ALONE IN HIS OLD QUARTERS, THE TINY GREEN-WALLED
room, Noren thought it through. He knew that he would
receive no help from Stefred, much less any pressure; his
decision was to be entirely free. It would be freer than it
could ever have been while he hated the Scholars. Of all
the strange things that had happened to him in the City, to
have been granted this freedom was the strangest.

He had no idea what depended on whether or not he recanted, although reason told him that something must,
some aspect of his personal future. "You're not permitted
to know yet, Noren," Stefred had said. "As I told you,
there'll be difficulties either way, but I can't explain them
in advance."

"Why not?"

"You tell me why not," Stefred had replied, smiling.

"I'd say it'd be—well, the wrong basis for a decision."

"Anyone who's come this far has a better basis," Stefred
had agreed. "You don't need any advice from me; your

own mind is more than adequate to determine your course."

"If you believe that, Stefred," Noren had challenged, "then why do you make heresy a crime?"

"We don't. Heresy isn't forbidden by the High Law; the villagers ban it themselves." He'd hesitated. "The reason they do is complicated, and I can discuss only a little of it now. Later you'll learn more."

Stefred had gone on then to tell what had happened after the First Scholar died. The Book of the Prophecy, and with it the High Law, had been given to the villagers the next year. That had been possible because in accordance with the First Scholar's instructions, all those who'd originally come from the Six Worlds had been admitted to the City as Technicians; it had been announced that only the "dictator's" insanity had kept them out in the first place—which was the last lie ever told by the Scholars. In the role of High Priests they had practiced no form of deceit.

The first-generation villagers had been warned that once inside the City they could never leave, but all the same they'd been happy, for they had missed the kind of life they'd been born to. The native-born, on the other hand, hadn't wanted to live in the City. They'd always been skeptical of their parents' claim to have been reared in such a place, and they'd known that with the elders gone, they would be the undisputed village leaders. So they'd been quite content with the distant promises of the Prophecy, which they had believed without question. There'd been nobody left who could refute anything it said—nobody who could distinguish symbols from science—and after all, it had been the first book they'd ever seen; they had learned to read and write by means of slates. Most had thought reading and writing a silly waste of time. Still, the Book of the Prophecy proved that the elders' insistence on school had not been entirely foolish, for if the Scholars themselves said the future would be unlike the past, was it not well to look ahead to that future? The Scholars that appeared as High Priests did not act like the "dictator" who'd been thought mad, and besides, the people knew that they were dependent on those Scholars' good will; they weren't anxious to jeopardize village welfare by letting anybody disobey the High Law, which set forth the same rules they'd been taught as children in any case. As time went on, however, they made rules of their own and became more and more intolerant.

"I don't quite see why," Noren had confessed.

"You'll have to study a good deal before you do. Essentially it was because village society reverted to a more primitive level not only as far as technology was concerned, but also in other ways. Attitudes that had been outgrown by the time the people of the Six Worlds built their starships came back, just as tallow lamps did."

"Couldn't you Scholars have prevented that?"

"No, no more than we could have prevented technological skills from being lost. Societies, like people, cannot be controlled without destroying their ability to grow and develop. All we can do is maintain an island of light amid the dark." With a sigh, Stefred had added, "Those of us on the island are not just basking in that light, you know. We're working against time to bring about the Prophecy's fulfillment."

Thinking about it, Noren knew that it was that—the research work—about which he really had to decide.

The Prophecy was true. He would gladly admit that publicly, though his reasons for doing so would be misconstrued by everyone but the Scholars themselves. He would affirm the Prophecy with pride; he knew that the First Scholar had created it in those painful last hours because only such a promise could ensure that the Dark Age would be temporary.

The High Law was also valid, and it too was necessary; it contained no provisions that were not essential either to the survival of mankind or to prevention of harm that might be caused by people's wrong interpretations. Stefred had given him a copy to review and, reading it in the light of his new knowledge, he'd seen that. The decree that convicted heretics must be turned over to the Scholars, he realized, had been placed there not to ensure their punishment, but to provide them with an avenue to the truth! The rules about Machines were all concerned with keeping people from damaging those Machines, or from going to the opposite extreme and worshiping them. There was nothing in the High Law that he was not willing to obey.

But recantation meant more than affirming the Prophecy and the High Law. It also involved affirmation of the system under which Scholars had privileges unavailable to others. It meant agreeing that they must remain supreme until the Prophecy's promises had been fulfilled: giving up all thought of changing the world immediately, letting people think he approved of things as they were . . . was that right?

It was not right! Yet the First Scholar had known better than anyone else that it was not; he'd established the system not because it was right, but because it was the lesser of two evils, and he had died at the hands of men whom he'd allowed to misunderstand him.

For the Prophecy was true only as long as the system was upheld. *The ancient knowledge shall be free to all people*—that couldn't happen unless the Six Worlds' knowledge was preserved. The Scholars were working to extend that knowledge so that men could survive on this world as they had on the old ones. They were striving desperately to create the kinds of metal needed to make the Machines essential to the support of life. They must finish the work; the world couldn't begin to change until they did. To try to make it perfect overnight wouldn't make it perfect, it would only cause all that had been salvaged from the burn-

(206

ing of the Six Worlds to be lost. Mankind would perish just as surely as if the First Scholar's plan had failed. Even revelation of the secret would be fatal, not for the same reasons as in his time, but because people were now as dependent on their belief in the Prophecy as they'd once been on the Six Worlds' culture. Through its fulfillment alone could the world be successfully transformed.

Between the dreams and what Stefred had told him, Noren knew something about why the research work was taking so long. It was harder than anything that had been achieved on the Six Worlds. There, they'd had plenty of metal; they had found it in the ground. Even people like the villagers had found it and had used it to make tools and Machines of their own: slowly, generation by generation, they had improved them, before either Technicians or Scholars had ever existed, and by doing so they had learned more and more, until finally they *were* Technicians and Scholars. His theory about savages becoming smarter and discovering knowledge for themselves had been quite true on the mother world. That was the way human beings were meant to progress, and that was how all the knowledge in the computers had been accumulated.

But normal progress couldn't occur where there could be no technological innovation. On the mother world, tribes of people who never learned to get metal from the ground never improved their ways of doing things; once they'd gone as far as they could with stone, they stopped changing. And because this world's ground had no metal at all that was suitable for making tools, the villagers' situation was very similar. They could not develop better ways to use their limited resources, since their ancestors had already known the most efficient methods there were for everything from the fashioning of household implements to the building of bridges. Only within the City did the conditions for new discoveries exist. And the discovery that must be made was extremely difficult even for the

Scholars: they must learn how to create metallic elements through nuclear fusion. Noren hadn't really grasped what nuclear fusion was, but he could see that although it involved combining several substances to get a different one, it was not just a matter of stirring those substances together. The Six Worlds' scientists had known how to achieve nuclear fusion to get Power. Nuclear fusion to get metal had been beyond anyone's hopes. Here, however, it was the only hope there was.

No one knew when that hope would be realized. Conceivably it could be soon, and in that case new Cities would be built immediately; the Prophecy did not say that there would be no changes *before* the Star appeared! In the meantime, the Scholars must retain their stewardship if hope was to continue.

You would have died in spite of us, Stefred had told him, *if you had not been brave enough to live.* The words had been puzzling, but all at once Noren understood them. A person who'd seen the world through the First Scholar's eyes had to be brave, for no one who wasn't could face the hard truth about the world. But there was more to it. Only a brave person could face the awareness that his own honest attempt to fight injustice, if successful, would have accomplished the opposite of what he'd been aiming for.

Noren faced it. He admitted to himself that overthrowing the Scholars would not have helped the villagers, but would instead have prevented Machines and knowledge from ever becoming available to them. To capitulate and recant would not be a defeat, he realized with surprise. His goals had not changed; his beliefs had not changed. What he'd wanted all along was for the world to be as the Prophecy said it would become. He would merely be conceding that it could not be that way before the time was ripe.

That evening he told the man who brought him food that he wanted to see Stefred. The Chief Inquisitor had been quite correct, he reflected ruefully, in predicting that in the end his innate honesty would leave him no choice.

It was dusk; the City towers were shafts of silver thrust skyward between the orange moons. Noren sat by the window in Stefred's study and watched the stars come out. "Will people ever travel between the stars again?" he asked wistfully. "Will there be more worlds to settle someday?"

"Someday," Stefred said, "if we don't fail on this one. It's the only permanent answer to our lack of resources here. The starships' design is stored in our computers, and in fact there are still stripped hulls in orbit; but there is much else we must accomplish first. It can't happen in our lifetime."

"Neither can the things I wanted people to fight for."

"No. There are some things fighting can't achieve."

"Is it always wrong to fight, then?"

"Not always. That can be necessary, too. If you study the history of the Six Worlds, you'll find that there are no clear-cut answers."

"There's a time to fight, I guess . . . and a time to surrender. I—I've come to surrender, sir." Noren sighed, glad that he had finally gotten the words out.

For quite a while Stefred was silent. Then, in a troubled voice, he asked, "Have you ever witnessed a public recantation, Noren?"

"Yes." Noren's heart chilled at the recollection.

"For some people it's worse than for others," the Scholar said, "and I can spare you nothing."

"I—I don't suppose you can."

"I must be sure you understand," Stefred persisted. "If you recant, I shall preside at the ceremony. You may think that because we know each other, trust each other, it will be less difficult for you; but it won't. It will be more so. You have never knelt to me, and I've never asked it; in fact I'd have thought less of you if you had. Can you do it before a crowd of villagers who'll think I've broken your spirit?"

"It's a form, a symbol, as the words of the Prophecy are symbols," Noren said. "It doesn't mean I'm your inferior. It means only that what you represent is worth honoring."

"Yes, you know that now. But the people in the crowd will not."

Noren swallowed. "It's necessary."

"Why, Noren?" demanded Stefred suddenly. "You know I won't force this on you. You must also know that you won't be punished for not doing it. Why take on such an ordeal? You came here seeking the truth, and you found it; what more do you hope to achieve?"

"I wanted truth not just for myself, but for everyone. I can't accept it without giving."

"Giving what? You won't be allowed to reveal anything of what you've learned; you'll stick to a prepared script."

"There won't be any lies in the script, will there?"

"No. The words you say will be literally true. But they'll be phrased in the language of the Prophecy, and the people have already heard those words."

"They've also heard me deny them. They've heard me ask *them* to deny them, and every heretic who does so strikes at the thing the First Scholar died for. I was wrong, Stefred! Would you have me conceal my error to save my pride?"

"No," answered Stefred, "I wouldn't have you do that. But though you were wrong, you were not without justification; and when a heretic recants no justification can be claimed."

"That doesn't matter. Truth is truth, and it's more important than what people think of me. Don't you see? I stuck to my heresy because I cared about truth; now I've got to recant for the same reason."

"I see very clearly," Stefred admitted, "but I had to satisfy myself that you do. This is no mere formality. It will be harder than you realize, Noren, and there will be lasting consequences."

"You warned me about consequences before," said Noren, smiling. "You thought I'd beg to be let off. You underestimated me after all."

"Don't be too sure. Your problems aren't over yet." The Scholar pulled a sheaf of papers from his desk and looked through them, handing one to Noren. "This is the statement you'll make. Read it."

Noren did so with growing dismay. He had not remembered the specific wording of the ceremony; the tone of it was something of a shock. Phrases like "I am most grievously sorry for all my heresies," and "I confess my guilt freely; I am deeply repentant, and acknowledge myself deserving of whatever punishment may fall to me," stuck in his throat. He went through it again, slowly and thoughtfully, before raising his eyes.

"Is it more than you bargained for?" Stefred inquired.

"Yes," said Noren candidly. "I thought I wouldn't be expected to say anything I didn't mean. Well, I was mistaken about the Prophecy and the High Law, and I'm willing to admit it; but I'm not *sorry* for having been a heretic. At the time I couldn't have been anything else."

"You agreed that there can be no self-justification."

"There'll be no self-abasement, either! To say my opinions were wrong is one thing, but to declare that I was morally wrong in holding them would be something else entirely."

"We will not ask you to lie," Stefred said slowly. "If there are things in the statement that are untrue, strike them." He held out his stylus.

Noren took it and did a thorough editing job; then, without comment, he handed the paper back. The Scholar perused it carefully. "You've removed all references to penitence," he observed.

"I'm not penitent, sir."

"You will wear penitent's garb, and your hair will be cropped short."

"I'll submit to whatever indignities are required of me, but I will not proclaim guilt I don't feel, Stefred."

Stefred eyed him. "What happens to an impenitent heretic, both during the ceremony and afterwards, is not quite the same as what is done with someone who repents," he said evenly.

"I can't help that."

"Aren't you being inconsistent? You tell me you must recant because heresy strikes at the cause for which the First Scholar was martyred; surely you're aware that a display of repentance would be far more convincing than the mere admission of error—"

"I've been perfectly consistent right from the beginning," Noren declared obstinately. "I said at my trial that keeping things from the villagers was wrong, and it *is*. I'm recanting only because I've learned that there's something worse. There will always be heretics, and there should be; I won't tell people that heresy's a sin. To affirm the Prophecy and the High Law is as far as I'll go."

"So be it, Noren," said Stefred. He rose, Noren following, and for a few minutes they stood side by side looking out at the darkening sky. "I know you're wondering what's going to become of you when this is over," the Scholar continued, "but I can tell you only that though the difficulties will be greater than you imagine, I think you'll prove equal to them. I must say no more until after the ceremony three days from now." As an afterthought he added, "You will not understand the whole ceremony at first; remember that I'm on your side, and that I'll have reasons for what I do."

"Three days?" faltered Noren. "I—I'd rather get it over with tomorrow."

"No doubt you would, but a little time for reflection will be good for you. You've shifted your whole outlook at a very rapid pace; this is a major step, and you mustn't rush into it."

Noren shuddered. Stefred was right, he knew; yet he was inwardly afraid that if he didn't rush into it, he would never have the courage to carry it through.

The next days were the longest Noren had ever spent. He was left entirely alone; the Technicians who brought his meals did not speak to him. At least he was now trusted to see Technicians, he realized; it was no longer feared that he'd tell them any secrets. What, he wondered, would happen if he ever encountered the one who'd befriended him? It would be hard to remain silent, but he knew that he would do so, although the man would be bound to draw the wrong conclusions.

Noren dared not speculate about the future in store for him, the mysterious fate about which he'd as yet been given no information. It would not be easy to face; Stefred had often warned him of that, and so far everything Stefred had said had proved to be true. He could not be forgiven and released. It had been clearly stated that the secret could not go outside the City walls. The Scholars themselves never went out, and if they didn't, they certainly wouldn't let *him* do it. To be sure, he'd been told that he would be allowed to go on learning; that was some consolation. It was also consoling to know that Stefred thought him equal to whatever was going to happen.

What was going to happen during the ceremony was inescapably grim, and he had apparently made it grimmer by refusing to declare himself penitent. He could understand that; though the Scholars themselves tolerated heresy, they could not do so publicly, and it was Stefred's duty to persuade heretics to repent. An example must be made of those who would not. Yet Noren still wasn't sorry; only if he had yielded before learning the truth would he have felt guilty. The fact that the system was the lesser of two evils might excuse the Scholars for establishing it, but that couldn't excuse a person who didn't know the facts for accepting such a system!

On the third morning two Technicians came to him. "The Scholar Stefred sends you a message," one of them said formally. "First, you are offered a final opportunity to withdraw."

"No," said Noren steadily, inwardly angry. Did they want him to recant or didn't they?

"Very well," the Technician replied. "In that case, you are reminded that you must obey us implicitly, remembering that you have chosen to submit of your own accord."

Noren nodded, his indignation growing. There had been no need for such a reminder.

"Finally," concluded the Technician, "you are informed that there will be a departure from the script. After you read your statement, the Scholar will question you; he asks that you be told that he is relying on you to reply with absolute honesty."

Stefred ought to know by now, Noren thought, that he would scarcely do anything else! But why the change in plans? It had been emphasized that the ceremony would be formal and that no departures from the script would be permitted. Still, he'd sensed from Stefred's manner that he must expect further surprises; there was no guessing their nature.

The Technicians ordered him to change into the clothes they provided, the gray, unadorned penitent's garb that to the spectators would be a badge of shame. He did so grimly, then sat in stoic silence while they cropped his hair. But when they proceeded to bind his wrists behind him, using not ropes but strong inflexible bands, Noren protested vehemently.

"It's unnecessary," he raged. "You know I'm not planning to run away from you."

"We know, but all the same it must be done. It's a matter of form."

It was a matter of appearances, Noren realized miserably. The impression would be given that he was a criminal who had been browbeaten into submission; his voluntary choice of this course, his pride in honesty that overrode the sort of pride that could admit no error, would not be permitted to show. Abruptly he grasped the full import of Stefred's remark that he could be spared nothing. To the crowd, there would be no difference between his recantation and that of the man whom he himself had held in such contempt! And perhaps there was no difference. Perhaps that man, too, had experienced the dreams before capitulating; Stefred had never said that his case was unusual.

They walked through passageways Noren had not seen before, descended in the cubicle that he'd learned was called an elevator, and crossed a small vestibule, finally emerging into the courtyard that surrounded the closely-placed towers. Looking back, he recognized the entrance of the Hall of Scholars from the last dream; he had been inside it all the time, he thought in wonder. He had been in the same tower in which the First Scholar had lived and died. In there were the computers, the awesome repository of the Six Worlds' knowledge, which he longed fervently to glimpse; would he ever be allowed to enter it again?

When they reached the dome through which one must pass to leave the City, Noren's guards did not accompany him into the broad, high-ceilinged corridor that stretched ahead; different Technicians took over, enclosing him within the formal rank of an escort of six. The eyes of the passers-by were all upon him. Noren straightened his shoulders and raised his head, trying not to notice. This was nothing, he knew, to what he must face outside the Gates, where he would be viewed with derision and scorn.

215)

The Gates appeared before him all too quickly, and to his surprise he recognized their inner surface; the First Scholar had gone through those doors to his death. The memory was so vivid that he found himself shivering. A Technician pushed a button set into the corridor's wall and the huge panels began to slide back. At the same time another spoke, raising his voice to be heard above the rumble. "One more reminder: in public, the Scholar Stefred is to be addressed as 'Reverend Sir.'"

Noren pressed his lips tightly together, holding back the ire that rose in him. His own words echoed in his mind: *It is a form, a symbol, as the words of the Prophecy are symbols. . . .*

He stepped forward into brilliant sunlight reflected from white pavement. Immediately a shout arose from the crowd, a hostile, contemptuous shout. And Noren froze, stricken by a terror he had never anticipated. It was like the dream! He was to stand in the very spot where the First Scholar had been struck down; he was being led directly and purposely to it. The sun, the noise, the enmity of the people: they were all the same—but this time there was no possibility of waking up.

The Technicians, after proceeding all the way to the platform's edge, moved back slightly, exposing Noren to full view. There was no barrier any more. Before him was the wide expanse of steps, the steps up which the First Scholar's assailants had come, where he himself had been immobilized at the time of his recapture. Men and women were swarming to the top. *Blasphemer,* they had called him then, and their mood had been one of shock; now they used more vulgar epithets. Their mood was not shocked, but ugly, as on the night in the village. The crowd was far larger, however, and the hecklers were bolder, knowing him to be helpless because of his manacled wrists and the vigilance of the Technicians. Noren struggled to master his panic, realizing that, ironically, the

Technicians were there not to guard but to protect him. Whatever else happened, they would not allow him to be murdered.

As he looked around, he saw to his dismay that there were no Scholars anywhere. The people would not act like this in the presence of Scholars; why had Stefred sent him out alone before he himself was ready to appear? And why, when he was doing what they had wanted him to do all along, should he be deliberately terrorized by being forced to re-enact the dream? The likenesses were too precise to be accidental.

When the first clod of mud struck him, Noren was so stunned that he nearly lost command of himself; but he quickly regained his poise and stood erect, taking it impassively. That was the only way to take it, he saw. He must not flinch from anything to which he was subjected. The sun dazzled him and the heat of it shimmered from the glaring pavement, so that the steps, the crowd, and the markets beyond the plaza all blurred into a hazy mist. He focused his eyes on nothing and tried not to think. He'd been aware that he would be despised, reviled; but having watched only the latter part of the other recantation, he had not foreseen that he would be the target of such abuse as this. The significance of the prisoner's filthy garments had escaped him despite the traders' then-cryptic remarks. Yet looking back, he could see that exposure to the crowd prior to the Scholars' entrance must be a traditional part of the ordeal.

Why? The Scholars, he knew, did not believe that he or anyone else deserved punishment of this kind, and they could easily prevent it. Why didn't they, if they disapproved of the villagers' attitude as Stefred had claimed? Noren cringed inwardly as more and more mud was flung at him, but he let his bearing show no sign. He was meant to understand, he felt, and concentration on the effort to do so was the only defense open to him.

The Scholars could not prevent people from hating, he realized. They could only provide occasion for the hatred to be vented in relatively harmless ways. In the beginning, the First Scholar had taken it upon himself, and when it had become dangerous, he'd discharged it by allowing the villagers to throw not mud, but stones and knives.

Most villagers no longer hated Scholars. Now they hated heretics; they hated anyone who was not like themselves, either for daring to be different or simply for being so. What would happen if they were given no outlet for their hate, if those turned over to the Scholars suffered no public humiliation? Fewer heretics would reach the City! More of them would die as Kern had died! So it had to be this way, but the role of scapegoat was not forced on anyone. Stefred had not forced him; on the contrary, in the end he'd tried to dissuade him. Like the First Scholar, he stood in this spot only because he had given free consent.

As that thought came to him, Noren glimpsed a little of Stefred's design. The similarity to the dream was not intimidation; instead, it was meant to bolster his self-esteem. The villagers hated him, misunderstood him—but they'd hated and misunderstood the First Scholar, too, and he was facing them for the First Scholar's own reasons. The people who'd once been on his side now despised him most of all, for they thought recantation a coward's act, a sellout; and though he knew better, it was hard not to feel that the surrender he'd fought so long would diminish him. The carefully arranged comparison was a reminder that it would not. Moreover, it was Stefred's subtle means of bestowing on him a status that the Scholars could not openly confer. To them, it must seem honorable to walk in those footsteps; the assumption that he too would find it so was a tacit endorsement of his inner equality.

With sudden insight Noren perceived that all he had ever believed, all he had ever done, had led inexorably to this moment. This, not the inquisition, was the true trial of his convictions. It was easy to uphold them when to do so meant merely to defy authority. To do so in secret, when not even his fellow-rebels would give him credit for it, was the only real proof that they meant more to him than anything else—and that he could trust himself to follow his own way.

He waited in silence, and the people went on pelting him with mud until his bare arms were splattered with it and the penitent's garb was no longer gray, but brown. He did not move; he did not bend his head; and somewhere inside he began to know that he was not really suffering any indignity. Dignity came from within; it could not be affected by a barrage of insults and filth.

And then, with cold shock, he glanced down at the steps and saw Talyra.

She had climbed more than halfway up them, heedless of the jeering mob, and she stood staring at him, her shawl pulled tight around her shoulders; in her face was more pain than he had ever seen in anyone's. His first thought was that he could endure no more of what to her would seem degradation, nor could he bear to have her think he'd betrayed the beliefs for which he had been willing to sacrifice their love. But at the sight of her grief he realized that he did not care about anything except the fact that she too was suffering. That she would witness the ceremony had not entered his mind; it hadn't occurred to him that she would ever know.

How could he have been so stupid? He'd known she was near the City, for she had told him she was going to the training center; and recantations were announced in advance. Talyra would have been heartbroken by his recapture, but relieved by the news that he was still alive. Yet her feelings must be mixed, for he'd convinced her that he would never recant of his own free will. Since she could not suspect the truth, there was only one thing she could possibly think: that he'd been tortured and had given in. There was no way he could tell her otherwise. She would think it for as long as she lived, and living with such a thought would be harder than resignation to his death.

Their eyes met. Talyra's face was wet with tears, and the anguish Noren felt surpassed anything he had previously undergone. She had come just to see him once more; she couldn't have stayed away; yet what was happening would hurt her far more than it was hurting him. He would break down, he thought in terror; he would lose all self-possession and run to her. . . .

Just then, however, there was a loud surge of the City's overpowering music, and Scholars emerged from the Gates, taking their places on the low dais at the opposite side of the platform. At the last came Stefred, who, unlike the others, wore not solid blue but the presiding Scholar's ceremonial vestments with white-trimmed sleeves. He crossed to the central position and raised his hand. The people, instantly hushed, fell to their knees. The Technicians closed again around Noren, escorting him away from the mud-stained steps to the clean stone base of the dais.

He knew what was required of him. Keeping his back very straight he approached Stefred and, in a gesture more of courtesy than of obeisance, he knelt.

The ritual words, the formal words of invocation, were said; Noren scarcely heard them. Then Stefred looked down and his eyes were cold, a stranger's eyes. "You come before us as a self-confessed heretic," he announced. "Are you ready to admit the error of your beliefs?"

"Yes, Reverend Sir." Noren spoke out clearly; if he was going to do it, he was not going to be backward about it.

The script was placed in front of him by a Technician. It was, he noted with indignation, the unedited version; all of the self-abasing statements he'd crossed out were still there. Stefred's face remained absolutely impassive. Noren began to read, his voice sounding hollow and distant in his own ears. It made no difference whether those statements had been struck or not; he remembered the phrasing well and omitted them as he spoke, though the words swam dizzily before him.

"I confess my heresies to be false, misconceived and wholly pernicious; I hereby renounce them all . . . I no longer hold any beliefs contrary to the Book of the Prophecy, which I acknowledge to be true in its entirety and worthy of deepest reverence . . . I have blasphemed against the Mother Star, which is our source and destiny; I abjure all fallacies that I have uttered and freely affirm my conviction that this Star will appear in the heavens at the time appointed . . . I retract all criticisms I may ever have made of the High Law; I admit the error of my opinions and declare myself submissive"—he altered the phrase *most humbly submissive*—"to all of its requirements, affirming it to be necessary to the Prophecy's fulfillment. . ."

It went on and on; Noren's voice broke several times, and he began to wonder if he would ever get through it. But all the words were true words; not once did he let an expression of penitence slip out. He felt suddenly triumphant. If they'd thought they could trap him, they'd been mistaken!

There was a long silence after he finished; then finally Stefred spoke. "You have made no proclamation of repentance," he said levelly. "Do you feel no remorse for these many heresies?"

"None, Reverend Sir," replied Noren with equal coolness.

A murmur arose from the crowd; such shameless lack of contrition would surely call down dire retribution indeed. It was a pity, most felt, that the Scholars never imposed their mysterious forms of chastisement in public.

"Do you not agree that you deserve to be severely punished for having held such beliefs?" Stefred demanded.

"No, Reverend Sir, I don't."

"But you know that you must take the consequences in any case, do you not? If you were to show sorrow for the things you have confessed and plead our mercy, it might make some difference in your fate."

"I will not do that," Noren declared, forgetting the honorific in his anger. One of the Technicians clamped a firm hand on his head, pushing it slightly forward. Fury consumed him; just in time he recovered his wits and repeated with no audible irony, "I will not do that, *Reverend Sir.*" For the first time it occurred to him that Stefred, who had known perfectly well that he wouldn't do it, was checking his self-control in preparation for some more formidable challenge.

"Why are you so obdurate," the Scholar persisted, "when we offer you the chance to redeem yourself in the sight of the people?"

"Because, Reverend Sir, I have done only what I had to do. I was mistaken, but I thought my beliefs were true."

"You were not asked to think, but only to accept what you were told. Was it not wrong of you to set your own judgment above that of your betters?"

"It was not, Reverend Sir. What but his own judgment is to tell a man who his betters are?"

That was too much for the spectators; there were shouts of disapproval and several loud suggestions of advice as to suitable punishment. Stefred raised his hand, silencing them. "At your trial," he went on, "your accusers testified that you had claimed that even Scholars were no better men than yourself; and you did not deny it. In your recantation you have made no mention of this. Why?"

Noren frowned, perplexed. He had not been asked to mention it, and he could not imagine why it would be brought up without warning. Surely Stefred knew that he could not retract that particular opinion! If to answer truthfully would do any harm, that was too bad; there was no help for it. "Scholars know more than I do, Reverend Sir," he said without faltering, "and some of them may indeed be better; but they are not so by virtue of their rank. All men have equal right to earn the respect of others."

The crowd, scandalized, waited with hushed horror to see what the Scholar would do. Stefred addressed them, his voice heavy with sarcasm. "Behold the man who thinks himself as wise as a Scholar!" he exclaimed. "No doubt he fancies that he would manage more successfully than we do; it would be amusing to see how he'd proceed."

There was no sound; the people were confused, for this reaction was not at all what they'd expected. Relentlessly Stefred pressed on. "Perhaps we should be kneeling to him instead of the other way around," he said; and, mockingly, he laughed. They laughed with him: at first tentatively, unsure as to whether it was proper, and then in an uproarous release of tension that turned their outrage to mirth.

Noren's face burned crimson. The ridicule was even harder to bear than the hate. Why was Stefred doing this? It could not be mere cruelty; there was no cruelty in Stefred, and this derisive tone was totally unlike him. Always before he had treated Noren with respect. *I'm on your side,* he'd said; *I'll have reasons for what I do.* And, in the message given by the Technician, *I am relying on you to reply with absolute honesty. . . .*

"Observe," Stefred continued, raising his hand once more, "that it *is* the other way around. This man's words are arrogant, yet despite his superior wisdom he kneels to me and acknowledges the truth of what he has been taught. I could humble his arrogance if I chose, but I do not so choose. He will receive discipline enough as it is."

All at once Noren understood what was taking place. Stefred was humiliating him, yes; impenitence could not be allowed to pass unnoticed. But in raising the question of the Scholars' alleged superhumanity, he was also doing other things, and he was doing them very cleverly. That idea was not part of either the Prophecy or the High Law; the Scholars themselves had never encouraged it, and to deny it was blasphemous only in the eyes of the villagers. To them such a denial merited not derision, but wrath. They would not have been surprised if Stefred had immediately pronounced an unprecedented death sentence. By forcing him to take the apparent risk, Stefred was demonstrating his own tolerance for the sort of "heresy" that should not be so labeled. Furthermore, he was vindicating him before the few who had ears to hear: those to whom such replies indicated not blasphemy, but human dignity and courage. Proof was being produced that the recantation had not been made from cowardice, and thus, perhaps, the seeds of faith would be planted in those who'd doubted its sincerity.

He met Stefred's eyes, and for the first time the Scholar responded; there was no overt smile, but Noren knew that whatever further ordeals might lie ahead, as far as Stefred was concerned he had done no wrong.

The ceremony resumed. This, the sentencing, was in the standard script, Noren realized; but it was a portion he had not seen. "We pronounce you an impenitent heretic," Stefred declared with austere formality, "and as such you are liable to the most extreme penalty we can decree; yet since we bear you no malice, we hereby commute your sentence to perpetual confinement within the City, subject to such disciplines as we shall impose. Look your last on the hills and fields of this world, for you will never again walk among them."

Noren gazed out past the plaza and the markets to the countryside beyond. He had known beforehand, of course, but he had not really taken it in. The purple knolls; the scent of ripening grain; nights when Little Moon shone like a red glass bead overhead while he and Talyra lay side by side looking up at it . . . farmhouse kitchens, lamp-lit, with bread baking on the hearth . . . the fresh touch of free air . . . his whole being ached at the thought that he was forever barred from those things. Perhaps he would never see sunlight again! A few rooms in the towers, like Stefred's study, had windows; but there was no reason to suppose that he would receive such accommodations, or that he would be permitted access to the courtyard that was open to the sky. The domes of the Outer City were roofed over. Perhaps he would never see the stars.

A sharp cry broke in on his desolation. "No, oh no!" a girl's voice screamed. He turned; it was Talyra, who knelt at the topmost level of the steps, and she was sobbing violently, her face hidden by her hands. He could not comfort her. He could never touch her, never even see her from this day forward; and though he had known that, too, it suddenly became the greatest deprivation of all.

The music blared out again, drowning her sobs; Technicians surrounded him, and she was hidden from his sight. Stefred left the platform, followed by the other Scholars. But Noren remained kneeling, his own head bowed for the first time, and he did not even notice the jeers of the dispersing crowd. The sun shone hot on his shoulders, and overhead the sky was vast and blue. He made no move until his guards helped him to his feet and led him back into the City, closing the heavy Gates irrevocably behind.

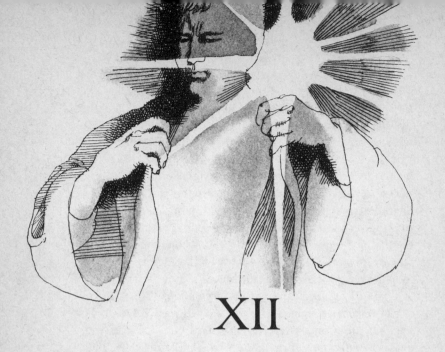

XII

ONCE INSIDE THE CITY GATES, THE TECHNICIANS WHO
formed Noren's escort silently removed the bands from
his wrists and, to his amazement, departed, leaving him
alone in the wide inner corridor. Then he saw that Stefred
was waiting for him. The Scholar came forward and gripped
Noren's hand. "That took a great deal of courage," he
said quietly.

Noren forced himself to smile. "I understood what you
were doing, sir," he said. "And going through the paces
of the dream—helped."

"I'm glad," Stefred declared, in a manner oddly more
like a friend and equal than a Scholar. "The spectators
despised you; I did not want you to despise yourself. Have
you any regrets?"

"No. I was wrong about the Prophecy, but I was right
to question it! I was right not to believe before I had proof!
If I could start all over, I'd do just the same; you'll never
get me to repent."

"I've never tried to, Noren."

"But the statement you wanted me to make—"

"Did I say I wanted you to make it?"

He hadn't, Noren realized suddenly. Stefred had not wanted him to make that statement any more than he'd wanted him to yield during the inquisition! He couldn't have, for never once had he implied that doubt was wrong; on the contrary, he'd endorsed it. He had achieved his end not by coercion, but by requiring Noren to live up to his own way of looking at things, and he had too much respect for honesty to want anyone to repent for the sake of appearances. The whole issue had been another calculated challenge. With surprise, Noren became aware that he'd been enjoying Stefred's challenges and that he was going to miss them.

"What happens to me now?" he asked resolutely, as they walked along the corridor and through the inner gates into the courtyard surrounding the towers.

"What do you think will happen?"

"I—I'm not sure. I can't leave the City, I know. And in the sentencing you mentioned discipline." Noren hesitated. He was guilty of no crime in their eyes, yet what could they do with him? The time had come when he could no longer put off facing the question. "Stefred," he burst out, "there's just no easy answer, is there?"

"No, there isn't." The Scholar's tone was very serious. "Much will be demanded of you."

Imprisonment, thought Noren in despair. There was no alternative. Weeks, years, in the small room in which he'd found a mere few days so trying, unless perhaps they made some arrangement whereby he could perform useful work. There must be other heretics somewhere; would he be allowed contact with them? Could discussion by non-Scholars of the secret truths be risked even within the City, when the Technicians weren't privy to those secrets? Solitary confinement was more likely, not as punishment but simply as a necessary precaution.

He would be well treated, he knew. He'd have every physical comfort, and would undoubtedly be permitted to read. All that recorded knowledge of the Six Worlds: he had been promised that more of it would be given to him, and the prospect was exciting. Yet to be shut up forever, alone . . .

He had been warned. All the ultimatums that he'd once considered threats had been true warnings. No Scholar had ever lied to him; when they'd told him he was incurring grave and irrevocable consequences, they had meant it. They would have to do what must be done to keep their secret.

Upon entering the Hall of Scholars they paused. Noren looked down at the mud-spattered penitent's garb in which he was clad, painfully aware of the glances of the people who passed to and fro in the vestibule. Stefred, watching his face, said compassionately, "Put this on. You'll be less conspicuous, and I want to talk to you for a while before we go upstairs." He handed Noren the robe he'd been holding: an ordinary blue Scholar's robe aparently carried to replace the ceremonial vestments that Stefred himself was wearing.

"*Your* robe? It's—not fitting, sir," Noren protested.

Stefred smiled. "I never expected to hear a statement like that from you!" he said. "Forget it, Noren. We're not stuffy about such things."

Noren put the robe on, reflecting bitterly on the irony of it. Talyra would think such an act the height of blasphemy, yet the Scholars themselves did not consider it so. How he'd misjudged them—still in guessing them to be men like himself, he'd not gone far enough. They had minds like his. He'd never met anyone who shared his views as closely as Stefred! If he'd been born a Scholar, he wouldn't have been such a misfit; why had fate made him a villager instead?

(228

"Noren," Stefred was saying, "you've taken some big steps, but there are bigger ones ahead. You haven't yet been told everything."

Noren looked up, startled. More secrets? His spirits rose despite the cold tingle that spread through him.

"The dreams were edited," the Scholar announced bluntly, "edited not merely to remove thoughts too complex for you, but because before your recantation we could not give you the whole truth."

"Edited?" cried Noren furiously. "You—you didn't trust me after all; you got me to recant on false grounds?"

"No!" Stefred exclaimed, grasping Noren's arm. "Don't you see that we must have trusted you a great deal to send you out before the public as we did? What you were shown was true, and you could have betrayed it."

"How did you know I wouldn't?" Noren asked slowly.

"You had proved that you value the same things we do. If you'd been penitent, we could never have taken the chance; the heretics who show repentance publicly are those who agree to recant before learning any secrets. And only rarely can we rely on someone's quick wits enough to depart from the script as I did with you."

"I don't understand—"

"Think it through," the Scholar said.

Noren thought. "If I'd been penitent, it would have meant I valued something higher than truth. And it might have meant I cared more about what people thought of me than what happened to them; in that case I might have given away the facts to justify myself."

"Yes. But there's more to it. What if you'd refused to go all the way through with the ceremony? We made it a bit rougher than it needed to be, you know."

"I didn't know," Noren began with renewed anger, and then he stopped, perplexed. Many of the seeming ordeals —the re-enactment of the dream, the questioning, and even the use of the unedited script—had not made it rougher, but had served to give him the status of a free agent instead of a helpless victim. Still, the whole thing would have been less trying if Stefred had explained it in advance. Why hadn't he? "I couldn't have refused, because I want the Prophecy to come true," he reflected. "But a person who didn't care—"

"Would have missed the significance of what was happening and balked at allowing himself to be humiliated unjustly."

"If you already trusted me," Noren protested, "what point was there in putting me to such a test? My recantation was all you needed, and to be sure of getting it, you should have made it as easy for me as possible."

"You're holding to false premises again. Do you really think I've devoted all this time and effort merely to getting your recantation? Would I have engineered your arrest in the first place just for that?"

"What else could you have wanted from me?" questioned Noren in confusion.

"You of all people shouldn't have to ask that, you who've maintained from the start that your mind is as good as a Scholar's! Don't you realize how desperately such minds are needed if we're to transform this world by the time the Star becomes visible?"

"The research work . . . me?" Noren felt a rush of astonished joy. He had never dared hope that they would let him assist them; hadn't the Founders believed that villagers couldn't be trained as scientists? But that, he recalled, had been because they'd known most villagers wouldn't care about knowledge. All at once the system's logic became clear to him. No wonder the Scholars saw to it that the few who did care were arrested! Yet there was one thing that didn't fit.

"Sir," he continued, still baffled, "if you thought me worthy to do that work, why did you keep warning me that my future would be so hard to face? And why did you edit the dreams?"

Stefred paused, considering his words carefully. "I can't answer that until you've figured out what we concealed. I'll give you a clue: we showed you the true origin of the Prophecy, yet the key to its fulfillment was withheld from you. You haven't sensed that flaw because you've always thought of us as a group and not as individual people. But you're intelligent enough to frame the right questions; ask them now. You have nothing to lose by frankness."

Noren frowned. The fulfillment of the Prophecy obviously hinged not only on the completion of the work and the appearance of the Mother Star, but on the willingness of the Scholars to give up their power when the Star did appear. The mere fact that it was real and that the original Scholars hadn't wanted power did not disprove his long-standing doubts as to the present ones' motives. Why hadn't the First Scholar had such suspicions? What way had he had of knowing that the generations to come wouldn't decide that they liked being supreme; why hadn't he worried about it? He must have! His fears along those lines must have been in the edited portion, for men were men, and the First Scholar had known only too well that those who'd held power in the past had often misused it. Only because his personal loathing for tyranny had been so strong—and because Stefred had seemed so honest— had the omission not been apparent.

"I was right all along," Noren whispered in horror. "You deceived me; you knew I wouldn't recant unless I was distracted from your own aims by those of the First Scholar."

"You don't believe that, Noren."

Their eyes met. No, thought Noren, he didn't; not of Stefred. But what of the rest? How could any of them be sure of each other, much less of those who would follow them? Merely experiencing the dreams wouldn't have much effect on someone who didn't share the First Scholar's ideas to begin with.

Stefred went on looking at him, and the right questions began to rise in Noren's mind.

"What's to prevent a Scholar from having selfish aims?" he demanded. "Why couldn't some of you do just what I used to think you were all doing?"

"There's a safeguard," Stefred replied gravely. "We must prove ourselves, you see; we must stand up for our values in a series of situations where it costs something."

How, Noren wondered, did they ever encounter such situations? It couldn't happen unless it was deliberately arranged. "Are people simply born Scholars," he asked, "or must your children pass qualifying tests?"

"Neither one. We are not permitted to rear our own children; they are given to village families who want to adopt babies, and no one ever knows their true parentage."

"Wards of the City? *All* your children?"

"Yes; otherwise they would grow up believing they had the right to succeed us, and they don't."

"But sir, if they don't, then how does anyone become a Scholar?"

In a sober voice Stefred said, "There is only one way, Noren. He must follow the same path you have followed, and become first a heretic."

Incredulous, Noren could only stand frozen, incapable of speech, as the Scholar added with feeling, "That's not my robe you are wearing now; it is yours."

Later, after his first meal in the refectory of the Hall of Scholars, after Noren had been greeted as an equal by blue-robed dignitaries as well as by many younger men and women who were less formally dressed but apparently of equivalent rank, after he had received with stunned embarrassment the congratulations of countless people and

(232

was alone with Stefred in the elder man's study, he stood at the window and painfully, haltingly, said what he felt must be said. He had been too overwhelmed, too bewildered, to say it initially; he had, in fact, uttered scarcely a word, and Stefred had not pressed him. But once the shock started to lessen he knew there was only one course.

"Look," he began, "I'm honored . . . I'm—well, overcome . . . but—but this isn't right, Stefred. I can't accept it." He held out the robe, which he had not worn since bathing and dressing, but had carried over his arm.

Stefred regarded him thoughtfully. "The status, once earned, cannot be revoked. No one will force you to do anything against your will, but you won't be able to take part in the research work unless you at least accept training."

"I guess not. But I still can't become a Scholar."

"I thought you'd say that," Stefred said. "In fact I rather hoped you would; it seems the courageous thing to do at this stage, doesn't it?"

There was silence. Noren thought miserably of what he was rejecting: the chance to study not merely a small portion of the Six Worlds' science, but all of it; unlimited access to the computers and the films and perhaps to more dreams; exciting work that would be of real value to the world; exciting people to work with, all of whom looked at things his way, the searching way, and all of whom cared. . . .

"At this stage," Stefred repeated. "Now we're going into it a little deeper. You haven't analyzed the issues as well as you think."

"I know you're my friend and you want to help me," Noren said determinedly, "but I can't let you."

"Have I ever led you anywhere except to truth?"

Noren sat down. It could do no harm to have one more talk with Stefred. He would be challenged to explore all the ramifications of his decision, but this time he was on firm ground, as he'd been in the matter of impenitence, and Stefred would respect his stand.

"You believe you're making a noble sacrifice for the sake of your principles," Stefred went on, "and I admire you for it. Once again, however, you happen to be dead wrong."

"But—"

"You will hear me out, Noren."

"Yes, sir. But you don't understand. I don't want to out-rank anybody! I certainly don't want anybody kneeling to me! I see why Scholars have to control what's here in the City, but I still don't really approve of the system."

"Of course you don't. If you approved of it, you wouldn't be fit for the job." With a sigh Stefred declared, "Noren, there's just one kind of person who can safely be entrusted with power, and that's someone who's proven his contempt for tyranny by staking his life in opposition to it. From the very beginning this system has been made to work by one unbroken rule: the secrets are passed to those, and only those, who have done so. The First Scholar planned it that way; that was the decision we edited out of the dreams."

"From the beginning? What about the Founders' own children?"

"They had no contact with their parents; they were reared by teachers, in one of the domes, and became the first Technicians. The Founders chose successors as we do, from among people with what it takes to recognize and defy the system's evils."

Slowly absorbing this, Noren mused, "Some of the orig-inal research station workers must have qualified by de-fying the man they thought a dictator. And all Scholars since—even the women, like the girl who operates the Dream Machine—have been brought here for heresy? They've been through the whole process and have remained impenitent?"

(234

"Yes. They weren't called heretics in the early days before the Prophecy; those of the First Scholar's time entered the City as hostages for the land treatment equipment's return, which was the means he used to determine their worthiness. He took only volunteers, you see, and naturally those who offered themselves did so with the hope of learning something that would help to defeat him. There have always been rebels, and every one of them has faced an inquisition believing himself destined for death."

"Even you?" It was a startling idea, yet not so hard to imagine, Noren found. Stefred's defense would have been worth listening to!

"I myself was a year or so younger than you are," Stefred told him, "and I was guilty not merely of heresy, but of having taken part in a most irreverent demonstration of my feelings toward Scholars. In my particular village some rather grisly rumors had gotten started; I was fully convinced that I was to be burned alive." With a grim smile he added, "My partners in the escapade weren't caught; they were present at my recantation and all of them, even my closest friends, assumed I could have just reason for making it."

"Oh, Stefred—"

The Scholar drew his chair closer to Noren's. "It's hard to give up one's visions of glorious martyrdom," he said quietly. "Even during recantation we're martyrs—we endure hatred and abuse, and picture ourselves dying not as we originally intended to, but as the First Scholar did. There's satisfaction in that, for we're still pitting ourselves against society. To become its respected agents is a far greater switch."

Noren bent his head. It was spinning; he felt unreal and without familiar footholds. "Do you suppose I wanted to accept the very role I had always despised?" Stefred continued. "I took it on only because I knew that if I didn't, I'd be betraying every conviction I'd upheld during my trial; and that's what you will be doing, Noren, if you refuse the trust that has fallen to you."

"Wait a minute. Isn't it the other way around?"

"What were you speaking for if not fulfillment of the Prophecy? You claimed we had no intention of fulfilling it, and we proved you wrong; still the promise cannot be kept unless the people who are qualified are willing to work toward that end. There's a lot to do, and though the time may seem long, it's barely enough for what must be accomplished. *'Cities shall rise beyond the Tomorrow Mountains,'* remember? Without suitable metal we can't build those cities! We can't even produce the machines to keep future generations alive! We've made progress, but we don't yet know how to synthesize it; new techniques—techniques different from anything the Six Worlds ever attempted—must be developed. The training for such work is very long and very difficult, and it's hardly surprising if you're not anxious to devote yourself to it—"

"You know I don't mind *that!*" Noren interrupted indignantly. "If being a Scholar meant only that, without—"

"Without the responsibility? Without the burden of representing a system you know is not as it should be?"

"I just don't think it's right for one group of people to be placed above another group," Noren maintained stubbornly.

"Neither do I, Noren. But you see, I don't consider myself better than the villagers; they merely think I do, just as they once thought me a coward who'd recanted to save my life. Which is more important: ensuring the survival of those people, or making sure they see me as I really am?"

There was no argument to that; the First Scholar himself, after all, had faced the same choice, and the living of it had been harder than the dying. Yet the First Scholar had been hated as an apparent villain. Even he had not been required to let people venerate him, kneel to him, under the impression that he agreed that was good! In desperation Noren switched tactics. "But everybody should have a chance to be a Scholar," he protested.

"Everybody does have a chance. The way is open to anyone whose motives are sincere, but there is no great surplus of heretics pounding on the gates of the City demanding to be let in. How many people did you try to enlist in your cause, Noren, before you resorted to that last desperate gambit of yours?"

Noren dropped his eyes. "Most of them either weren't interested, or weren't willing to risk anything. And there were a few who wanted to destroy what they couldn't have or else to seize power for themselves. If questioning things were encouraged, though, maybe more children would grow up caring."

"Encouraged by whom? The village leaders? You stood trial before a village council, so you must have a fairly realistic idea of the way they think. Yet they're elected by the people and we can't interfere with them. We don't tamper with democratic government in the villages; to do so would be exceeding our bounds. As High Priests we exert no influence beyond the sphere of the Prophecy and the High Law."

"Well, by Technicians, then. Some Technicians use their minds."

Stefred smiled. "A Technician encouraged you, didn't he, when you were still in school? A young man who spent the night at your father's farm?"

"I never told you that," Noren gasped. "I never told anyone!"

"The incident wasn't accidental," explained Stefred. "Neither were some of the less happy ones; there's more than one kind of encouragement, and at times we gave you cause to hate us. We've been watching you since you were a small child."

"You—you set me up for this . . . from the beginning? I didn't have free choice after all?"

"Oh, yes. You had free choice. We encourage every person who shows any spark of initiative, but most of them don't follow through. And the risks you took were real; if you'd fallen into the hands of certain fanatics, we might not have been able to save you. We failed with your friend Kern, for whom we had great hopes."

"You were watching Kern, too?"

"Of course," said Stefred unhappily, "but we were helpless; he was rash and spoke before we anticipated, before we'd arranged protection. Can you imagine how I felt when I heard you'd eluded yours?"

"That really was why you got those Technicians to trick me into getting myself arrested!" exclaimed Noren, realizing that despite the suspicions of the young man who'd switched places with him, Stefred had told them the literal truth.

"Yes. It was necessary for your safety that the time and place be of our choosing, but the decision to respond as you did was yours alone."

Noren frowned. "What if a Technician doesn't like the orders he's given?" he inquired, unable to forget the man's anguished remorse.

"It's a violation of the High Law to disobey. He is free to become a villager if he wishes, but otherwise he's subject to our authority and can be convicted of heresy by the Council of Technicians if he defies it."

But that was awful, Noren thought. And then he saw the implications of what Stefred was saying. Technicians too could be heretics, and could therefore go on to become Scholars! There must be more than one of them who opposed the system; yet like the villagers they were reared to believe in the Prophecy and the High Law, and by the same token must believe that they could be killed for refusing to recant—which was as it should be if offering one's life was the only way to qualify.

"The men sent on such missions are very carefully chosen," Stefred went on. "Often the encouragement of heresy is intended to be mutual. You may have thought you weren't convincing anyone at your trial, but I suspect you convinced the Technician whose clothes you took; it was evident afterwards that he was tormented by the thought that he'd betrayed you. Someday soon, Noren, you'll be able to tell him that you weren't harmed by what he did, for the next time I give him such orders, he'll refuse them."

Stefred had painstakingly avoided the question of what that Technician had been doing in his cell in the middle of the night, Noren noticed; no doubt he'd guessed the truth from the beginning. Probably the man had never been given any instructions to pretend, but had simply not known how else to interpret the Chief Inquisitor's suggestion that he sympathize.

Torn, Noren struggled inwardly with the significance of what he had just heard. If Scholar status could be attained by anyone with the right sense of values, the scheme of succession was fair; and yet . . .

"I'm not trying to soften this," Stefred said, "because you want and need to face all its implications. But actually you are not going to be plunged abruptly into a position where people will worship you. I have not urged you to wear the robe, for the obligations it represents can't be imposed on anyone. The blue robe is a symbol of full commitment. It's your right to assume it whenever you choose, provided you're ready to make such a commitment formally. Most Scholars don't do that until they've passed through the first phases of training and seen what our work is really like. A few never do it at all."

"You mean I needn't become a High Priest?" asked Noren, relieved and yet confused.

"That's up to you to decide. You'll be ineligible for certain types of work unless you commit yourself; you will not even have a vote—and we Scholars vote not only to elect leaders, but on many issues that affect fulfillment of the Prophecy. Your fitness to participate is conditional on

239)

your being willing to share the accountability."

There was another distinction between novice Scholars and fully committed ones, Noren learned; a novice's true status was not revealed to the Technicians. He hadn't realized that there were Technicians who lived permanently in the Inner City. Stefred, however, explained that since they did not wear uniforms except for special duties, any more than committed Scholars wore their robes, and since everybody mingled freely outside the Hall of Scholars itself, a person's rank could not be determined by looking at him. Nor could it be determined by the kind of job he did, for not all heretics who earned Scholar status had desire or aptitude either for scientific research or any other field of study, and some did less skilled work than some of the Technicians, who also had opportunity for education. The difference lay in knowledge of the secrets. Technicians admitted to the Inner City had to remain because they knew Scholar rank wasn't hereditary; yet they didn't know anything about the process whereby it was conferred, so they too were eligible to attain it, although some were candidates who had failed.

"You realize, don't you," Stefred said, "that that's what would have happened to you if you'd recanted before learning the truth?"

"I'd have become an Inner City Technician?"

"Yes."

"What if I'd refused to recant after I learned? Or if I'd been penitent?"

"It very rarely happens, Noren. We don't enlighten anyone we're not sure of. Still, we're fallible, and your freedom of choice was real."

"You'd have had to isolate me."

"Unfortunately we would. The conditions wouldn't have been harsh—you'd have had our companionship whenever possible—and you'd have retained eligibility for a second chance, as does any person who's disqualified, for that matter."

"I might not have wanted one if I'd known what was ahead."

"No candidate knows; his incorruptibility can be proven only if he takes all the steps without expectation of personal gain."

"That still doesn't make accepting a Scholar's role *right*," Noren insisted.

"The question's not whether it's right for a special group of people to control the knowledge and equipment brought from the Six Worlds," Stefred said. "We're agreed that it isn't. Yet you conceded, when you decided to recant, that for the time being that's how it's got to be. You did so only because you'd been convinced that the Founders didn't want the job, and that those of us who are like them would prefer to be rid of it. Would you throw the whole burden on us—on me? Is it to be condoned only as long as you yourself can wash your hands of any involvement?"

Wretchedly Noren admitted, "If I refuse an active part, I'm condemning you all; I'm right back where I started. What's wrong with me, Stefred? Why do I feel this way, when only this morning I was willing to do anything that might be required of me?"

"If you don't know, you've less honesty than I've been giving you credit for."

Noren pondered it. "Some of the people hated me this morning," he said slowly, "because they thought I'd sold out. I could face that because I knew it wasn't true . . . but now I'm afraid it is true."

Stefred nodded, understanding. "You don't have to be," he said. "Why do you suppose we waited until after the ceremony to tell you, if not to spare you that fear? We were already sure of you; our final decision had been made; you were, in fact, a Scholar when you were exposed alone to the crowd, for we don't allow disqualified candidates to become targets of abuse. The final tests were not for our benefit but for yours, Noren! Would we have let you suffer them without good cause?"

"I thought maybe you wanted to see how much I could take before rewarding me with honor."

"This is not a reward. We kept you unaware because we knew you could accept nothing from us that was offered as payment."

"Sometimes I think you read my mind," Noren confessed ruefully.

"You forget that we've all traveled the same route. Every one of us, having refused to back down under pressure, has recanted for the sake of the future we're working toward; and that experience is just the beginning, for when we re-enact the dream, we assume all the responsibility it implies. I took part in this morning's pageant, too, after all. I stood there and let the villagers kneel to me, pay me homage, while they despised and reviled you; and I well knew that the one was no more deserved than the other. Did you think I was enjoying myself?" Stefred's voice was sorrowful as he continued, "Noren, I watched you and looked back on my own recantation almost with nostalgia, thinking how simple life was for me then! Yes, we were judging you. No man who was secretly longing for my role could have borne yours as you did. But the reverse doesn't necessarily hold true."

He rose and walked to the window, looking out across the shining towers of the City. "Before I revealed the secret of the Prophecy to you, I asked if you would accept the consequences without protest; and when you declared you would, I predicted that a day would come when you'd go back on those words. I warned you that in the end the consequences would seem so terrible that you'd be willing to give up all the things you cared most for in order to escape them; that you would stand here in this room and tell me so. You laughed. Even this morning you'd have laughed; you felt that by your voluntary participation in that ceremony you were proving me wrong. But you can't laugh now, Noren, for you have just fulfilled my prediction. If I'd made a bet with you, you would have to pay off."

"You meant—these consequences? All along?"

"Yes," Stefred said gently, "all along. They are the consequences not merely of your acts, Noren, but of everything you are."

"I—I can't escape, can I?" Noren said resignedly. It was more a discovery than a question, and Stefred did not reply; no reply was needed. Both of them already knew the answer.

For a while it was as though he were still in the dreams: he was himself no longer, but a Scholar; and he would be a Scholar forever. The idea was overwhelming, yet not entirely unwelcome. Looking around Stefred's familiar study, with its shelves of books and its many still-incomprehensible Machines, Noren felt a tremendous surge of excitement. All the mysteries were to be revealed to him! Whether or not he ever chose to wear the robe, he had both the right and the duty to understand them and someday to pass them on.

The training would be more challenging than anything he could imagine, Stefred warned. It would not be like the village school; there would indeed be discipline, rigorous discipline, for he would be given tasks that would tax his mind to the utmost. "There will be problems beyond any you've yet conceived," the Scholar concluded, "but though our life's far from easy, I think you'll find that it suits you."

Noren nodded; knowledge was what he'd longed for, and he could not believe that the process of absorbing it would be anything but a joy.

"It is not a life of comfort. Like the Founders, we endure greater hardships than the people whose heritage we hold in trust, and we are confined here, remember. The decree that you can't leave the City still stands; that is one of the things we renounce. There are others."

"Marriage," murmured Noren, thinking again of Talyra.

"Not at all," Stefred assured him. "We are free to marry among ourselves, and fully committed Scholars, who have revealed their rank, can even marry Technicians."

"I—I won't ever want to marry anyone, Stefred."

"You don't mean that. You mean you don't want to marry anyone but the girl you're in love with." At Noren's astonished look he went on, "Yes, I know how you feel about Talyra, but even if I didn't, it would be easy enough to guess. The situation's not exactly unusual. Many of us, both men and women, have been very deeply hurt by it."

"I could bear that myself," Noren said unhappily, "but when I think of *her*— She was there this morning. She suffered more than I did; that was the worst part of the whole thing."

"I saw," Stefred said. "Her instructors forbade her to attend, but she disobeyed them." He hesitated, then added with abrupt candor, "Noren, there is one more fact you must know. There's no need for Talyra to go on suffering on your account. If she loves you enough to share your confinement, she can become a Technician."

Noren drew a breath of surprise. "Is that what happens to the people who vanish from the training center?" he asked, beginning to piece things together.

"Yes. That's one reason I appointed her to go there: so that if it worked out as I hoped, her disappearance from the village could be explained."

"But . . . we can't marry unless I accept the robe?"

"Would it be fair to make her your wife without telling her that a barrier of secrecy must always stand between you?"

(244

No, reflected Noren, and certainly not without letting her know that they'd be unable to rear their own children. Besides, Talyra wouldn't want to be a Technician! The idea would shock her. She had been happy in the village, but in the City she'd be terrified and miserable. "Don't bring her here," he said resolutely.

"I couldn't even if you wished it," Stefred told him. "In a case like this, a village woman must come of her own accord; she must request audience to plead clemency for the man she loves and show herself spirited enough to see justification in his acts as well as to adapt to the Inner City. As a Technician, she'll always believe that we made him a Scholar not because of his heresy, but in spite of it; yet she must sense that he has proven himself worthy."

Then it was hopeless, Noren thought. He must put it out of his mind. Talyra was so very devout, so unwilling to question; she would never challenge the Chief Inquisitor! As he sat silent, remembering things she'd said, a new doubt came to him.

"Stefred," he began hesitantly, "there's something that bothers me. Lots of people believe in the Mother Star and it—well, comforts them. They've got the idea that it's a power that takes care of things. If they knew the truth, they might feel . . . lost. There'd be nothing up there any more. Mightn't that happen when the Time of the Prophecy comes?"

There was a long pause; Stefred, for the first time in Noren's memory, seemed at a loss for an answer. "That's a complicated question," he said finally, "and a very serious one. Men have always looked toward something above and beyond them; they always will. They've called it by different names. Throughout the history of the Six Worlds there were many, and by the time of the Founding the right of each person to choose his own was almost universally accepted. The High Law still grants that right, but few villagers exercise it; most of them have forgotten all

245)

names but that of the Mother Star—which, used in such a way, would have seemed blasphemous to people of the First Scholar's day."

"I don't understand," Noren admitted.

"No, and you won't until you have studied much of the wisdom that is preserved here. What you can grasp now is that it's the idea that's important, not what it's called: the idea that there is something higher and more significant than we are. You, I think, would call it Truth. Later you may find another name more meaningful, as many of us do."

Comprehension stirred in Noren, making him glance again at the blue robe set aside. Stefred smiled. "Don't try to solve everything at once. You have quite a few surprises coming—even Talyra may surprise you—and in the meantime, there's plenty of work to get started on."

Noren raised his eyes to the window. Beyond the wall of glass, beyond the bright towers and beacons of the City, he could see the far-off rim of the Tomorrow Mountains. A whole new earth, and beyond the earth, a universe! One day, above those ridges, the Mother Star would appear in radiant splendor, and the annunciation of the old worlds' tragedy would become the confirmation of the new one's faith. *"And the spirit of this Star shall abide forever in our hearts . . ."* What did it matter if the truth was cloaked in a little symbolism? The idea behind it was the same! With sudden elation, he found himself looking forward to the tasks ahead.

Author's Note

THOSE WHOSE HORIZONS ARE WIDER THAN NOREN'S WILL have noticed that not all the mysteries of his world have been revealed. How can its resources be so limited that the people cannot even make wheels? How can the Scholars have been working for generations without finding a way to manufacture tools and machines; why isn't the planet's metal suitable, and if it's not, can't they invent some substitute? And what do they think will happen when the Prophecy comes true? Surely they don't, like the villagers, expect a sudden magical solution to all the problems.

Readers who are asking these and other questions may rest assured that their curiosity will be satisfied. Noren's search for truth is not yet finished. He still has a great deal to learn: not only about the City's secrets, not only about the past achievements of the Six Worlds and the coming ones of his own, but about the universe in which all worlds exist. And he still must decide whether to commit himself fully to the role he has barely begun to understand. Much, therefore, remains to be told in the second volume of this story, BEYOND THE TOMORROW MOUNTAINS.

247)

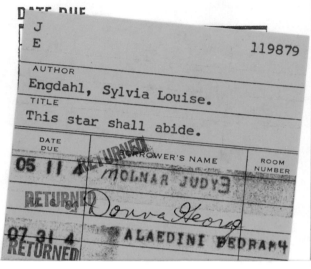